THE MONSTERS
WE MAKE

THE MONSTERS WE MAKE

KALI WHITE

W★RLDWIDE

TORONTO • NEW YORK • LONDON
AMSTERDAM • PARIS • SYDNEY • HAMBURG
STOCKHOLM • ATHENS • TOKYO • MILAN
MADRID • WARSAW • BUDAPEST • AUCKLAND

WORLDWIDE™

ISBN-13: 978-1-335-48425-3

The Monsters We Make

First published in 2020 by Crooked Lane Books, an imprint of
The Quick Brown Fox & Company LLC.
This edition published in 2021.

Recycling programs
for this product may
not exist in your area.

This edition published by arrangement with Harlequin Books S.A.

For questions and comments about the quality of this book,
please contact us at CustomerService@Harlequin.com.

Harlequin Enterprises ULC
22 Adelaide St. West, 40th Floor
Toronto, Ontario M5H 4E3, Canada
www.ReaderService.com

Printed in U.S.A.

For my children:
Drake, Seth, and Gauri
My best stories.

So now the national media, the television networks and the national press are fascinated with an unlikely tale: terror in Des Moines, of all places. We are on display, each one of us bit players in a drama that examines what's wrong in a place that's supposed to be so right.
—James P. Gannon, Editor, *The Des Moines Register*,
August 15, 1984

SUNDAY, JULY 18, 1982

IT STARTED WITH a boy, and a wagon.

He left his spacious white brick home shortly before sunrise, in darkness. A humid Iowa morning. Dewdrops clung to blades of grass. Condensation ran down windowpanes in watery rivulets. The manicured West Des Moines neighborhood was still drowsy, quiet.

He towed an empty red Radio Flyer wagon with his faithful corgi, Lucy, trotting alongside him. He walked at an easy pace, occasionally passing through the pale-yellow circles of dimming streetlights. Sleepiness tugged at his eyelids.

Shortly before six am, he reached the corner where he waited for his newspaper bundles to be dropped off. He was only twelve years old but took his paper route seriously. In a sales contest the year before, he'd finished second and won the red wagon. This year he wanted the grand prize: an eight-track tape player.

Within a few minutes the delivery van arrived, and the driver unloaded the boy's bundles of the *Des Moines Register.* The van pulled away and the boy started rolling and binding the papers with rubber bands.

As he worked, a dark-blue car stopped at the corner. A man, asking how to get to the mall. Strange, the boy thought, because the mall wouldn't open for several hours. But he did his best to give directions. *It's that way.* He pointed. *On Valley West Drive.* The exchange lasted mere minutes, and the man in the blue car left. The boy returned to his task and finished rolling. He set out on his route pulling his now-full wagon, Lucy at his side.

Streetlights sputtered out against the rising sun. A car door slammed. An engine revved. Lucy barked for a few moments, then stopped.

The neighborhood returned to silence.

As the tip of the sun peeked above the horizon, the boy was gone.

In the blink of an eye. A brief turn of the head.

Only his red wagon remained, just a block away from the corner, where his father found it still full of rolled newspapers an hour and forty-five minutes later, after Lucy returned home, alone.

Matthew Michael Klein
"Matt"
Case #82–2745

By Sunday, August 12, 1984, when another boy disappeared under identical circumstances, Matthew Klein had been missing for seven hundred and fifty-six days.

ONE

SUNDAY, AUGUST 12, 1984

One hour missing

IN THE EARLY-morning darkness of a South Side Des Moines neighborhood, twelve-year-old Sammy Cox ran down Clark Avenue as fast as his short, thick legs would take him. He glanced over his shoulder and saw that no one was following him anymore but continued running anyway. He clutched his empty canvas newspaper delivery bag to his side, and the keys hanging around his neck on a string bounced wildly off his chest. His heart hammered until it felt as if it were going to punch a hole right through his ribs, but he kept running. If he stopped, he might get caught again.

At the New Hope Baptist Church on the corner of Clark and Tenth Street he crossed the yard, the dry grass crunching beneath his sneakers, and ran straight to the east door of the church. The east door was always left unlocked on Sunday mornings by the pastor, who arrived without fail by eight am to sit in his office and practice his sermon.

Sammy had hidden in the church before. He knew it would be safe.

He opened the door and soundlessly entered the hall-way, tiptoeing by the pale shaft of light illuminating the

bottom of the pastor's office door, and let himself into
the dark fellowship hall. There, he crawled beneath one
of the linen-covered tables and waited.

He tried to make himself invisible. Stinging beads
of sweat dripped into his eyes.

The fleshy skin of his upper arm was already starting to hurt where fingers had squeezed and pinched.
Sammy gently brushed his fingertips over the tender
spots, just below the sleeve hem of his shirt, and winced.
He'd barely escaped this time by wrenching his arm free
and making a run for it.

Sammy touched the fabric at the crotch of his shorts.
He'd wet his pants again during the struggle.

He knew he was never supposed to run away, that
he'd probably be punished for it later, but he didn't care.
Sammy hated Sundays, and he hated the Sunday paper
route. He constantly begged his mother to let him quit,
but she'd gently remind him that he needed the exercise
to lose the weight he'd put on recently, that some extra
responsibility one morning a week was good for him,
that he should be grateful to even have the job.

She would just repeat what someone else had told
her.

A door banged in the hallway, and Sammy tensed.
He removed a pair of his mother's orange-handled scissors from the bottom of his canvas bag and gripped the
blades, ready.

He held his breath, straining to listen. A cough. It
was only the pastor, moving around. The office door
closed, and Sammy exhaled. He slipped the scissors
back into the bag.

Sammy crawled out from beneath the table. The fellowship hall was still empty. He scanned the trays of

cellophane-covered cookies the church ladies usually put out the night before Sunday services. The choices today: Fig Newtons, generic vanilla-cream sandwiches, and an assortment of homemade chocolate-chip cookies. A small platter of Keebler Fudge Stripes caught his eye. He lifted a corner of the clear plastic and grabbed a handful. He then artfully rearranged the remaining cookies to cover the bare spots.

Back beneath the table, he slipped his index finger through a center hole and began to nibble bits around the edges, the best way to eat a Fudge Stripe. He would eat his cookies and then go.

On several of the Sunday mornings before he'd begun to hide in the church, he'd considered trying to make a run for home but knew he couldn't make it. He got winded easily and barely ran fast enough to make it to the church. His house was still several blocks away, and the streets on the South Side were hilly. His older sister Crystal was a pretty good runner, but Sammy was chubby and weak and slow. It wasn't fair.

Sammy rubbed the tender marks on his arm once more. For a brief moment, he thought about knocking on the office door and asking the pastor for help. Telling him what had been happening since last fall.

He imagined the pastor calling the police. Or maybe even the FBI. There would be questions, *interrogations*, and Sammy would have to talk about it. He'd be forced to tell all the terrible details that made his stomach feel slimy just thinking about them.

Sammy wiped cookie crumbs from his chin and wrapped his arms around his belly.

No. He could never tell anyone again. It was a secret.

He'd promised. Crossed his heart and hoped to die. And he didn't want to die.

And besides, when he'd tried telling before, nothing had happened, nothing had changed. So, he would keep trying to get away whenever he could. He would keep carrying the scissors on Sunday mornings. Maybe one day he would finally be brave enough to use them.

Sammy slid another cookie over his finger and peeked beneath the tablecloth to check if the coast was clear. When he emerged, he noticed a long chocolate-milk stain bisecting the front of his white *I'm a Pepper* T-shirt from drinking out of the carton earlier that morning. His father used to drink out of the carton. He said chocolate milk somehow tasted better that way. Sammy agreed.

He missed his father. Florida was so far away.

He pulled his white-and-red-striped tube socks up to his knees and left the fellowship hall as quietly as he'd entered. He needed to get home, or he would be late. And if he was too late, his mother would notice and scold him for dawdling and taking too long on his route.

Outside, the full sun crested the horizon. The streets were busier at this hour than normal. Passing cars, several people out walking, calling to each other. Sammy clutched his canvas bag in front of the wet spot on his crotch and dashed across the churchyard to the sidewalk. As he was about to cross the street, he stopped and waited for two speeding motorcycles to pass. They slowed at the top of the hill, then stopped. A group of people crowded around the corner of Tenth and Hillcrest, where one of the other paperboys had his bundles delivered.

Sammy started running again to make up time. But

instead of turning right on Tenth and walking just one block north to Cutler Avenue where he lived, the shortest and most direct path home, he crossed Tenth and continued west on Clark. It took him in a wide, circular route to his street.

His safety route.

A route where no one would think to look for him. Where he would be a little safer.

TWO

One and a half hours missing

CRYSTAL COX HUNCHED over the kitchen table reading the *Des Moines Register* about the latest news from the Olympics in Los Angeles. Everyone was stewing over a big controversy the day before when an American runner got tripped by a barefoot South African and fell, losing the race she was favored to win. The ensuing debate was whether the South African had run a dirty race. Crystal slid a pen from behind her ear and opened a red spiral notebook. She jotted down a possible article idea for her school paper on cheating in the Olympics. Or maybe an article on spectators' need for heroes and villains in competitive sports. When she started her senior year in a few weeks, she would be editor of both the yearbook and her high school newspaper, *The Railsplitter*, with a weekly column and regular feature stories, so she was always on the lookout for good story ideas.

With no new article ideas gelling, Crystal closed the newspaper and shuffled to the sink. The basin was still full of cold, stagnant water, dirty plates, and tumbler cups. She was supposed to have done the dishes last night but had forgotten. She reached into the water, her hand breaking the greasy layer floating atop, and fished around for the dishrag. She'd get them cleaned up quickly, before her mother awoke.

As she washed, Crystal switched on the police scanner sitting on a shelf above the sink set to the Des Moines frequency. Her father had left the scanner behind when he moved out after the divorce three years ago, and listening to it was her favorite pastime. An odd interest for an eighteen-year-old girl, but it was a great source of local breaking news. Whenever Crystal was in the kitchen, the scanner was on. She was so used to its chatter filling the background of the house that she'd learned most of the police ten-codes. Ten-eleven, dog case. Ten-seventy, fire alarm. Ten-fifteen, civil disturbance.

Crystal clamped a pair of pliers around the hot-water valve of the sink and pulled until the water ran. The handle had broken months ago, but as usual her mother didn't have the money to fix it.

As Crystal rinsed dishes under the tap, she yawned again. She'd been unable to sleep in late because her bedroom was too hot and uncomfortable, even with the box fan blasting on high three inches from her head. A dispatcher's voice crackled through the speaker, her voice hurried, urgent.

"Ten—thirty-five, major crime alert. Suspected ten—forty-one A at corner of Hillcrest Drive and Tenth Street. Available officer in the area, please respond."

Ten—forty-one A... Crystal didn't recognize the code. She turned up the volume.

"APB thirteen-year-old male, brown hair, brown eyes, five feet two inches, one hundred and five pounds, last seen at corner of Hillcrest Drive and Tenth Street on paper route between five forty-five and six am wearing blue jeans and gray tank top. Name is Christopher Thomas Stewart. Father just called it in."

The frequency squealed and clicked. A male voice now. "Unit 22 responding."

"BOLO silver or gray Camaro reported in vicinity of Tenth and Hillcrest where child was last seen."

Crystal pulled the faucet off and tapped the pliers head against her chin, thinking.

They were looking for vehicles. *Child last seen... 10-41A...*

They were looking for a missing paperboy.

Hillcrest and Tenth was just three blocks away.

She dropped the pliers on the counter and stepped outside onto the damp, seeping pavement of the driveway. Dewy air blanketed her.

The corner of Hillcrest and Tenth was just blocks from Sammy's paper route, too. He should've been finished with his route and home by now.

Multiple police sirens wailed in the distance. Crystal squinted her eyes behind the thick lenses of her glasses, trying to make out a pair of blurry figures at the end of the street. It was two uniformed cops, stopping and searching every passing car.

Several neighbors had also noticed the commotion and peeked out between curtains or poked their heads through the cracks of front doors. Crystal walked farther down the driveway. Next door, old Mrs. Murley was standing in the middle of her yard in her floral housecoat and curlers, shading her eyes against the sunrise as she watched the police work.

This missing-kid thing was for real. A current of worry for Sammy rippled through Crystal's gut but was quickly replaced by excitement. This could possibly be a topic for her YJWA scholarship application. The Young Journalists Writing Award was a national essay-writing contest for journalism majors with a $2,000-a-year renewable college scholarship, and Crystal desperately needed that money if she had any hope of going to college next fall. This year, the topic for the journalistic essay was "Issues of Contemporary Societies," and this missing kid could be a promising lead. All good journalists had to follow promising leads, and Crystal was serious about becoming a journalist. She wasn't some lookie-loo or rubbernecker like all her gawking neighbors.

Crystal rushed back into the house and grabbed a pad of paper and a pen from the junk drawer and hastily scribbled down what she'd heard on the scanner moments ago.

She stuffed the notebook and pen into her back pocket and ran up the stairs two at a time, leaping over piles of clothes and discarded shoes, and pushed open the door to her mother's bedroom. Tina lay sprawled on her stomach across her queen-size water bed, a thin top sheet tangled around her body.

"Mom," Crystal whispered, nudging Tina's shoulder. "There's something on the police scanner."

Tina didn't move. She'd worked late again last night at her second job: waitressing at a Chi-Chi's restaurant on weekends. During the week she cut and permed hair at a Haircrafters Salon in the mall, so Sundays were her only morning to sleep in.

"Mom! I just heard something on the police scanner," Crystal repeated.

"Ten more minutes," Tina murmured, and pulled the sheet over her head.

"No, listen to me." Crystal peeled the sheet back. "A

kid went missing. I heard it on the scanner. I'm going to go look for Sammy and check out what's going on."

The old family cat, Mr. Tibbs, who often slept curled in a ball on her pillow, stirred and stretched, burying his claws in Tina's long, ratted hair that still smelled like fried food from the restaurant.

"Did you do the dishes yet?" Tina asked, her eyes still closed.

"I'll finish them when I get back. This could be a breaking story."

"Seriously, Chrissie?" Tina cracked one eye open. "Give the reporter shit a rest. It's barely seven in the morning." She rolled onto her side away from Crystal, sending waves rippling through the mattress. Mr. Tibbs meowed and irritably flicked his tail.

Crystal dropped the sheet and left the room. Despite her mother's stinging words, she went back downstairs and slipped on a pair of flip-flops. She wasn't going to miss this chance to chase a story. And, she guiltily checked herself, to find her brother.

In the carport, she mounted her red Schwinn bicycle and pedaled down their uneven driveway to Cutler Avenue, past the police barricade, where she turned onto Tenth. She stopped one block away from Hillcrest where a large group of people milled about the corner. No sign of Sammy yet.

Crystal straddled her bike and pulled out her notebook and pen to write down a few notes about the scene. She even attempted to ask a passing police officer what was going on, but he blew her off, telling her to go home and stay out of the way. She ignored the order and kept writing. Good reporters weren't scared off that easy.

"Hello, Cree-*stahl* Cox."

Her heart instantly pulsed at the familiar accented voice behind her. She twisted around to see Mr. Kovacs, or Mr. K they called him, Sammy's weekly math tutor, walking up the Tenth Street sidewalk. She'd been so focused on getting a piece of the action that she hadn't realized she was sitting on the corner of Tenth and Southlawn right in front of his house.

She instinctively touched her short, bobbed hair to make sure it was smooth and that no childish cowlicks were sticking up anywhere.

"Hi, Mr. K." She pulled her shoulders back to make herself look taller and, hopefully, to make her breasts look bigger.

He stopped in front of her bike and touched the handles. "What are you doing out here so early in the morning?"

"I'm looking for Sammy," Crystal said. "Have you seen him?"

Mr. K gestured to the fat roll lying on his front stoop. "No. But I see he already delivered my paper." He wore dark jogging pants, a dark hooded sweat shirt, and, Crystal now noticed in the rising sunlight, a pair of binoculars hung around his neck. Strapped over his shoulders was a black backpack.

"What are *you* doing out here so early in the morning?" she asked, trying to make her voice sound playful, but it only came out weird and awkward.

Mr. K swiped the back of his hand over his perspiring brow. "Oh, I, uh, walk the neighborhood every morning, for the exercise. And I like to bird-watch." He lifted the binoculars. "At the park."

"Bird-watching. That's cool." Crystal nodded and

touched her own forehead to make sure it wasn't sweaty and shiny.

While Crystal would rather die before admitting her crush out loud, she privately thought Sebastian Kovacs was the smartest, most interesting man she'd ever met. He was only twenty-four, so he wasn't *that* much older than her. She'd been eighteen since the first of August, as she'd pointed out to him a few weeks ago.

A trio of paperboys passed, talking excitedly, but no Sammy.

Mr. K's gaze continually darted to the corner a block away, and he shifted from one foot to another, seeming fidgety.

"What's going on up there?" he asked.

"A paperboy went missing this morning," Crystal said. "From that corner, I think."

He wiped his brow again, still perspiring, and Crystal wondered why he'd worn heavy sweats in the humidity. "What's the boy's name?"

"Christopher Stewart. Do you know him?"

Mr. K shook his head. "That's terrible," he said quietly.

"I know." Crystal rolled her bike a few inches closer. "I'm trying to find Sammy, but I'm also trying to get some information for a possible story. You know, taking notes and stuff." She held out her notebook.

"Mm-hmm." Mr. K's eyes drifted over her head to the corner again. He didn't appear to be listening, and didn't even glance at the notebook.

Crystal tucked it back into her pocket, grappling for another topic to keep him talking to her a while longer.

"Are—are you going to the State Fair next weekend?" she asked. "Because we're going. On Saturday.

Well, Saturday night. After my mom gets off work at the restaurant. She has to work the day shift." She dug her nails into her palm. She hated it when she babbled.

"I don't know yet," Mr. K said. "I might go to the concert on Saturday."

"Maybe we'll see you there!" She dug her nails in harder. She'd sounded too excited.

As a police cruiser approached the corner, Mr. K abruptly turned and hurried toward his house.

"I have to go," he said, jogging across the lawn. "See you later."

"Oh, okay," Crystal said. "See you tomorrow for Sammy's tutoring!" But he'd already gone inside and closed the door.

Crystal wanted to kick herself. She'd sounded like a desperate idiot.

The police cruiser bleeped its siren, and the cop gestured for her to keep moving away from the corner. Officers were now staking out yellow crime-scene tape. They weren't going to let her get any closer.

Disappointed that she hadn't gotten anything significant on the missing paperboy, Crystal mounted her bike to look for Sammy. She pushed off in the opposite direction, pedaling faster toward Clark Avenue. Sammy always walked home from Clark to Tenth to Cutler, so they should cross paths at any moment. As she coasted down the hill, warm wind caught her hair and lifted it off her neck, cooling her flushed skin.

At the corner of Clark, she squeezed the brake handles and did a quick glance in both directions without stopping. Just as her front tire rolled onto the street, car tires squealed behind her on the right and a horn blared, startling her. She wobbled and nearly lost her balance.

"Hey! Pay attention, kid! I damn near hit you!" the driver shouted at her.

Safely across on the other side, she stopped and planted her feet on the ground, her heart racing. She hadn't seen the car, even though she'd looked. She removed her large, clear, square-framed eyeglasses—her expensive new ones with the gold, low-temple earpieces—and cleaned the lenses with shaking hands on the hem of her shirt.

She should've come to a full stop and looked more carefully. She knew better.

Crystal had been born with colobomas in each eye, a condition that caused small sections of her pupils to leak downward into her irises, giving them a tadpole shape and seriously impairing her vision. Legally, she was considered blind and couldn't even pass the eye exam to get a driver's license. Her only means of transportation was her bicycle, and even that was dangerous sometimes.

Crystal slipped her glasses back on and caught a flutter of movement on Clark Street in her peripheral vision. She squinted harder, and the flutter came into focus. A short, round figure, running west on the sidewalk. It was Sammy, going in the opposite direction of home. She frowned.

"Sammy!" she called. "Hey! Sammy!"

He kept running.

She pedaled after him, yelling, "Sammy! Stop, you dumbass!"

Sammy glanced over his shoulder. When he saw it was her, he finally stopped, breathing hard.

Crystal dumped her bike next to him and flopped onto a lawn, also panting.

"Why were you running so fast?"

"I don't know. Exercise, I guess."

"Why didn't you stop when I yelled at you?"

"I didn't hear you." He tried to discreetly slip a pair of their mother's scissors into his canvas bag, but Crystal saw them in his hand.

She narrowed her eyes at him, but he wouldn't look at her. Instead, he kept glancing up and down the street.

"What's with the scissors?" Crystal asked. "Why are you going home this way? Why are you so late this morning?"

"Just… I was… I don't know. Stop asking me so many questions!" He fidgeted with his canvas bag, holding it awkwardly in front of him. "Why are *you* out here?"

Crystal stood and brushed off her backside. "Haven't you heard? Cops are looking for a missing paperboy."

Sammy stopped fidgeting and stared at her. "Who?"

"A kid named Christopher Stewart. He lives on Sheridan, I think."

Sammy watched another car speed by. "Why is he missing?"

"Who knows. Maybe he was kidnapped. Like that Klein kid."

Sammy's eyes grew wide. "What Klein kid?" he whispered.

She swatted a biting fly off her leg. "That West Des Moines paperboy from two years ago."

Sammy shifted his gaze away from her. "Oh, yeah," he said slowly. "I remember now."

"Did you notice anything this morning while you were on your route? There's cops all over the place. Up on the corner of Tenth and Hillcrest."

"Why are they up there?"

"That's where he was kidnapped, dummy!"

"Oh."

"So, did you see anything this morning? Your route goes right by his."

Sammy stared down the street in the direction of Hillcrest. He didn't respond for a long moment, his expression blank and glassy.

"Hello?" Crystal said, snapping her fingers in front of his unblinking eyes.

Sammy jerked his head back to her. "I didn't see… I just… I saw a lot of cars and stuff. A few people yelling, but that's it." He averted his eyes once more and lifted his arm to scratch the top of his head. The sleeve of his shirt slid up to reveal a series of angry red circles on his upper arm.

"What happened?" Crystal started to touch the marks, but he slapped her hand away.

"Nothing," he said. "I bumped into a door."

"Why are you acting so weird?"

"I'm not," he said, and ground his fists into his red, puffy eyes.

She took a step toward him, but he recoiled from her.

"If you saw something," she said carefully, "don't be scared to say so."

"I didn't see anything!" he yelled, and a nearby dog started barking from a backyard.

Sammy jostled the bag again, and Crystal caught a glimpse of a wet spot on the crotch of his shorts.

He was lying about something, she could tell.

"Let's go," he said, his gaze darting up and down the street once more. "I wanna get home."

Before she could respond, he started jogging again.

Crystal stood her bike up and mounted the seat.

He was definitely lying.

Something had happened this morning that he didn't want to tell her. Something that scared him.

Or someone.

As she started to pedal, she glanced over her shoulder to make sure no one was following them.

THREE

Two hours, ten minutes missing

SERGEANT DALE GOODKIND sat at his desk in the Crimes Against Persons Section on the second floor of the downtown Des Moines Police Department. He typed the last lines of the daily patrol assignments, hunting and pecking around the keys with his index fingers.

He glanced at the wall clock again. He should've been off twenty-six minutes ago, but as the weekend shift watch commander, he couldn't leave until his senior police officer for the day shift arrived. SPO Bradley. Now twenty-seven minutes late.

He tucked a pair of I-Cubs baseball game tickets into the front pocket of his sports coat and counted out twelve quarters from the loose change in his desk drawer, gifts for his son Curtis's golden birthday. Twelve on the twelfth. The party started at one, and Dale needed to squeeze in a nap.

He switched off the humming electric typewriter, yanked the patrol assignment schedule from the carriage with an angry *zzzzp*, and laid it in his *Out* basket. Finally, SPO Bradley hurried through the door, brushing past Dale's desk without a single word, not even bothering to offer an apology or excuse for his tardiness. Dale dramatically held up his wrist and made a show of checking his watch, but Bradley ignored him. No love lost between them. Dale was new to the DMPD and new to the CAP Section. He'd transferred from the West Des Moines PD four months ago with a promotion to sergeant. A promotion that had gone to him, not Bradley.

Dale organized a small pile of office memos to deal with tomorrow—a special crack cocaine task force the chief was putting together, the annual "Law versus Fire" baseball tournament faithfully sponsored by Midwest Heating and Cooling, and a volunteer sign-up sheet Dale had created for the DMPD booth at the Iowa State Fair next week.

He paused at the fair sign-up. Only two names so far, and someone had scrawled *Sergeant Goodgirl* into a slot.

Even though Dale had spent the later part of his youth here and was, like most South Siders, a genetic mutt of Irish, Italian, and Russian, the guys in his precinct made fun of him behind his back with the nickname, coined because of his aversion to swearing and alcohol. And even though he'd worked hard for that promotion and earned it, their swipes at him still bruised his ego. So much for their famous *South Side Pride*.

With his paperwork finished, Dale opened the sketchbook he carried with him everywhere and flipped through pages of doodles—Spiderman shooting webs from his wrists, animals in funny hats, caricatures of friends and family members—until he found the composite sketch of a robbery suspect he'd created a few days ago, tucked in the back. Dale was a natural artist and had volunteered to do a new Smith & Wesson witness facial composite training last year, one of the reasons behind his promotion to sergeant. He removed the sketch from the binding and clipped it to a corresponding report. Finally, he was done for the day.

"Goodkind." Lieutenant Duff loomed over Dale's desk and thrust a form in his face. "Get out to Southwest Tenth and Hillcrest," he said. "Missing kid."

Dale took the paper from Duff's hand. "I'm about to go off the clock," he said.

"I don't care," Duff answered, already walking away. "This one's right up your alley."

"I'll take it," Bradley said, swiveling his chair around. "I'm on today."

"It's already assigned, Bradley." Duff slammed the door behind him.

Bradley eyed Dale for a moment before returning to his desk.

Dale settled back into his chair and skimmed the limited information on the intake sheet.

8-12-84
0830
MISPER 13 yr old boy
Dark brown hair, brown eyes, 5' 1" app. 105lbs.
Last seen wearing blue jeans, gray tank top, white
Converse LA84 Olympic sneaks w/ blue stars.
Scar above right eye. Speaks with slight lisp.
Report filed by Bud Stewart, father.
1905 Sheridan Ave
LKL corner of 10th St. & Hillcrest Dr. while on
paper route
Christopher Thomas Stewart
"Chris"
Case #84–5482
Status: Open

His eyes snagged on the words *paper route*, and a small bean of dread dropped into the pit of his stomach and began to sprout vines.

A missing paperboy.

It couldn't be happening again.

AFTER EIGHT HOURS of shoe leather, the sun slid behind the houses in the west. In the fading light, Dale and Lieutenant Duff stood on the street corner where Chris Stewart had last been seen at sunrise, sitting on a patch of grass, rolling his newspapers.

Images between the two cases had been overlapping each other in Dale's mind all day. A warm, early morning. A quiet, middle-class neighborhood. A pile of undelivered newspapers. A boy who had seemingly vanished into thin air.

The prickly vines in Dale's stomach now pressed against his organs. At least that was how he described his anxious feelings to Dr. Smith. Like something crowding out his insides.

"FBI wants all the van delivery routes and drivers for the entire South Side," Duff said. "You'll be working with Agent Miller from the Omaha bureau." He stared at Dale. "Write it down."

"Sorry." Dale refocused and scribbled the note in his sketchbook.

Duff ran his fingers through his salt-and-pepper hair and spit on the ground. "What a shit deal this is."

After interviewing and clearing every member of the Stewart family, after searching the Stewart home, yard, and neighborhood, after putting up roadblocks around the entire South Side and conducting hundreds of traffic stops, they still had little more than the basics: Bud Stewart reported that Chris left their house just before five am. The van driver from the *Register* said he dropped off three bundles a few minutes after five, where Chris was waiting alone at the corner. About an hour later, calls started coming in from customers complaining they didn't have their papers yet. Route manager got to the corner around six fifteen and found a half dozen rolled papers in a delivery bag, but not a single paper delivered. No Chris. Manager took the bag and delivered the papers himself. Once finished, he went to the Stewart home around seven thirty to give Chris hell for oversleeping. But when Bud searched the house, no Chris. Concerned, Bud hopped on his motorcycle and searched the neighborhood for about fifteen minutes. After finding no sign of the boy, he called it in, and Dale was handed his second missing-paperboy case in less than two years.

Duff shouted at a patrol officer to move a group of onlookers away from the scene. He turned back to Dale.

"Give me the witness timeline again."

Dale read from his notes. "A few passersby saw Chris talking to a man in what appeared to be a friendly conversation around five fifteen. Another said five thirty. Another still said five forty. One said the man looked thirty to thirty-five. Clean-cut. Neat dark hair parted in the middle. One had him with something around his neck, maybe Walkman earphones; another said a black sweatband."

"We'll get the witnesses in tomorrow, and you can start sketching," Duff said. "Who's this again?" He pointed to the small brick house on the corner of Tenth and Hillcrest.

"Guy named VanZante," Dale said. "Retired Polk

County sheriff, if you can believe it. Didn't see or hear a thing. Broke down when I told him what happened this morning. Both he and the wife checked out. Said we can use the house for anything we need."

Duff looked hard at Dale. "The kid disappeared in the front yard of a goddamned retired sheriff?" He yanked on his tie. "No time off till this kid is found. He's already been missing nearly twelve hours. The clock is ticking."

"Yes, sir," Dale said.

"I'm heading back downtown to get a hotline set up. Pull everything you have on the Klein case. All your old notes, interviews, everything. And get in touch with the West Des Moines guy still on it."

Dale wrote *notes from Klein case* and stared at his handwriting. There wasn't anything in the Klein file or in his old notes that would help them.

He'd thought the move and promotion would be a fresh start. He'd promised Connie it would be.

"Goodkind!"

"Yeah. Sorry."

"I know the Klein deal is sour for you, but you're the only man in our department who worked on it and has experience with a missing kid."

"Of course."

"I'm taking the parents downtown."

"Yes, sir."

Duff clapped his hand on Dale's shoulder. "Finish up here, then meet me back at the station."

Dale agreed, and Duff walked away.

He checked his watch. He should've called Connie hours ago before he left the station. He never meant to do this—completely forget about his wife and son for hours at a time, standing them up without so much as a phone call because he got preoccupied by a case—and no amount of apologizing ever helped.

He climbed the small hill of the VanZantes' yard and knocked on the door. Mrs. VanZante answered, and Dale asked to use their phone again. She ushered him inside to the telephone in the kitchen.

First try, the line was busy. Dale hung up and waited a minute, then dialed the rotary again. This time, it rang once and Connie answered.

"Where have you been?" she snapped, assuming correctly it would be Dale calling. "You missed your son's birthday party and he's heartbroken. We've talked about this a hundred times, Dale. I'm done making excuses—"

"Connie, listen," he said. "Don't be mad. I'm working a case. I caught it this morning right before my shift ended and I didn't have time to call."

She exhaled loudly into the receiver.

"Another paperboy went missing early this morning," he said.

He waited, strained to listen. Trying to read her silence was like trying to read air.

"Con? Are you there?"

"God have mercy," she whispered. "The poor family. Who is it?"

"Bud and Cindy Stewart. They live over on Sheridan."

"That's barely four blocks from us!" she cried.

"I know. Don't let Curtis out of the house alone for any reason," he said. "I'll be home as soon as I can."

"Dale."

"Yeah."

She hesitated, the line clicking between them. "Never mind," she finally said, and hung up.

Back outside, Dale finished taking notes of every nearby side street where a car could've been parked for a quick getaway. He rubbed the back of his neck, trying to work out a hot muscle just above his left shoulder. He walked along the Tenth Street sidewalk, slowly, scrutinizing every inch of pavement he could see in the fading light.

Someone across the street shouted for a flashlight. The neighborhood was noisy and still buzzing with officers from the department, guys from the Iowa Division of Criminal Investigation, and a half-dozen suits from the Omaha FBI field office. It was hard to concentrate.

Dale stopped at a street gutter and flipped to a fresh page. He sketched a new map of storm drains and made a note in the margin:

Maps of city drainage system, abandoned cisterns & old coal mines—5 mile radius?

That kind of search could take weeks, even months. Geographically, the South Side was the biggest area of the city. It started south of the Racoon River, stretching east to Easter Lake and west all the way to the airport. At the southernmost fringes, it turned to vast, flat fields of corn. The South Side had once housed the largest coal mine in Polk County, and now the underground was like a block of Swiss cheese, dotted with old, abandoned mines. Hundreds, possibly thousands, of places to hide a body.

Dale continued moving the pencil over the paper, and soon it was filled with his meticulous sketches and labels.

His chest ached, the muscles tight with stress, and he

drew a long, deep breath to try to stretch them out. He should bump up his next appointment with Dr. Smith. Get a refill on those sleeping tabs she sometimes gave him.

A suit approached him. "Goodkind? I'm Agent Miller." One of the FBI agents from Omaha. "Got any nearby rap sheets for me?" He snapped a piece of gum in his mouth. Dale hated it when adults chewed gum. It made them look juvenile and unprofessional. He ignored the chomping and opened his sketchbook to the first page, squinting at his notes, now barely legible in the thickening darkness.

"Several guys with records in the neighborhood. Two for sexual assault, but they've already been interviewed, alibied, and cleared. We're still working on the pervert list."

Miller bit the gum between his front teeth. "Give me vehicles again."

"BOLO went out early for a car seen in the vicinity, but the witness descriptions are sketchy. One saw a light-blue two-door sedan, then another described a gray or silver Camaro. Possibly late seventies."

Miller handed him a sheet of paper. "Routes and names of paper carriers on the South Side. Start interviewing them first thing tomorrow. Newspaper is working closely with us on it. Fully cooperating."

"Thanks." Dale tucked it between two pages of his sketchbook. "I'll work on the van drivers for the drop-offs first thing in the morning."

"Good." Miller planted his hands on his hips and stopped chewing. "I hear you worked on the West Des Moines case two years ago."

Dale closed his sketchbook. "Yeah."

"So, what's your take on this one?"

Dale stared at Miller. "Honestly? We haven't got jack shit. Just like last time."

Miller looked sharply at him. "Then *find* something, goddammit," he muttered, and walked away.

Dale slapped his sketchbook against the side of his thigh. He shouldn't have said that. It wasn't helpful.

He dug his fingers into the back of his neck again. Two nearly identical cases, two different jurisdictions, and he'd been assigned both.

Impossible.

"Are you a cop?" a small voice called.

Dale turned around. A young boy straddled a red ten-speed bicycle on the corner across the street. He was heavyset, and the bike looked too big for him. He had to balance on his tiptoes.

"I am," Dale answered.

"Are you looking for the Stewart kid?" the boy asked.

"Yeah." Dale glanced around. "You know him?"

"No."

"Are you out here by yourself?"

"I live nearby." He jerked his head south. "That way." A dark stain streaked the front of his white T-shirt. *I'm a Pepper. He's a Pepper. She's a Pepper.* The jingle played in Dale's head.

"You should go home," he said. "You shouldn't be out here alone, especially after dark."

"You won't find him," the boy said.

"Who?"

"Chris Stewart. He's probably dead already. Like that Klein kid."

Dale crossed his arms and widened his stance. "Why would you say that?"

The boy looked away. "I just know." He looked back at Dale and pointed at his holster. "Is that your gun?"

Dale touched the hard pistol butt resting against his hip. "It is."

"Have you ever shot anyone?"

"No. Luckily, I haven't had to."

The boy bit his lip, considering Dale's answer. "Would you ever kill a bad guy? Like the guy who took Chris?"

Dale frowned. "What did you say your name was?"

He started to cross the street, but as soon as Dale stepped off the curb, the boy abruptly turned the bike around and began pedaling, his chubby legs pumping furious circles. Within seconds, he was coasting down the hill.

Dale stopped and watched, perplexed, until the boy made a left-hand turn onto a street near the bottom of the hill. He jotted down a note:

Heavyset boy on red bike, light brown hair
Age: Possibly 11? 12?
Lives south of Hillcrest. On Clark or Cutler?

He glanced back in the direction the boy had ridden. He needed to figure out where the kid lived and pay him a little visit as soon as possible.

FOUR

One day, fifty minutes missing

AWAKE BY SEVEN AM, Crystal studied a trio of college applications and brochures spread across her desk. She'd narrowed down her choices to two in-state journalism programs, Iowa State and the University of Iowa, but her first choice was the University of Miami. On a whim she'd toured the campus last summer while visiting her father and had fallen in love with everything about it, but especially their journalism department and student-run paper *The Miami Hurricane*. Ever since, she'd been dreaming of eventually working as an investigative journalist at a major newspaper in a big city, like the *Miami Herald*.

Crystal laid her hands over the application and felt a knot of anxiety twist deep in her gut. U of M was a private school, and out-of-state tuition was something like $5,000 a year. She looked up from the papers and sighed. Just above her desk on a low shelf was an unnerving row of porcelain dolls, gifts from her mother. Tina had ordered the collectibles from the Sunday flyers and given one to Crystal for three consecutive birthdays. So far, she'd received Dorothy from *The Wizard of Oz*, Scarlett O'Hara from *Gone With the Wind*, and Holly Golightly from *Breakfast at Tiffany's*. Their fixed expressions and creepy glass eyes stared back at Crystal.

On the floor next to her desk was the latest doll for Crystal's eighteenth birthday a few weeks ago: Princess Diana in her wedding gown, still in the box. It was Tina's prized purchase and had cost a fortune. Money that could've been saved to help Crystal with school. The dolls represented just how much her mother didn't understand her. Crystal switched on her clock radio, rolling the AM dial until she found a news report. She sipped lukewarm coffee from a chipped ceramic mug and read the headline of the *Register*:

```
MISSING PAPER CARRIER BELIEVED KIDNAPPED
   Boy, 13, disappears early Sunday. His
      partly folded papers left behind.
```

With a special magnifying glass for reading small print, she scrutinized a grainy photo of Christopher Stewart's shy smile on the front page, his dark, shaggy bangs falling over his brow. The caption beneath read *Christopher Thomas Stewart didn't talk to strangers*.

She opened a red spiral notebook and started taking notes—the Stewarts' home address just a few blocks from her own, Chris's timeline from yesterday morning, scant witness statements. The reward for any information was already up to $5,000.

She scrawled an idea for the scholarship: *Paperboys and Strangers: The Hidden Dangers of Kids Delivering Newspapers*.

Hadn't there been a couple of paperboys murdered in Omaha last year? She made a quick note to look it up. She vaguely remembered something about a military guy getting convicted last winter. Maybe there were more child-abduction cases in the Midwest. Or even nationwide.

Child Abductions: A Growing Epidemic.

This could be a good angle. She could write about the most high-profile cases and their effects on cities, do in-depth research. Research looked good. Maybe she could even interview local people about how these cases made them feel, whether it had changed their habits or routines. Crystal chewed on the top of her pen. She could walk to the mall this afternoon, talk to shoppers about the missing paperboys. The mall would be busy. Moms doing back-to-school shopping. She started a list of questions.

And she'd run the YJWA story idea by Mr. K when he came to tutor Sammy. He sometimes helped her with her writing. It was always a good conversation starter.

Crystal quickly made her bed and tucked her pajamas away in a bureau drawer. She always kept her room neat as a pin, with her books organized by subject and alphabetized, her clothes grouped and hanging in the closet according to season, and her bed made when she wasn't in it. She changed into a clean pair of shorts and a nice polo shirt and brushed out the tangles of her overgrown bob. She licked her index finger and pushed the hairs of her eyebrows upward because she'd once read in one of her mother's beauty magazines that brushing the eyebrows up gave the appearance of intelligence and maturity.

She wanted to start saving every article about the Stewart case, so she crossed the hall and silently entered Sammy's dim bedroom to get their mother's scissors, which Sammy was always taking on his route. As Sammy slept, she tiptoed through a stew of clothes, shoes, toys, candy wrappers, and partially assembled model cars spread out across the floor on newspapers. She lowered to her hands and knees and checked under the bed. More dirty clothes and trash, but also his canvas newspaper delivery bag. She slid the bag out and stuck her arm inside. Sure enough, her mother's scissors were in the bottom. But beneath the scissors, she felt another item and pulled it out.

A Polaroid picture.

She turned it over and squinted at the image.

It was of a boy from the waist up with his shirt off, striking a goofy pose, flexing his arm muscles and laughing at the camera. He looked to be about Sammy's age, skinny, with shaggy golden-brown hair. Crystal held the picture closer. She recognized the boy. His name was Corey Collier and he'd lived a few streets away near the library. Tina had worked at Haircrafters with Corey's mother until the Colliers moved. The picture had to be at least a few years old. Corey would be around sixteen now.

She didn't recognize the background of the photo— an unfinished room of some kind, with exposed wooden studs and plywood walls. Corey's basement or attic, maybe. Crystal hadn't realized Sammy had ever played at Corey's house. Probably where Sammy got his hands on a Polaroid camera. Their mother certainly couldn't afford one. The flash bars alone were $2.99 apiece.

Crystal returned the picture and shoved the bag under the bed where she'd found it, leaving Sammy undisturbed and still sleeping. Her mother banged around in the bathroom, getting ready for work, so Crystal went back to her bedroom and grabbed the two in-state college applications. She'd start with those. Ease her way into the conversation.

Crystal took a deep breath, knocked once, and opened the door. Tina stood in front of the small medicine cabinet mirror with a Capri super slim pursed between her lips as she crimped a section of her long hair in a smoldering iron. She took one last puff of the cigarette and tossed it into the toilet with a flush. When the tank kept running, Crystal entered and jiggled the handle several times to make it stop. She closed the lid and sat, the knot in her stomach pulling tighter.

"Can Sammy and I go to the mall today?" Crystal asked.

"Sure." Tina set the iron down and ratted her bangs with a comb, then sprayed them stiff with an aerosol can of hair spray. "But don't forget that Sammy has a tutoring session this morning."

"I know," she said. "We'll go this afternoon."

"What do you want to go to the mall for?"

"Um, just this school thing I'm working on. An article." Crystal dangled the applications between her knees.

"For your little newspaper deal?" Tina squirted a mist of knockoff designer perfume and grimaced as the droplets landed on her chest.

"Well, sort of. But also this other project. That's actually what I need to talk to you about. I've been think—"

"Shit!" Tina muttered. She leaned closer to the mirror and touched an infected bump just above her collarbone. Sometimes when she gave men haircuts, tiny pieces of hair landed on her chest and worked their way just beneath the surface of her skin, causing painful, pus-filled bumps, which Crystal found disgusting.

Tina grabbed a pair of tweezers and pulled the foreign sliver out. She fluffed her hair once more and moved to her bedroom to change, the conversation about Crystal's article already forgotten. Crystal felt like Tina treated her passion for journalism as if it were a cute hobby. She loved to tell the story of how Crystal, at age thirteen, wrote dozens of letters to then-president Jimmy Carter, criticizing his handling of the Iran hostage crisis, and how Carter wrote back, politely thanking her for the "advice." It was a battle to get her mother to see that she took journalism seriously.

Crystal reluctantly followed Tina into the bedroom, where she uncomfortably perched on the padded edge of the water bed, trying to muster the courage to broach the topic of college.

From her closet, Tina selected a black jean skirt, a hot-pink tank, and a black mesh top—the type of outfit all the younger stylists at the salon wore. It was hard to fathom that Tina had just turned eighteen when she'd gotten pregnant with Crystal, the same age Crystal was now. A shotgun wedding, divorced after fourteen mostly miserable years, working two jobs she hated and still struggling to pay the bills. For Crystal, her mother's life was a road map to a destination she never wanted to visit. It refueled her determination to forge a different future for herself.

She took a deep breath and started again. "Mom, I need to talk to you about something."

"Okay, I'm listening," Tina said, as she rummaged through her jewelry box on the bureau.

"I'm going to the mall today to work on a story that I'd like to submit to this scholarship. It's a big scholarship that could help me pay for college next year."

Tina slipped on a row of bracelets over her wrists

and frowned. "Chrissie, we already talked about this. There's no way we can afford to send you to school."

"I know. That's why I'm applying for this scholarship and some other things."

"There's no guarantee you'll get it. Then what?"

"But I can at least try, right? I have a really good story idea that involves these paperboy cases—"

"Crystal, this conversation is pointless." Tina jabbed a large white hoop earring through her lobe. "College is too expensive and out of the question. I can barely pay the bills I already have! You need to get a job after graduation. Learn a useful trade. Like doing hair. Peggy already said she'd give you a job at the salon even with your eye problems. Then you could just ride to work with me every day and you wouldn't have to worry about driving."

"Mom," Crystal said quietly, "I don't want to do hair. I want to be a journalist."

Tina searched the floor for her other black satin heel, kicking around discarded articles of clothing until she found it. "Well, I wanted to be an airline stewardess and travel the world, but life doesn't always work out the way we want it to, does it?" Tina sank into her rickety bamboo papasan chair and struggled to shove her swollen feet into the heels.

She rested her head in her hands for a moment and sighed. "God, I'm already tired."

The bedroom door pushed open and Mr. Tibbs darted inside, followed by a bleary-eyed Sammy wearing an old T-shirt and underwear, his arms awkwardly crossed over the front of his white briefs.

"I wet the bed again," he said quietly.

Tina stood. "It's okay, sweetie," she said, patting his

back. "You're drinking too much water before you go to bed. Chrissie will help get you cleaned up. I gotta get downstairs to make breakfast." She kissed the top of his head and hurried out of the room.

Crystal slowly folded the college applications in half, the paper heavy in her hands. So that's how it would be. Now she knew. She'd have to find a way to pay for college herself. Pell grants. Disability grants for her eye condition. Student loans. Work-study jobs, if she could find one that accommodated her poor eyesight. And scholarships like the YJWA. But she had to get accepted first. One problem at a time.

"Come on," Crystal said, and led Sammy back to his room.

He changed his clothes, and she stripped the soiled bedsheets. When he lifted the T-shirt over his head, she noticed that the line of red dots on his upper arm had turned to dark bruises. Sammy saw her staring and hastily slipped on a fresh T-shirt, covering the bruises.

"How'd you get those again?" she asked, as she pulled a clean fitted sheet over the edges of the mattress.

"Some boys," he said. "Horsing around. Giving me a hard time."

She scowled. "What boys?" Yesterday he'd said he'd bumped into a door.

"Just some boys from the neighborhood. I don't know their names."

"Why didn't you say that yester—"

"Can you just drop it? It's not a big deal. I'm fine." He grabbed an unfinished model car from the floor and stalked out of the room.

"What is your problem?" Crystal called after him, balling up the dirty sheets.

Downstairs in the kitchen, Tina was already whisking eggs in a bowl. Crystal opened the folding louvered doors of the laundry closet and put the sheets and clothes in the washing machine with a cup of detergent.

Sammy slumped in a swivel chair at the table and stuck a racing-stripe decal on a door. He was always bringing home some model kit to put together in his room, stinking the house up so bad with the glue it nearly made Crystal high from the fumes. He seemed to spend his paper route money faster than he made it.

"How about scrambled today?" Tina asked. "I have just enough time."

"I'm not hungry," Crystal said. Sammy silently bobbed his head.

As Tina poured the eggs into a skillet, a knock rattled the screen.

"Now what," she muttered.

Crystal hurried to answer the door, assuming it was Mr. K for Sammy's tutoring session. Instead, a broad-shouldered man with a dark moustache waited on the stoop.

"Can I help you?" Crystal asked.

"Sorry to bother you," he said. "My name is Sergeant Dale Goodkind, and I'm with the Des Moines PD." He brushed his jacket aside to show a silver badge clipped to his belt, and Crystal squinted at the letters. She recognized his name from the newspaper article this morning.

"I need to speak with Sammy Cox," he said. "Is your mother here?"

Tina moved behind Crystal. "Yes, I'm Tina Cox."

"I need to speak with Sammy about his Sunday paper route."

"I'm sorry," she said, "but I only have about ten minutes before I have to be at work."

"It won't take long."

Tina glanced at her fake-gold watch. "Um, sure." She pushed the screen open for him to enter. Mr. Tibbs hissed and sprinted from the room. "Is this about the Stewart boy?"

"Yes," Goodkind said. "We're interviewing all the delivery boys in the neighborhood."

Tina scooped the eggs onto plates and handed them to Sammy.

"That's Sammy, and my daughter, Crystal."

Goodkind squeezed his long legs beneath the small table and Crystal moved to the chair next to him, her interest piqued. She would've loved to get a closer look at his badge, and wondered if he carried a gun on his other hip.

"So, Sammy Cox," Goodkind said. "We meet again."

Sammy eyed him warily, cutting his eggs into small, precise pieces.

"Have you two met before?" Tina asked.

"Sammy and I kind of met yesterday evening. While I was working the scene. One of the other paperboys gave me his name and address."

"I see," Tina answered, but Crystal could tell she was barely listening as she filled the sink with soapy water.

Crystal's eyes pinballed among the three as they spoke.

"Do you play any sports, Sammy?" Goodkind asked.

"No," Sammy answered quickly.

"Yes, you do," Tina said. "He plays baseball with a neighborhood rec league."

"Oh, yeah? My boy loves baseball."

"I *hate* baseball," Sammy said. "It's stupid."

Tina propped her hands on her hips. "What is your deal today?" She helplessly shrugged at Goodkind.

"It's fine," he said. "Sammy, I just need to ask you a few questions about your paper route. Would that be all right?"

"Whatever," Sammy answered.

Goodkind removed a pen from his front breast pocket and opened a large notepad. Crystal discreetly rolled her chair closer to see what he wrote down. At the top of the page she read, *Samuel Cox, age 12, Cutler Ave. (Boy at crime scene w/ questions.)*

Boy at crime scene with questions? Crystal glanced at Sammy, curious as to why he'd been at the crime scene last night and what exactly he'd asked the cop.

Goodkind unfolded a map and traced a line around the neighborhoods of Sammy's route. Crystal tried to study the upside-down pencil markings.

"I spoke with your route manager last night, and he said you cover these streets over by the library, not far from Christopher Stewart's route."

Sammy looked at the map and nodded.

"Did you walk your route yesterday morning by yourself?"

"Yeah. I always deliver by myself."

"Did you see anything unusual? Hear anything unusual?"

"No."

"See any strangers out and about? Anyone you've never seen before that early in the morning? Anyone acting funny in any way?"

Sammy pushed his plate away after eating only half his eggs. He seemed to hesitate before answering. "No."

Goodkind leaned his elbows on the table. "Did you know Christopher Stewart?" he asked. "When I saw you at the corner yesterday, you said something peculiar about him."

Tina was busy wiping down the counters and hadn't heard Goodkind's comment, but now Crystal was dying to ask what the "peculiar" thing was that Sammy had said to a cop about a missing boy. Though she didn't dare interrupt.

Sammy stared at Goodkind for a long moment, unblinking. "I told you, I don't know him." He laid his head down in the crook of his arm and rolled his model car back and forth on the table.

Goodkind watched him closely. Crystal held her breath, waiting for his next question.

"Sammy," he said slowly, "yesterday morning a woman on your route saw you running down Clark Avenue, toward Tenth Street. Not far from where Christopher Stewart was last seen."

Sammy kept rolling the car. Tina banged the skillet around in the sink as she rinsed it out.

"The woman thought it looked like you might be running from something," Goodkind pressed. "Or someone. Why were you running?"

Sammy stopped the rolling and lifted his head. "A dog was chasing me," he said.

Crystal looked sharply at Sammy, but he kept his gaze on the car. This was the third version of yesterday morning she'd now heard. Why all the lying?

Just as Crystal opened her mouth to call out his changing story, there was another knock at the door. Tina dried her hands on a towel and opened the screen.

"Hi, Mr. Kovacs," she said. "Come on in."

"Good morning." Mr. K entered, carrying a fat math workbook. He smiled warmly at Tina.

"We're a popular place today," she said. "Sebastian Kovacs, this is Officer Dale Goodkind. He's here asking questions about the missing paperboy."

The smile on Mr. K's face dissolved when he saw Goodkind at the table. He clutched the math book tighter to his chest, keeping his gaze locked firmly on the floor.

"Nice to meet you," he finally said.

"Mr. Kovacs is Sammy's math tutor," Tina said to Goodkind. "Someone struggles with long division." She gave Sammy a stern side-eye.

Sammy abruptly stood. "Because I hate math, too!" he shouted, and went into the living room.

"Sammy!" Tina said. "You're being really rude today. I'm sorry."

"It's fine," Mr. K said, and hurried after Sammy.

Tina leaned against the counter and rubbed her forehead. "I hope you were done," she said to Goodkind, lowering her voice. "He's had a really hard year. He flunked several classes last year. That's why I hired Mr. Kovacs to tutor him a few times a week."

"I see." Goodkind also spoke more quietly. "Does he always tutor Sammy here?"

"Yes. Occasionally Sammy goes to his house. He also gives piano lessons to kids in the neighborhood."

"How do you spell his last name?"

"*K-o-v-a-c-s*," Tina answered.

Goodkind wrote it down. "Married?"

"No. He lives alone."

"Where?"

"Southlawn Drive."

Goodkind glanced over his shoulder toward the living room. "Is he Russian or something?" He lowered his voice to match Tina's. "The accent...the dark skin?"

"Mr. Kovacs is Hungarian," Crystal said, irritated by the cop's nosy questions about him. "He's of the Roma people. They're sometimes called gypsies in Europe, but that's a derogatory term. He's very smart. He was a professor when he lived in Budapest. He's also really into bird-watching. He walks the neighborhood every morning."

Goodkind swiveled his chair toward her, as if noticing her for the first time. "How do you know all this?"

Crystal's cheeks flushed. She didn't know why she'd just blabbed so much personal information about Mr. K. "I—I interviewed him for the school paper last year. And he proofreads my writing for me sometimes."

"He's really good with kids," Tina said. "Though you wouldn't know it by how Sammy's been acting toward him lately."

"Interesting. He walks the neighborhood every morning, you say?" Goodkind looked over his shoulder again and stared at Mr. K with an intensity that made Crystal inexplicably nervous.

This time she kept her mouth shut and looked down at Sammy's unfinished eggs, now cold and rubbery. Her stomach soured.

Crystal read Goodkind's final note over his shoulder: *Background check on Sebastian Kovacs, tutor, Southlawn Dr.*

FIVE

One day, seven hours missing

THAT AFTERNOON AT Southridge Mall, Crystal planted
herself in front of Montgomery Ward with her red notebook and pen in hand and a memorized list of questions.
Sammy sat on a nearby bench, playing with a blob of
gray Silly Putty he'd bought at a toy store after getting
some tip money from Tina at the salon next door. Crystal approached only the shoppers who smiled and made
eye contact and found that mentioning _school newspa-
per_ seemed to be the golden ticket to getting people to
stop and chat. The mothers were the most forthcoming,
anxious to talk about how they weren't going to let their
kids play outside unattended or allow them to walk to
school alone anymore.

By two o'clock, she had a dozen pages of material
and decided it was enough. She treated Sammy to a
basket of waffle fries, a cheeseburger, and a Coke from
the food court. They ate in silence, watching the mall
carousel turn slow circles at the periphery of the tables
and chairs.

Crystal sipped the Coke and watched her brother
devour his burger. The marks on his arm peeked out
below his sleeve.

"You lied to that cop about a dog chasing you yesterday morning," she said.

Sammy bit off the end of a fry and looked away.

"Why do you keep telling different stories?"

"I don't want to talk about it."

"About what? A group of boys picking on you?"

Silence.

"Who is it? Other paperboys? You should tell me."

Sammy stopped chewing. His eyelids fluttered and turned red-rimmed. For a moment, Crystal thought he was going to start crying.

"I don't want to talk about it," he repeated.

"Just tell me *why* they're giving you a hard time."

He sighed. "Maybe because I'm fat. I don't know. Just drop it, Chrissie. It's not a big deal."

Crystal balled up her napkin and tossed it onto the table. He was still lying, but it was clear she wasn't going to get the truth out of him today. She'd keep working on him. Sammy never kept secrets from her for long.

"Maybe Mom will finally let me quit the paper route because of what happened to Chris Stewart," he said.

"I doubt it."

"Why not?"

"She's convinced it's good for you and teaches you responsibility."

He smashed a fry with his thumb, pushing the mushy innards out of the crispy sides. "It's not good for me."

Crystal leaned forward and laid her hand on his. "I'll start going with you."

Sammy perked up. "Really? You promise?"

"Yeah, I promise."

Sammy smiled for the first time since yesterday morning and ate another fry.

Crystal crossed her arms and looked around the food court, trying not to notice a group of girls from her grade eating and talking at a nearby table. She'd recognized several kids from her high school hanging out, but they hadn't given her a second glance, especially the boys. Not that Crystal cared. They were incredibly immature and stupid compared to Mr. K. Crystal told herself she was ignored by boys her age because she was so studious, not because of her eye condition and thick glasses, or her plain hair and cheap clothes. Her friend Somphone had once told her that high school wasn't meant to be experienced but instead merely survived.

At the mall entrance, a group of people gathered on the sidewalk handing out flyers. Curious about what they were doing, Crystal tucked her notebook and pen into her bag.

"Let's go," she said.

"I'm not done with my soda."

"Take it with you."

Sammy grabbed the cup before she emptied his tray into the trash.

Outside in the blinding sunlight, Crystal approached a woman in the center of the group wearing slacks and hiking boots and tapped her on the shoulder.

"Excuse me," she said.

The woman whipped around. She wore a silver whistle around her neck and held a stack of papers in her hands. "Yes?"

"What are you all doing?"

"Organizing a search party for Christopher Stewart." The woman handed Crystal a map and flyer with Christopher's picture on it. "We've targeted a list of nearby parks and woods and created search grids."

Crystal immediately liked how the woman talked.

Search grids. She sounded official. And taking part in a search party. Another great angle for a story.

"Can we help?" Crystal asked. "We live on the South Side and know this area well. I'm eighteen."

"Sure," the woman said. "We need all the help we can get."

"Chrissie," Sammy whined, "I don't want to. It's too hot."

"I don't care," she hissed in his car.

The woman handed Crystal a black plastic whistle and pointed at a nearby group. "You can go with them," she said. "They're searching the Fort Des Moines Park."

"Okay."

"Stay close together, go slow, and take small steps," the woman continued. "If you see something that might be evidence, just blow your whistle until the group leader can come and mark the item with a flag. We're looking for any kind of clothing, large garbage bags, boxes, weapons, or areas of disturbed dirt."

Crystal couldn't wait to write all of this down as soon as she had a chance.

She and Sammy melded into the group and set out on Army Post Road.

Once they entered the park, the group headed to the west side of the pond, but Crystal veered onto a trail around the east side. She knew the park well, as their father used to take them fishing there. She wanted to search on her own. That way, any discoveries of evidence would be all hers. The east side seemed more promising anyway, since it was more remote.

Crystal showed Sammy the flyer with the description of Chris's clothes, then explained the other items they should be on the lookout for. She picked up two sturdy sticks to part the tall grass as they walked.

"Scan the ground as far as you can from left to right and back again so that you don't step on anything important. And go slow. Take small steps."

"I *know*, Chrissie," Sammy said. "I heard the lady."

Together, they started walking, slowly, swishing their sticks through the weeds in front of them.

After barely an hour of searching, Sammy started complaining. It was hot. He was thirsty. The bugs were biting him. The weeds were cutting his legs. Despite shushing him, Crystal was growing discouraged herself. So far, they'd found only empty soda cans, a car tire, and a squirrel carcass, and it was straining her eyes so much it was starting to give her a headache.

Sammy's whining eventually forced them to stop in the shade to rest.

Crystal removed her backpack and lay back in the grass, staring up at the branches above her. Sammy flopped next to her and stretched out his legs. The air was hot and thick, like soup. Voices from the rest of their search group echoed across the surface of the pond.

Crystal plucked a deer tick off her shin and pinched it between her fingernails.

"Chrissie?" Sammy asked.

"Yeah?"

"What do you think the kidnapper wants with Christopher Stewart?"

"What do you mean?"

Sammy scratched the crest of his belly and adjusted his legs. "I mean, why did he take him? What's he going to do with him?"

Crystal narrowed her eyes at the sky. She'd thought a lot about this when Matt Klein was kidnapped.

"It could be a number of reasons," she said. "Maybe it's a crazed psycho killer who took him. Or someone wanting money. Sometimes people are kidnapped and held for ransom, like the Lindbergh baby." She remembered reading a comic book like that once, with a picture of a little kid chained to the wall in a basement by a madman demanding a million dollars from the mayor of the city. "But that's unlikely, 'cause the Stewarts aren't rich."

Sammy stayed silent.

"Or maybe it's some crazy dad whose son died, and he took Chris to replace him," Crystal said, half joking. "That happened to Laura on an episode of *Little House on the Prairie*." She shaded her eyes and looked at him. "What do you think the kidnapper wants with him?"

He lowered his hand to let an orange beetle crawl up his arm. "I think he wants him for something else."

"Like what?"

"Just…something else."

Crystal laid her head back. "We'll rest for five more minutes and then get back to work."

Sammy was quiet for a moment. He slid his house keys back and forth along the string around his neck.

"Chrissie?"

"Yeah."

"Where do pickles come from?"

"What?"

"What are pickles made of?"

Crystal opened one eye. "Cucumbers, dummy!"

"Really?"

She laughed. "Yes. They're little cucumbers put in jars of vinegar. Everybody knows that."

She shaded her eyes again. From the expression on his face, she knew she'd hurt his feelings, and she felt bad.

"I didn't mean that you're stupid, Sammy. I only meant that you should know this by now. You're twelve."

Sammy gently brushed the beetle back into the grass and stood. "I know a lot more about the world than you think I do." He walked to a tree several feet away and struggled onto a low-hanging branch. There he sat with his back to her, a punishment.

Crystal closed her eyes. She'd let him have his sulk for three more minutes.

"What are you doing out here?"

Crystal's eyelids snapped open.

A man in cutoff shorts and a plain white tank top cast a long shadow over her. Crystal sat up and adjusted her glasses.

"Huh?" she said.

"What are you doing?" he repeated. He wore a black whistle around his neck identical to hers.

"I'm in the search party," she said, and lifted her own whistle as proof.

"I see that." The man smiled and planted a hand on his hip. "I've seen you before." His mouth slowly stretched into a grin, and he snapped his fingers. "You're Tina Cox's kid. I seen you at your house once. Last year, when I helped your mom with her furnace."

Recognition sparked in her as well. The feathered hair. The lopsided smile.

"You got them weird cat eyes." He pointed at her face. "My name's Kenny Harris. I coach your brother on my baseball team." He held out his hand, and Crystal limply shook it.

Now she remembered him.

Tina had briefly dated Kenny last year. He did something with heating and cooling because he'd fixed their furnace for free, like he said, when it quit during a cold snap.

"How's your mom doing?" he asked.

"Fine," Crystal said unenthusiastically.

During their brief, one-time meeting, Crystal had found Kenny annoying. He'd bragged about his glory days as the star pitcher on his high school baseball team and said cringey things like "Righto!" with a thumbs-up. She vaguely recalled her mother only casually going out with him for a few months before breaking it off, lamenting to Crystal that he was really nice and had a great job, but there was zero chemistry. Tina had remained friendly with him, though, because he'd let Sammy play in the recreational baseball league his company sponsored and he'd gotten Sammy the paper route job. He apparently had some pull around town, and Tina was thrilled about any positive male influences in Sammy's life after their father left.

"I'm helping with the search, too," Kenny continued. "Haven't found anything, though. Real shame about that Stewart kid."

"Yeah." Crystal blew a flyaway strand of hair from her face.

"You shouldn't wander around by yourself. It ain't safe."

Crystal stood and brushed off the back of her shorts. "I should get home," she said.

"Okay, then," he said. "'Bye now."

Kenny followed the trail to the other side of the pond, and Crystal waited until she was sure he was gone. She walked to the tree to tell Sammy they were leaving, but the branch was empty, and Sammy was nowhere in sight.

SIX

One day, eleven hours missing

SAMMY LOWERED HIMSELF into the bathtub. The scratches on his arms and legs burned the instant they contacted the scalding water. A mosquito bite swelled angrily on the backside of his knee.

He was filthy from walking around the park, the bathwater already turning dull gray. He searched the ledge of the tub but found no bar of soap. He stepped out of the tub, dripping water across the bathroom floor, and got the bar of soap himself from the cabinet beneath the sink, then jumped back into the tub and made sure to create an extra splash.

Sammy rolled onto his belly and plunged his face beneath the surface, counting the heartbeats pulsing in his eardrums, *one, two, three*, fighting to overcome the urge to lift his head. *Four, five, six.* He struggled against the growing discomfort and ache in his lungs. Every inch of his body screamed for a breath. *Thirteen, fourteen, fifteen.* If he could just open his mouth and inhale the water, it would be over quickly.

He popped back up and gasped, gulping delicious, soothing mouthfuls of air.

Failure, again. He always wimped out.

He rolled onto his back and tried to float in the cramped tub. He loved the sensation of floating, of being weightless and unattached to anything physical. When he floated, his mind went to a nowhere place where nothing was good, and nothing was bad. Sometimes he could re-create this nowhere, floating sensation when he needed it, like during school, or on the paper route. He could trick his mind into not thinking about bad stuff and instead just think about floating in the nowhere place.

The thought of a new school year beginning in a few weeks was like a boulder sitting on his chest. He hated school so much. He hated the teachers, he hated the classes, and he hated all the other kids. When everything went wrong last year, and he gained weight and missed day after day staying home sick and nearly flunked sixth grade, he'd become the fat, dumb kid overnight. The kid with cooties. Untouchable. If a girl accidentally brushed up against him, she would smack the person closest to her and cry, *Sammy's germs! Not it!*

Sammy sat up and touched the tender bruises dotting his arm. He placed four fingertips over the line of purple circles, like the holes on a flute.

Sammy grabbed the new bar of Irish Spring, lathered it inside a frayed washrag, and began to scrub. Feet, legs and arms, belly, face, and neck. Last, he scrubbed his privates, his eyes clenched shut, scrubbing hard enough to tear skin away onto the terry cloth. When he finally opened his eyes, he expected the bathwater to be tinged pink with blood. But it was still dingy gray. Dirty.

He set the Irish Spring in the little soap nook and spread the rag atop the water, where it floated for a moment, then disappeared beneath the surface. He draped his arms over the cool porcelain sides of the tub and rested his chin on the ledge. The bathroom mirror was already completely fogged over from the steam.

His soiled clothes lay in a pile on the floor at his fingertips. From the back pocket of his shorts he removed the folded flyer and map that Crystal had picked up at the mall. Mindful of his wet fingers, he carefully opened the paper by the corners. On the backside of the map was a picture of Chris.

Chris Stewart was a *handsome boy*, a phrase Sammy's mother liked to use. He had nice brown eyes and hair. Were these the things the kidnapper liked about him? Chris's eyes, or his hair? Or maybe he'd done something else that made the kidnapper notice him, like him, *choose* him from among other boys.

Sammy thought about Crystal's crazed psycho killer theory.

He held Chris's face closer to his own, staring into the brown eyes.

A crazed psycho killer hadn't taken Chris. Or Matt. Sammy was too stupid to know about pickles, but he knew plenty of other things.

He dropped the paper to the floor and rooted around in the other pocket. There he found the gift Mr. K had given him this morning during their tutoring session, when no one else was around.

I'm sorry you're angry with me, he'd said. *I want to make it up to you.* In his hand he'd held out a small cloth pouch he called a *bujo*, a medicine bag. *I made it special for you.*

He'd said the Roma believed *Mamioro*, their little grandmother spirit, brought disease and fed on filth, but that she left behind powerful *johai*, ghost vomit, that could heal ills when mixed with flour and special herbs and baked into hard pieces.

Put it in your pocket to help protect you.

Sammy sniffed the *bujo*. It smelled strange. Both spicy and rotten. Even though he was still upset with Mr. K, he would put it in his newspaper bag. He needed all the help he could get.

Sammy got out of the tub and wrapped a towel around his waist like his father used to. He wiped the condensation off the mirror above the sink with a tissue and combed his hair carefully, making a deep part on the left side, and swept it forward across his brow, like Chris's hair in the picture. Maybe he would let his hair grow a little longer. He turned his face from side to side. His cheeks were fatter than Chris's. But so far, being fat hadn't kept him safe.

The bathroom door flung open and hit Sammy.

"Hey!" he shouted, cradling his shoulder.

"Where were you?" Crystal yelled. Tiny hairs around her face curled from sweat, and her large glasses had slipped down her nose.

"I walked home," Sammy said.

"You didn't *tell* me you were going home!" She punched him on the arm, square in the line of bruises.

"Ow! Stop it!"

She crossed her trembling arms as tears filled her eyes. "I couldn't find you, and it scared me."

Self-conscious of his exposed belly and the patches of skin he'd rubbed raw in the tub, he picked up his shirt from the floor and held it in front of himself.

"Why did you leave like that?" she asked, her quiet voice sounding so much like their mother he sometimes couldn't tell them apart.

Sammy slipped the T-shirt over his head and grabbed his shorts. "I just didn't want to be there anymore," he said.

Crystal blocked the door, studying his face. He waited nervously for her to challenge his answer.

"You just should've told me," she finally said.

"I'm sorry."

She gently touched a fingertip to a particularly raw patch of skin on the side of his neck. "Stop scrubbing so hard," she said. "I keep telling you."

"I know." Sammy left the bathroom before she noticed him blinking back tears.

In his bedroom, he changed into a fresh pair of cotton pajamas, even though it was hot and he wouldn't go to bed for several more hours. He just wanted to wear pajamas. Pajamas made him feel better.

He sat on the floor and resumed working on his latest model. A 1968 GT500 Shelby Mustang, dark green with orange-and-yellow stripe work. The top of his bureau was crowded with car models he'd assembled. Sammy's favorite was a bright-yellow 1957 Chevy Bel Air sport coupe with orange flames across the doors.

He was nearly finished with the Mustang. He glued on the chrome side mirrors and set the model aside to let it dry.

Sammy retrieved the soppy flyer and the *bujo* and stepped into his closet. He closed the bifold doors, shutting himself inside with his smelly shoes and toys he didn't play with anymore. From the top shelf, he removed a small cardboard box and sat on the floor. He opened the flaps and rummaged through the contents by the light coming through the door slats: his hidden stash of candy bars. He started with a package of Reese's Peanut Butter Cups, then a Hershey bar, then two Kit Kats, and finished with two more Hershey bars, even though his stomach now hurt.

Sammy studied Chris's picture on the flyer once more.

Did he try to run? Fight?

He refolded the paper and tucked it inside the box beneath the empty candy wrappers. He dug deeper into the box and removed a set of brand-new walkie-talkies. Expensive ones. A special gift. He hadn't used them yet because he didn't have a friend to give the other one to. He put them back where his mother wouldn't find them and ask questions, and closed the flaps.

Remember, the dead don't talk.

Sammy could recite the words in his sleep, he'd been warned so many times.

Chris Stewart was never coming home, like he'd told that cop with the funny name.

If he'd been faster, he would've been able to get away *every* Sunday morning. If he'd been tougher, he would've had something better to carry than a dumb pair of his mother's scissors. If he'd been smarter, he would've known that wolves can hide in sheep's clothing, and none of this would even have started.

At least Crystal had said she would go with him from now on. Sundays would be safe again.

Maybe Mr. K's magic medicine bag was working after all.

SEVEN

Five days, nine hours missing

"TELL ME HOW you've been sleeping the last few days," Dr. Smith said.

Dale removed his sports coat and tugged at the knot in his tie to get a little air to the damp skin around his neck.

"Um, not great," he answered. "But I've been working long hours because of the new case."

She scratched her pen across a notepad on her lap. She wore her long, white hair in a loose bun held haphazardly in place with what appeared to be two chopsticks. Pull out one of the sticks, Dale sometimes imagined, and it would tumble down like a river of spilled milk.

Dr. Jane Smith. Her name was so commonplace it sounded like an alias. Even her office was commonplace. A nondescript brick building a few blocks away from the university campus. No sign denoting her services. Just her name on a small placard next to the door: *Dr. Jane Smith, D.O.* He'd found her name buried in the yellow pages of the phone book.

Her office was forty-five minutes north of Des Moines, in Ames, where Dale was unlikely to run into anyone he knew. If the lieutenant or other officers found out he was seeing a shrink, it would spell trouble for his job. Alcoholics were fine. Wife beaters even got second chances after guys in the department worked them over. But head cases? No hall pass.

"Any new blackout incidents since our last visit?" Dr. Smith asked.

A hot flush migrated up Dale's neck and into his cheeks. The blackouts were embarrassing. More embarrassing than hearing the words *clinical depression* and *medication*, which made him feel like a bored housewife. Even though nothing he said or did ever seemed to faze Dr. Smith, he felt humiliated by it all. He didn't know a single person who saw a shrink or took medication for mental problems.

"No blackouts since the last one at Christmas," Dale said.

"That's good," she said.

He'd told Connie the blackouts were from high blood pressure, and she'd taken him at his word without question. Cut his salt and caffeine intake. Put a banana in his lunch every day. He hadn't been able to tell her the truth yet.

The blackouts were hard to explain, anyway. He would go into a state where he felt disconnected from his body, like he'd stepped outside his own skin and was standing next to it, watching himself. Then a dark curtain would lower and he'd slip into a void. When he came out of it, sweating and disoriented, he'd have no idea how much time had passed or what he'd done. The first one had happened nine months into the Matt Klein case while he was interviewing another paperboy who'd seen a car speeding away from the neighborhood.

Dr. Smith set her pen down, her signal that she was about to say something big. "I think it would be a good idea if we increased the dosage of your Ludiomil by twenty-five milligrams. That would put you at one fifty."

"Why?" Dale asked.

She clasped her hands. "I know you can't talk about specific details of your work, but you mentioned that this new case is similar to the previous case. And we already know that case was a great source of stress for you. You're sleep deprived and clearly experiencing feelings of anxiety. So"—she tapped her index finger on her knuckles—"increasing the dosage now will be proactive. Preventative."

Dale briefly considered her argument but knew she was right. Between the medication and the talk sessions, he'd gotten better in the last few months. He didn't want to lose all the progress he'd made.

"All right," he said.

"Good." She picked up her pen and prescription pad and started writing again.

Still. More medication seemed like a step backward.

He scanned the bookshelves behind her, crowded with medical journals and encyclopedias. It amused him that discreetly tucked in one corner was a collection of Stephen King novels with titles like *Night Shift* and *Pet Sematary*. Rather ironic in a shrink's office treating people with mental problems. He couldn't imagine Connie even touching books with titles like that. She read women's magazines only for the recipes and decorating ideas. Dale himself didn't like to read anything. Too hard to sit still and focus.

"Now," Dr. Smith said as she finished writing, "remember to watch for side effects while your body adjusts to the new dose. Dizziness, dry mouth, nausea."

She tore the prescription from the pad and handed it to him. "And call me immediately if you experience any confusion, unusual thoughts, or hallucinations. Or if you have another blackout."

He took the paper and slid it inside his coat pocket. "You mean, call if I start acting crazier than I already am."

Neither of them laughed.

DALE ARRIVED HOME just in time for dinner. Connie was mashing a pot of potatoes to go along with baked pork chops, and Curtis was setting the table. A tiny breeze from the open window over the sink cooled the small kitchen.

"You're late," Connie said. "I wasn't sure if you were eating with us or not. You didn't call."

Dale kissed her cheek. "Yeah, I had a…last-minute interview to finish up before I could come home."

"You missed my baseball practice again," Curtis said, twisting a cloth napkin between his hands.

"I know, little man, I'm sorry. Big new case. You know how it goes." He ruffled Curtis's dark, wavy hair, identical to his own.

"You still need to eat and sleep," Connie said.

Dale laid his coat on the back of a chair and sat at the table, resting his elbows on either side of his empty plate. He was tired enough to fall asleep sitting up. He'd barely slept but for a few hours on a lumpy couch in the office before he'd had to get up at dawn to ride on the backs of garbage trucks around dozens of neighborhoods, digging through trash cans full of rotten food, dirty diapers, old newspapers, broken bottles, and crushed soda cans for any potential evidence. At one point he'd opened a bag full of rancid chicken meat crawling with maggots, and he'd gagged so hard he'd dry-heaved. And after four hours of searching thousands of cans, nothing.

Connie dropped a spoonful of potatoes onto Dale's plate. "Curtis and I are going school supply shopping tomorrow, so I'll need the checkbook."

"It's in the top drawer of my nightstand."

"I have to get a protractor this year," Curtis said. He perched on the chair next to Dale.

"Is that so?" Dale said. "I liked geometry."

"I hate math," Curtis said. "It's so hard."

Just as Dale started to answer, the wall telephone rang. Connie set the potatoes down and picked up the receiver.

Dale nudged Curtis's arm as Connie talked in the background. "If math gets tough again this year, I'll help you. I promise."

Curtis propped his chin in his hand and picked at the vinyl tablecloth. His small face was dotted with summertime freckles. "You'll be too busy with this case. I just know it."

"Dale," Connie cut in. "It's Chief Hagen."

She held out the black receiver and stretched the curly cord across the room to his chair.

"Yeah, Chief," Dale said.

Connie crossed her arms over her chest, waiting.

The conversation was quick. A tip had just come in on the hotline about a cornfield between north Des Moines and the little bedroom community of Ankeny. The team needed to gear up for another search. A woman, a psychic, insisted that Chris Stewart was lying injured in this particular field. She was having *vi-*

sions. She could *see* him. And since Chief Hagen took tips from psychics seriously, he wanted the team reassembled immediately.

Dale stood and hung up the phone.

"Let me guess," Connie said. "You have to go back to work." Irritation dripped from her voice.

"I'm sorry," Dale said, slipping his coat back on. He wasn't happy about it either. Tips from psychics were ridiculous. They never amounted to anything. The search would be a waste of time.

"I'll be back before you know it," he said.

"No, you won't." She turned to the stove and stirred the gravy. "You said you wouldn't get like this again after the last time."

Dale stopped. "Connie, this is my job. And it won't be like last time, I promise."

"We'll see."

He couldn't blame her for being angry. Cops' wives weren't saints, after all. They were just women who wanted to eat dinner with their husbands every night.

"Did someone find Christopher Stewart?" Curtis asked. "Do you have to chase a suspect? Will it be dangerous?" He twisted the napkin again.

"It's just a search, little man. Nothing serious."

Curtis became fretful when Dale worked the long, early days of a case, and Dale, in turn, worried about his son. Curtis was already an anxious kid without the added stress of his father putting in twenty-hour days on a case that had terrified an entire city.

Dale probably didn't do enough to ease Curtis's anxiety, because Dale himself was paranoid and overly cautious. The families of cops could be easy targets for any crackpot. He'd never allowed their home address and telephone number to be listed in the phone book, they never took family pictures for the church directory anymore, and Dale made Curtis tell his friends his father "worked for the city"—a protectively vague description—instead of telling them he was a cop. And after working on the high-profile Klein case, Dale had insisted that both Connie and Curtis start going by Connie's maiden name, Fuller, to further protect their identities. *Goodkind* was too distinct and easy to track down. Connie had thought Dale's request was crazy and they'd argued for weeks about it, but he'd finally worn her down and she'd registered Curtis at his new middle school as *Curtis Fuller* a few weeks ago.

Dale shoveled three bites of the potatoes into his mouth, grabbed a warm roll from a basket on the counter, and left without saying anything further to Connie. It was best to just let her be.

Thirty minutes later, he arrived at the outskirts of Ankeny as dusk settled. Starting at the north edge of the field, each team member walked the rows of eight-foot cornstalks with flashlights. Every patch of disturbed dirt, every depression in the ground, every broken stalk had to be examined.

Hours passed into inky darkness. In his rush, Dale hadn't thought to dress for hiking through a cornfield on a humid August night. His black wing tips were caked with dust and had rubbed blisters on the backs of his heels. He'd abandoned his tie and sports jacket and rolled up the sleeves of his dirty, sweat-stained shirt.

In the middle of a row, he bent over and rested his hands on his knees, feeling unsteady. How many fields had he searched during the Klein case? At least a dozen. He'd lost count.

The cases were an endless echo of each other.

Dale straightened and thrashed at a cornstalk with his flashlight. The razor-sharp edge of a leaf cut his cheek, and he winced.

He should've told Hagen on the phone that tips from psychics were a waste of time. They'd gotten hundreds of them during the Klein case, all worthless. But Dale hadn't been raised to talk back. He knew how to take orders. He'd been obedient his entire life. A good kid who rarely got into trouble. A soldier, and then a cop. His mother used to say he was such an obedient child that he'd been born on his due date.

Too obedient.

If only his mother had known.

Chief Hagen's voice crackled over the radio clipped to Dale's belt. He was suspending the search until sunrise.

Dale emerged from a row and stood in a dirt clearing. He mopped his forehead with a handkerchief and checked his watch. Four am. He now hadn't slept in nearly twenty-four hours.

He walked to his Cutlass, parked at the edge of the field. Agent Miller was sleeping in the back seat, snoring softly.

Dale opened the driver's door and slid onto the gritty maroon vinyl seat. Miller smelled like a dirty sock. Dale leaned his head back and closed his eyes, but they somehow snapped back open after only a few seconds. He tried again. Same result. Too tired to sleep. Connie used to say that about Curtis when he was a toddler.

Dale removed his sketchbook from the glove box and

opened it to a new page of notes from his last interview
with Bud and Cindy Stewart.

- *Small for his age but a responsible kid, no problems with anyone in the neighborhood.*
- *Youngest of two children. Close with his older
  brother, Dennis Jr., age 20.*
- *Several good friends from school. Likes baseball and plays Little League. Favorite subject
  is history.*
- *Turned thirteen last month and insisted on doing
  the route by himself.*
- *Saving up route money for the Iowa State Fair.*
- *Loves riding the sky glider and Ye Old Mill.*
- *Has a slight lisp and it makes him shy, not likely
  to talk to strangers?*

Over time, Dale would get to know the Stewart family better than his own parents and siblings. That was
how it had gone with the Kleins. With the Kleins, he'd
learned intimate details about their marriage and family, their jobs, their routines, daily habits and chores,
their vacations, bank accounts and bounced checks,
even fights over money and in-laws. He knew the layout of their home and street, which direction they drove
to church, which direction they drove Matt and his
younger sister to school. He'd gotten to know grandparents, aunts and uncles and cousins, pastors, former
babysitters, close family friends, and even Matt's be-
loved dog Lucy, who would sit on Dale's lap anytime
he came to the house.

As for Matt himself, he'd learned the names of every

one of the boy's friends and playmates, every place they liked to hang out, the games they liked to play. He'd learned Matt's likes and dislikes (chocolate ice cream, bratwurst), his fears (big dogs and deep water), his illnesses (scarlet fever as a toddler), and past injuries and scars (compound fracture of his left arm). He knew Matt's last report card by heart and could recite every detail of Matt's bedroom—the blue checkered bedspread and matching curtains, the Pinewood Derby car trophies on the shelf, the neatly folded cotton pajamas on the top of the bureau—all of which remained exactly as he'd left them that morning in July two years ago.

A boy he knew as intimately as his own son, yet had never even met.

This would happen with the Stewarts, and with Chris, too.

Dale was already growing particularly fond of Bud after discovering how much they had in common. Both had been Army sharpshooters in Vietnam. Bud from '66 to '68, Dale from '69 to '71.

As he continued reading his notes, his eyelids drooped and he nodded off, but he snorted awake after a few minutes. He ground his fists against his eyes and turned to a fresh page. In the yellow pool of the dome light, he doodled a quick caricature of Agent Miller with an oversized head, exaggerated ears, and a giant bubble gum bubble protruding from his lips.

In high school, Dale had created a comic book about an Iowa farm boy who was accidentally sprayed with fertilizer by a crop duster, giving him superhuman senses and strength, which he learned to use to secretly fight crime and solve his little sister's mysterious murder. It was pretty good. Dale's art teacher had encouraged him to think about art school after graduation.

He still fantasied about it sometimes—quitting the force and drawing a daily strip for a newspaper or the Sunday funnies. But after Dale's older brother died in '68 during the Battle of Khe Sanh in 'Nam, Dale had enlisted in the Army as soon as he turned eighteen. When he finished his tour in '71, he returned home, married Connie, and joined the police force. He needed a dependable job to support a family. He never talked about art school again.

Miller's radio screeched, and he bolted upright and looked around, disoriented. He clutched his balled-up sports coat to his chest. Dale closed the sketchbook.

"What's going on?" Miller said.

"Nothing new." Dale slid the book back beneath the papers.

His radio crackled again, and Miller climbed out of the back seat and walked away from the car to talk in private.

Dale rubbed his face. He badly needed a shower and shave. He needed to eat. He needed to refill his new prescription. He needed to stop at the bank. A week-old paycheck was sitting in his glove box, and he had to deposit it before their account dried up and Connie bounced a check tomorrow shopping for school supplies.

Miller returned and clipped the radio back onto his belt.

"We're done here," he said.

"What do you mean?" Dale asked.

"That was Hagen on the bitch box just now. Farmer

who owns the field is laying an egg that we destroyed forty acres of his crop."

Dale looked at the field in front of him, at the rows of broken and trampled stalks.

"We did destroy it," he said.

"Well, he's threatening to sue the city. Time to scram before the lawyers show up." Miller shook out his coat. "It was a bad tip. The kid ain't here. Go home. Get some rest."

No kidding it was a bad tip.

DALE ENTERED THE lobby of the Des Moines Brenton National Bank and squinted against the harsh fluorescent lighting. He walked to the deposit station and removed his latest paycheck from the breast pocket of his shirt. He unfolded the paper, smoothed it out on the counter top, and flipped it over to the endorsement line on the back.

As he was about to scribble his name, a flyer on the counter next to him caught his eye. He picked it up and found himself face-to-face with a picture of Chris.

Help Find Christopher Thomas Stewart Fund Proudly Sponsored by the Des Moines Brenton National Bank Donations accepted at teller windows Inquiries welcome

Dale set the pen down. After only five—no, six—days, he knew the boy's face as well as he knew his own son's. He closed his eyes and pictured Chris, sitting cross-legged on the corner, rolling his papers. Then a man, walking up Tenth Street. The man smiles. He says something. *Hey, son, can you help me?* He's friendly, chummy. Chris looks up, sees a clean-cut guy, someone's dad, someone's uncle.

I'm lost, the man says. *I'm trying to get to the airport.*

Chris is shy and doesn't like talking to strangers, but he's also a typical midwestern kid. Innocent. Trusting. Taught to respect adults and be polite.

Sure, Chris answers.

I have a map in my car. Could you take a look at it and show me?

Chris agrees and follows. He lives in a place where bad things don't happen to kids.

Dale swayed and opened his eyes. He steadied himself against the counter, the pain in his head ready to split his skull in half.

He stepped into the only open teller line behind an older gentleman talking to the cashier, telling her about his recent bus trip to Yellowstone.

Dale wondered how much the bank had raised for Chris. The *Des Moines Register* was reporting that their reward fund had jumped to $42,000 in the last three days. But Dale knew the Stewart family would easily spend double, triple that amount. Forty-two grand would be a drop in the bucket. Lost children were expensive. Just ask the Klein family.

Lyle and Marilyn had taken a second mortgage out on their house after the initial Find Matthew Klein Fund ran dry. They were hoping to hire a private detective because the police weren't doing anything anymore. The police being Dale.

Two years later, and Lyle and Marilyn were still waiting for Matt to come home. When Dale left the West Des Moines PD, he hadn't worked any new leads or evidence for that case in months. Marilyn had called the

Des Moines station a dozen times every day since the news broke about Chris Stewart. Dale hadn't had time to call her back. Or maybe he was just putting her off.

It was too hard to face them after all this time with nothing new to say.

The old man finally moved on, and the young teller greeted Dale from behind the counter.

"Good morning, welcome to Brenton National," she said. "Sorry for the wait."

"It's fine." Dale unfolded the check and realized he'd forgotten to endorse it.

As he picked up a pen to sign the back, he saw another Chris Stewart flyer taped to the side of the teller's booth.

Donations accepted at teller windows.

The first night at the corner, Sammy Cox had said, *He's probably dead already*.

Dale's vision clouded, and he rocked back on his heels, lightheaded.

"Sir? Are you okay?" the teller asked.

Dale blinked hard and tried to focus his eyes. He told himself it was just exhaustion, breaking his body down.

"Yes. Sorry. I'm fine."

He looked down at the blank line on the back of the check. Quickly, without another thought, he scribbled his signature and slid the check across the cool laminate counter top.

"For the Chris Stewart fund," he said.

The girl took the check and studied it for a moment. She looked back at Dale, her brow wrinkled.

"The whole thing?" she finally asked.

"The whole thing."

"Are you sure?"

The fogginess had cleared. "I'm sure," Dale answered.

He turned and walked out of the bank.

EIGHT

Six days, three hours missing

SATURDAY MORNING, BEFORE TINA had to work the day shift at Chi-Chi's, Crystal went with her to deliver a pan of funeral potatoes to the Stewart home. Funeral potatoes—a cheesy shredded potato dish—were a standard midwestern offering in difficult times, but Crystal privately wondered if, because of the name, it was bad form to give them to a family whose child was only missing and not actually declared dead. But she kept this worry to herself, because the food delivery was another opportunity to get closer to the case. Crystal didn't want to be insensitive, but she secretly hoped it might create a chance to talk to the family, ask some questions.

Tina parked her old brown Pontiac station wagon on the congested street in front of the Stewarts' modest ranch house. She cranked down the squeaky handle of her window and finished a cigarette, and Crystal waited with the glass pan warming the top of her thighs. She ran her fingertip over a strip of tape on the lid that read *T. COX* in black marker.

A steady stream of people came and went from the house, also carrying dishes, and Crystal hoped they weren't *all* funeral potatoes. One woman carried in a giant cellophane-wrapped tray of cookies.

"God, it's Rhonda Hansen," Tina breathed.

"What's wrong with Rhonda Hansen?" Crystal asked. "She's always so unfriendly to me."

Crystal had noticed over the years that her mother wasn't friends with many people on the South Side, even though she'd lived in Des Moines for well over a decade. Strike one against Tina was that she'd been born and raised in Miami, so she wasn't an Iowa native, and definitely not a true South Sider. Strike two, she was divorced, and married moms were rarely friendly with divorced moms, especially pretty divorced moms. Even Crystal knew that.

Her mother talked about moving back to Miami all the time, but Crystal's father, Randy, had beat her to it after their divorce. Tina had declared that she'd rather die than look as if she were following him. He had a serious new girlfriend, and his chartered fishing boat business was doing well. He'd recently sent Crystal and Sammy a picture of himself on the boat with the girlfriend, a younger woman with a tan as dark as tree bark, both of them smiling like dweebs. When Crystal had shown Tina the picture, she'd huffed, *I get custody of kids, he gets custody of a state*, which only made Crystal feel like her mother thought she was on the losing end of the deal. And even though the comment smarted, it also further fueled Crystal's determination to get out on her own.

Tina smashed her cigarette in the overflowing ashtray beneath the dial radio. "What should I say to them?" she asked. "I can't say I'm sorry for their loss, right? That sounds like I think he's dead."

Crystal thought about it for a moment. "We're sorry for their troubles?"

"Yeah," Tina said, "that's good." She exited the car.

Crystal followed, carrying the casserole across the freshly mowed yard. Blades of dried grass slipped through the holes in her white plastic jelly shoes and wedged between her toes. She stopped and removed her right shoe to shake it clean, juggling the dish in one hand. As she tugged the shoe back on and straightened, she nearly ran headfirst into a man's chest. She looked up. Kenny Harris.

"Hello again, Crystal Cox," he said. "Twice in one week. I'm a lucky guy."

"Hey," Crystal said, backing away.

Tina stopped and turned around. "Hi, Kenny!" she called with a wave. "How are you?"

Kenny approached and gave her a light hug.

"I'm groovy," he said. "How are you, pretty lady?"

Behind his back, Crystal rolled her eyes, but Tina laughed.

"I'm well," she said. "Just working my life away."

"I seen your daughter earlier this week," he said. "At Fort Des Moines helping search for this missing kid." He winked at Crystal over his shoulder. "Like a good little citizen."

Crystal set her mouth in a firm line, refusing to give him any encouragement. When he turned back around, she balanced the dish in one hand and stuck her finger in her mouth with the other in a mock gag. His jeans were so tight she wanted to gag for real.

"Do you know the family?" Tina asked.

"Negative," he said. "I just see him on his paper route sometimes. I brought a donation for the search fund." He fanned his face with a white envelope in his hand.

Crystal glanced down at the casserole, which now

seemed foolish. The Stewarts probably needed money more than they needed food.

Her mother apparently agreed. "Oh, yeah. That's a good idea," she said.

The hot bottom of the dish was starting to burn Crystal's forearms. She maneuvered the glass to hold it by the small handles. "Can we hurry, please?" she said.

"How's my little buddy Sammy?" Kenny asked Tina.

"He's good," she said.

Kenny moved closer with a concerned tilt of his head. "He's having a good summer?"

"I think so. I'm taking the kids to the fair tonight after I get off work."

More cars arrived, rolling slowly in front of the house, trying to find a parking spot. Crystal nudged her mother in the side with the corner of the dish. If too many people showed up, she'd lose her chance to try to talk to someone from the family.

"I love the State Fair," Kenny said. He reached out and touched Tina's shoulder. "Are you sure everything's okay with Sammy? He hasn't been to ball practice for a couple of weeks."

"I know, I'm sorry," Tina said. "I've been working so much that I haven't been able to take him. And he's been too lazy to walk. You know how he is."

"There's a charity ball game coming up in September. Policemen versus firemen. The one my pop sponsors every year at Easter Lake. Anyway, I'd be happy to take Sammy. It's a fun deal."

Again, Crystal had the urge to roll her eyes. Somehow, in addition to always finding a way to brag about his old baseball-star days, Kenny managed to work into every conversation that his father's business was a big deal.

"Sammy would love that. Thanks, Kenny." Tina began walking toward the house again. "I have to run. See you later."

"Later." Kenny started toward the street.

As he passed, Crystal muttered under her breath, "Sammy hates baseball."

Kenny stopped. "What did you say?"

"Nothing," she said, and walked faster to catch up to her mother.

When they reached the porch, a young man opened the front door and stepped outside to tie a satin yellow ribbon around the porch post. Crystal scanned the street once more, but Kenny was nowhere in sight.

"Hello," Tina said. "My name is Tina Cox. I live over on Cutler Avenue, and I brought this food to give to the Stewart family."

"Okay." He took the dish from Crystal's hands.

"It's cheesy potatoes," Tina said, and Crystal was relieved she didn't call it by the other name.

The young man stared but said nothing.

Tina adjusted her purse on her shoulder.

"I usually go with him," he said.

Crystal and Tina glanced at each other.

"What?" Tina asked.

"On his paper routes." He ran his fingertips over the strip of tape on the lid, just as Crystal had. "I always go with him, but I didn't last Sunday."

Tina reached out and hugged the young man, crushing the dish between them. "I'm praying for Christopher," she said.

He thanked her. When he turned to go back inside, Crystal sensed her opportunity was slipping away and opened her mouth to speak, but didn't know what to say.

She should've prepared something *before* she walked up to the house.

Disappointed, she followed her mother back to the car.

"What a crock," she said. "You've never prayed a day in your life." Her tone came out critical of her mother, because she was actually angry with herself for not thinking faster on her feet.

Tina fluffed her hair. "So what? It seemed like the right thing to say, and people around here always say it." She slammed the door and started the engine.

Crystal clamped her arms over her chest. As Tina pulled away from the curb, Crystal noticed an idling silver car on the opposite side of the street. Kenny sat behind the wheel, watching. When they drove by, he gave her a thumbs-up.

NINE

Six days, ten hours missing

THAT EVENING, SAMMY, Crystal, and their mother arrived at the west gate of the Iowa State Fairgrounds and performed Tina's traditional entry routine—one that Sammy dreaded. She paid for her ticket and got a paint stamp on the back of her hand, then immediately walked back out the gate to where Sammy and Crystal waited at the street corner, wet a tissue, blotted the stamp, and rolled the top of her hand over each of theirs, creating copies. The three then walked around the grounds to the north gate, where they entered with passable stamps.

Everything was so complicated when his mother didn't have money.

Back when his parents were still married, the State Fair had been one of their favorite yearly events as a family. They'd loved the free concerts, riding the sky glider, eating all the crazy fried food on a stick, and taking pictures with the Big Pumpkin, the Big Boar, and the Super Bull. But now, without his father, the fair wasn't the same. Nothing was the same.

After they walked through the crowded midway rides and saw the twenty-fifth-anniversary butter cow sculpture, which Sammy found boring, Tina bought him a funnel cake. They sat on an empty bench along the Grand Concourse in front of the Grandstands, where the thumping bass of a rock 'n' roll concert vibrated in his chest. Sammy shared the cake with Crystal while their mother smoked a cigarette.

Sammy licked the powdered sugar from the funnel cake off his fingertips.

"Can we go through the Hall of Flame under the Grandstands?" he asked. "I saw in the paper that they have a display of melted stuff from house fires, and they're giving away free Smokey the Bear T-Shirts tonight."

Tina crushed out her cigarette, slipped off a shoe, and flexed her swollen, red toes. "Yes, we can go look at the melted stuff, but then we're going home. I'm exhausted."

After she worked the lunch shift, they'd come straight to the fair and walked for hours. His mother was always so tired that Sammy sometimes worried she'd get sick and die. Last winter, she'd had pneumonia and coughed so hard the whites of her eyeballs became covered in spindly red lines that made her look possessed, but Crystal said they were just broken blood vessels and would go away and she'd be fine. Still, Sammy had checked on her every night for weeks to make sure she was still breathing.

Sammy folded the grease-stained paper plate from the cake and stuffed it in a nearby trash can while Tina struggled to get her shoe back on. They strolled into the cavernous Hall of Flame beneath the Grandstands, where Sammy examined the table of melted items carefully: a hot clothing iron that had been left on a bed and set the comforter on fire, a remote-controlled monster truck with a defective battery that had exploded into a fireball, and the most impressive, an old kerosene space heater that had been placed too close to a window and set the drapes on fire, burning down an entire house. All that from a little heater the size of a toaster oven.

As Sammy walked around the table and read the stories and warnings about each item, a gloominess descended over him and he lost interest in all the melted stuff. He'd barely enjoyed anything about the fair tonight. He hadn't cared about the butter cow or the midway rides. The sky glider had only made him nervous that the cable would snap and he and his mother would plummet to the ground below, and now the Hall of Flame just made him think of ways his house could catch on fire and kill them. His mother could forget to turn off her hair crimper, or fall asleep with one of her cigarettes still burning. Crystal could leave a burner on the stove going because she sometimes couldn't see the dials very well.

Everywhere Sammy went and everything he did just made him think about ways to die.

As they finished the Hall of Flame, a fireman offered Sammy a free Smokey the Bear T-shirt, size small, which he knew wouldn't fit. He reluctantly accepted it.

They moved on to the next room, the Hall of Law. A large display in the center caught Crystal's attention, and she elbowed her way through throngs of people to get to it. Sammy and their mother followed.

A poster of Christopher Stewart's face dominated the center of the display.

HAVE YOU SEEN ME?

Crystal grabbed a plastic bag and began gathering the free items on the table—pencils, key chains, magnets, and flyers with pictures of other missing people across the state. Sammy picked one up and stared at a photo of Matthew Klein.

Another boy. He looked like Christopher, with the same hairstyle Sammy had tried to copy.

"That's so sad," Tina said, reading the flyer over his shoulder.

"He's dead, too, you know," Sammy whispered. "Just like Christopher."

Tina cooled herself with a free paper fan from some insurance company and made a disapproving *tsk* noise. "Why would you say something like that?"

Sammy didn't answer. He folded the paper and tucked it into his back pocket.

"Hello, Cox family."

Sammy turned around and saw the cop with the funny name and slipped behind his mother. He didn't want to talk about last Sunday morning or his paper route again.

"Hi! Sergeant Goodkind, right?" Tina said brightly. "Are you working here?"

"Something like that," he said. He scratched the side of his jaw, and Sammy could hear the scrape of his nails over his stubbly whiskers. "We're handing out info on, you know, open cases. It's a good place to reach a lot of people…drum up new leads…" His voice trailed off, and he glanced around the large room.

"Do you have any leads yet?" Crystal asked.

The cop didn't answer. He stared over their heads at something in the distance.

"Sergeant Goodkind?" Tina said.

"What?" He snapped to attention. "No, I can't talk about an active investigation, unfortunately."

Sammy noticed a small brown stain on the front of

Goodkind's wrinkled white shirt and wondered if the cop drank chocolate milk from a carton, too. It was easy to spill and not know it.

"Are you interested in the case?" Goodkind asked Crystal.

"I'm thinking about an essay topic for—" She stopped and glanced at their mother. "An article for my school paper. I'm the editor."

"Is that so?" Goodkind raised his eyebrows. "Here, take what you like." He picked up several papers and pushed them into Crystal's hands. "Take more pencils, too. Oh, and this." He held out a navy, oval-shaped object to her. "It's a pocketknife. A pretty nice one."

"A knife?" Sammy pushed in front of Tina.

Crystal took the knife and ran her fingers over the gold lettering on the covering.

"*D-M-P-D*," she read aloud. She carefully extracted the thick blade, which had a surprisingly sharp tip. Sammy couldn't take his eyes off it.

"They're new this year," Dale said. "Special giveaways just for the fair. They're pretty handy on a key chain."

"Cool. Thanks." Crystal slipped it into her plastic bag.

"Can I have one?" Sammy asked. He leaned against the table, and it scooted a few inches.

Tina pulled on his shoulder. "Absolutely not," she said.

"Why not?"

"It's dangerous. You're not old enough to carry something like that around."

Sammy's posture wilted. All he'd gotten at the fair so far was the stupid too-small T-shirt. It wasn't fair. A girl would never use it.

Goodkind rubbed his forehead. "Sorry. I wasn't thinking. I should've known better than to dangle something like that in front of a twelve-year-old. I have a boy that age myself."

"It's fine," Tina said. "You look exhausted."

Goodkind sighed. "Yeah, the Stewart case has me pulling extra hours. Haven't slept much this week."

With his mother and the cop chatting and his sister still engrossed in all the missing-people stuff, Sammy moved on to the next law display—a table of pamphlets telling parents to *Buckle That Baby!* into a safety seat. Sammy wrinkled his nose. That was no fun. When he was little, he'd loved riding on his dad's lap and steering the car whenever they drove around the neighborhood.

Sammy laid the pamphlet down and felt sudden pressure on his bladder. He'd been holding it since the butter cow. He glanced at his mother, but she wasn't paying attention. She was still talking to the cop. The bathroom was close, so he slipped away and pushed through the door. No one else was inside. He tossed his Smokey the Bear T-shirt over his shoulder, got unzipped, and relieved himself at a urinal just in time.

The bathroom door squealed open, followed by slow, heavy footsteps. The hairs on the back of Sammy's neck prickled. His legs turned watery and his stomach cramped. He quickly zipped his shorts, dribbling pee on the front of the dark fabric.

He didn't want to turn and look, he told himself not to look, but he did it anyway.

How had he known Sammy would be here?

Are you having fun?

The voice echoed in his ears, far away, like in a dream. Sammy's feet grew roots holding him in place.

You ran from me again on Sunday. You know I don't like it when you run.

A hand grabbed his forearm above the bruises that had finally faded to a sickly yellow-green. Fingers squeezed. Sammy's body trembled and he tried to pull away. He prayed his mother would look for him, or for someone else to walk in.

Hot breath in his ear. *Don't be scared. You're always safe with me.*

Then, a woman's voice, shouting nearby. The hand let go, and Sammy sprinted to the door and outside, shouldering his way through the crowds of people, back to his mother. But she hadn't even realized he was gone and didn't notice his return. She and Crystal were too busy watching the scene in front of them.

A woman stood before the missing-people table, shouting at Goodkind.

"You could've prevented this!" she yelled. "Another boy is gone because of you!"

"Marilyn, please," Goodkind said quietly. "Please, don't do this."

More people gathered, watching.

"You didn't believe me for so long," the woman said. She was crying now. Black tears ran down her cheeks, like her eyes were leaking ink. "All those hours and days and months, you didn't believe me. You said he ran away. You said he'd come back." She pointed her finger at Goodkind. "When I told you someone took him, you told me I was being hysterical. You called me crazy."

Goodkind's moustache twitched.

The woman picked up a flyer with Christopher Stewart's picture on it and screamed, "I'm not so crazy now, am I?"

On the other side of the wall, a song at the rock concert ended and the crowd erupted into cheers. Goodkind stared at the woman but said nothing. He looked sad and Sammy thought he might cry, too, like the woman.

After a moment, she crumpled the paper, threw it at Goodkind's face, and walked away. The mob parted for her like the wake of boat, and she disappeared, swallowed up by all the people outside.

Another cop appeared and whispered something in Goodkind's ear. They hurried behind a velvet curtain of the display.

Tina puffed her cheeks and laid a hand on her chest. "Oh my god. That was intense."

"Who was that?" Crystal said, still craning her neck in the direction the woman had gone.

"That was Marilyn Klein," Tina said. "Matthew Klein's mother."

"Holy shit," Crystal muttered. "How do you know that?"

"I cut her hair at the mall once," Tina said. "Before the stuff with her son."

"She really gave it to that cop."

"Poor guy," Tina said. "Let's go. I've had enough of the fair for one night."

His mother grasped Sammy's forearm to direct him through the crowd, and he winced as she put pressure on the fresh marks forming beneath his skin.

Tina looked down at him. "Where's your free T-shirt?" she asked.

Sammy touched his shoulder where he'd draped it, but it was gone. He must've dropped it in the bathroom.

"I—I guess I lost it," he said.

He glanced back, relieved to see no one was following him.

TEN

Six days, twenty-three hours missing

BEFORE SUNRISE THE next morning, Crystal sat cross-legged on the driveway trying to read Sunday's *Des Moines Register* under the yellow glow of the entry light. Sammy sat on the damp pavement next to her, rolling papers from a large bundle. She was supposed to be rolling papers from her bundle, but she'd been distracted by the front-page story.

The latest article said that bundles were normally delivered directly to the house for most paperboys, like Sammy, unless the carrier lived on a dead-end street. Bundles for those carriers were dropped on a designated street corner instead. And Chris Stewart, she knew, lived on a dead-end street, so his bundles were dropped on a corner, where he picked them up and rolled them, alone.

Crystal set the paper down, thinking.

A victim of chance simply because he lived on a dead-end street.

Or maybe he was a victim of *circumstance*. Some stranger, some lone dark figure out and about early in the morning, had spotted him on the street corner with no adults anywhere in sight. It was barely light out at that time, so there was some camouflage in the lingering darkness. Snatching a boy his size would've been quick and easy. The plucking of a flower.

And it had probably been an impulsive act. Like buying unnecessary items from the rack in the checkout lane just because they were there.

Chris, and Matt, too. Victims because of specific circumstances.

She held the paper back up, inches from her nose, tilting it just so to catch the best light, and continued reading the article by crime reporter Herb Almeida.

Klein Parents Continue Their Struggle for Answers After 2 Years

In the two years since their son disappeared without a trace, Lyle and Marilyn Klein have spent nearly $100,000 in the search for Matthew, a boy whose name is familiar to thousands in Iowa and beyond.

What happened to Matthew Klein in the early morning hours of Sunday, July 18, 1982? More and more, the answers to the Matthew Klein mystery are looking to be the same answers in the Christopher Stewart case. The similarities between the dates and circumstances, Des Moines police say, are hard to ignore.

Crystal admired Herb Almeida's writing. Most of the articles she'd clipped and saved about both cases had been written by him. She wanted to be like that—respected in an important profession. Make a difference in people's lives.

"Stop reading and help me," Sammy said. He nudged her bundle with his foot.

Crystal reluctantly closed and rolled the fat paper and slid a rubber band around it. Moths fluttered around and clung to the security light, creating a flickering effect that had started to give her a headache.

"This sucks," she said, and jammed the roll into Sammy's canvas bag.

Because half the paperboys had quit in the last week, Sammy was now covering two routes. The route manager had telephoned the parents of remaining carriers and asked that they deliver with an adult for the time being, as well as carry flashlights and some kind of noisemaker. Sammy wore the black whistle around his neck that Crystal had been given during the search of Fort Des Moines Park, and both carried small plastic flashlights in their pockets.

It was going to be a long morning.

Crystal stuffed her last rolled paper into Sammy's bag as he topped off the pile in his rusted orange wagon. They set out into the lingering morning darkness on his route, with Sammy carrying the bag and tossing the papers as Crystal pulled the squeaky wagon. The wavering beams of other carriers' flashlights periodically sliced through the dimness. Many houses had left porch lights on, and every paperboy they encountered was accompanied by an adult or older sibling.

As they approached Mr. K's house at the corner of Southlawn and Tenth, Crystal's stomach flipped with nerves. Perfect timing. It was just after sunrise, and Mr. K should be leaving for his walk at any moment. It was the only upside to helping Sammy with his route. She switched off her flashlight and dropped it into the wagon.

Crystal grabbed a rolled paper and walked slowly toward his house. A small lamp blazed in the front window, so she knew he was awake. She lingered at the stoop, laying the rolled paper down in slow motion.

"Hurry up!" Sammy called.

She ignored him and ambled across the overgrown yard, even stopping at one point to fake-tie her tennis shoe. She continuously glanced at the house. Finally, the front door opened and Mr. K emerged.

"Hey, Mr. K!" she called.

"Oh!" He sharply looked up. "Hello." He carried the black backpack in his hands, which was packed so tightly the zipper bulged.

"No bird-watching this morning?" She gestured to his bare neck.

"Oh." Mr. K's fingers fluttered to his chest as if he was just realizing he'd forgotten the binoculars. "Uh, no, not today. Just…walking."

"I'm helping Sammy," she said. "All the paperboys have to go with an adult this week." She'd been planning ways to refer to herself as an "adult" for the last three blocks.

"I see."

"I'm also doing research," she added, "for that scholarship I told you about."

"Yes, that's wonderful." He glanced up and down the street and seemed to be only half listening.

She took a deep breath to get the words out. "Maybe you could take a look at it tomorrow when you come for tutoring?"

Before Mr. K could answer, Sammy nudged Crystal in the back. "Chrissie, let's go."

Mr. K blinked and focused on Sammy. "How are you this morning, Samuel?" he asked softly.

"Fine." Sammy stared at the ground and moved a rock around with the toe of his shoe.

"Did you have fun at the fair last night?"

Sammy kicked the rock hard, sending it rolling across the pavement. "I guess," he mumbled.

Mr. K reached out to touch Sammy's shoulder, but Sammy jerked away from him.

A siren bleeped behind them, and the three turned around in unison. An unmarked police car with a single flashing light stopped at the curb.

"*Szaros*," Mr. K whispered.

Crystal had heard him say it before and knew what it meant. *Shit*.

A plainclothes officer got out of the car. "Everything okay here, kids?"

"We're fine," Crystal replied.

Mr. K took a few steps away from her and Sammy.

"Who's this you're talking to?" the officer asked.

"It's okay, we know him," Crystal said. "He's on a walk. Bird-watching." She glanced at Mr. K. "Well, not today. Just walking."

He slung the backpack over one shoulder, his hand trembling. Crystal knew why he was nervous. When she'd interviewed him last year, he'd told her how badly people like him were harassed in Hungary. The Roma were treated like disreputable thieves and accused of black magic and sorcery. His grandparents had been executed during the Holocaust, and Mr. K himself had been arrested and beaten several times by Hungarian police.

The officer moved closer to Mr. K. "What's your name, sir?"

"Sebastian Kovacs," he answered quickly.

"Where do you live?"

"Here." He pointed over his shoulder at his house. "On Southlawn Drive."

The cop pulled a small notepad and pen from his front jacket pocket and flipped it open.

"Spell your name, please."

With a clog in his voice, Mr. K spelled out his first and last names as the cop scribbled it on a page.

"What are your names?" he asked Crystal, and then pointed his pen at Sammy.

"My name is Crystal Cox. I'm eighteen, and this is my little brother, Sammy. He's a paperboy, and I'm chaperoning him." Crystal lifted her chin.

The cop wrote another note. Even though she knew he was just doing his job, this was ridiculously unnecessary.

"May I ask what *your* name is?" She sounded gutsier than she felt. She was an adult, and they weren't doing anything wrong.

The cop looked at her with an amused expression. "I'm Senior Police Office Bradley," he said.

"May I see your badge, please?" she said.

The cop openly laughed. She never understood what adults found so funny about her.

Bradley unclipped his badge from the side of his belt and held it out in his palm. She leaned closer to read it.

"Looks legitimate," she said with a nod.

"Well, thanks for your approval," Bradley answered

dryly, replacing the badge. He flipped the notebook shut and slipped it back into his pocket. "All right," he finally said. "I'll let you folks get on your way."

"Thank you," Crystal said.

"Thank you, sir," Mr. K echoed.

As soon as the car rolled away from the curb, Mr. K audibly exhaled.

"Oh-*key*," he said, his face pale, "I have to go now." He hurried back to his house.

"Wait, what about your walk?" Crystal asked.

"I forgot about an appointment." He reached the stoop and fumbled to fit the key in the lock.

"Do you think you'll be able to help me with my essay tomorrow? Mr. K?" Crystal called, but he'd already closed the door. The dead bolt clicked.

She sighed. That hadn't gone at all like she'd hoped.

"Finally." Sammy hoisted his bag onto his shoulder and crossed the street. He resumed tossing the rolled papers from his bag.

Crystal grudgingly followed. As she crossed the street pulling the wagon, she decided she would start calling him by his first name. No more "Mr. K" like other kids, because she wanted him to think of her as an adult.

"Hey, Sammy," Crystal said. "Why were you so rude to… Sebastian just now?" His first name awkwardly slid across her tongue. It would take some getting used to. "He was perfectly friendly to you."

Sammy flung the last paper from his bag and stopped to refill from the wagon. "I wasn't rude."

Crystal gathered a handful of papers to help him. "Yes, you were."

"No, I wasn't!" Sammy snapped. He jammed a paper into the bag. "Maybe I just don't like him."

Crystal straightened, surprised by his comment. "Why on earth don't you like him?"

"Why do you care so much?" he shot back. Sammy closed his eyes and made a kissy-face at her, running his hands up and down his own arms. "Oooo, *Sebastian*!"

Crystal shoved him and dumped the papers into the wagon. "You're such a child." She turned away to hide her embarrassment. Despite her efforts to be cool about it, she'd exposed her feelings for Mr. K—*Sebastian*— so clearly that even her twelve-year-old kid brother had seen them.

She probably hadn't hidden it well. She'd had a crush on Mr. K ever since she'd interviewed him for a world history project. It had been a chilly evening, and he'd invited her to his house, where he'd made her a cup of hot, spicy tea from an ornate blue-and-gold-painted kettle on his stove. They'd sat at his kitchen table as he told her about his boyhood home in Felsőnyék, a small village a few hours outside Budapest, and how he'd fled Hungary for America in 1979 because the Soviet-controlled Communist government was brutalizing the Roma.

"Home is so far away," he'd said. Another lifetime, when he'd still been *Szebasztián Kovács*, a name too often mistaken as Russian, as enemy here in America. So he'd sanitized it of the suspicious marks and letters, because, like Americans, he despised Russians, and hated to be mistaken for one.

It was after the interview that she couldn't stop thinking about him. He was so worldly and smart, and always asked about her interests and pursuits. He listened to her, like a close friend. Other than Somphone, Crystal didn't have many friends.

Sammy finished refilling the bag, and they continued walking, silently fuming at each other. Finished with the extra route, they moved on to his regular route, east, near the library, down quiet residential streets. Crystal mentally noted details of the neighborhood: which houses left on porch lights for the paperboys, which had H.O.P.E. decals in the windows—houses vetted by the *Des Moines Register* as safe havens where paperboys could go if they were ever in trouble—a program that had started last year in response to the Klein case and two murdered paperboys in Omaha. Though it wasn't lost on Crystal that the H.O.P.E. program hadn't helped Chris Stewart.

She pieced the neighborhood map together in her mind. When they reached the corner, she read the cross-way signs. Southeast Southlawn Drive and Thirteenth Street. One block north was Clark and the library, then the New Hope Baptist Church to the west. All streets and neighborhoods she'd played in as a child. Ridden her old banana-seat bike around with Somphone when they were in elementary school, barely two blocks from the corner where Christopher Stewart had been abducted.

A new essay idea.

Mayberry No More: Living in the Era of Dangerous Neighborhoods.

Or, *Goodbye, Mayberry: The Lost Era of the Friendly American Neighborhood.*

She should've brought a pencil and notebook to write down ideas.

Crystal and Sammy made a left onto another street,

and Sammy abruptly slowed, causing Crystal to accidentally step on the back of his sneaker.

She poked him in the shoulder. "Hurry up. Why are you going so slow?"

He tossed a paper at a porch. It landed just short of the first step.

"I dunno," he said. Now he was the one dawdling, seemingly wasting time.

"Come on," she said. "We're almost done."

He tossed another paper and hit the shrubs next to the front door. His aim was suddenly terrible.

They approached the next house, a small white ranch with a H.O.P.E. decal dotting the front picture window. The door of the detached, single-car garage was open, and a naked bulb burned brightly from inside. Sammy flung a newspaper onto the grass several feet from the front stoop.

Crystal slowed too, studying the property. A white van with the words *Midwest Heating and Cooling* printed in red letters on the side was parked in the driveway. Inside the garage sat a silver car with its hood up.

Sammy was now several houses ahead of her. Not only was his pace erratic, but he was walking in the street instead of on the sidewalk. She opened her mouth to holler at him to slow down but was interrupted.

"There's my paperboy!"

Crystal snapped her head in the direction of the voice. A man stood in the opening of the tall garage as if he'd materialized from thin air. The overhead bulb cast a shadow across his face, and it took a few seconds for Crystal's eyes to focus.

Kenny Harris.

Smiling, Kenny started down the short driveway toward Sammy but stopped when he noticed Crystal. "Oh! And big sister is helping today, I see."

"Hi," Crystal said.

"Third time in a week. How about that."

Crystal kept taking small, slow steps. She didn't want to stand around and chitchat with him.

"Hey, little buddy!" Kenny waved at Sammy, who had now completely crossed the street to the opposite side. "What are you doing way over there?"

Sammy continued his brisk pace, haphazardly throwing the last of his papers from his bag into shrubs and flower beds.

"Are you a permanent team now?" Kenny asked Crystal.

"I'm helping because of that Stewart kid thing," Crystal said.

"Yeah, that's a bad deal."

Inside the garage, she noted a row of shelves lining the east wall containing several boxes with red block letters on the sides, just like the van. She recalled her mother once commenting that Kenny's father owned the largest heating and cooling business in central Iowa— big money—and that Kenny would one day take the business over and do well for himself.

Kenny wrinkled his brow. "Something wrong?"

Crystal looked away. "No, nothing. I should go. We're really behind."

"Sure thing." Kenny gave her a thumbs-up. "See you later, buddy!" he called to Sammy, and picked up his paper from the grass. He went back into the garage and pulled the door closed.

Crystal started jogging after Sammy, the old wagon rattling behind her.

"Slow down!" she yelled, growing breathless.

At the corner, he finally stopped and waited. A pair of older paperboys walked together on the opposite side of the street, talking loudly.

Crystal finally caught up. "What the hell's gotten into you?" she panted.

Sammy stared at the boys, breathing hard himself. "I just wanna get home." He swiped his wrist across his wet brow with something clutched in his hand.

"What is that?" Crystal asked.

Sammy tried to hide his hand behind his canvas bag, but Crystal caught his forearm and pried his fingers open.

It was their mother's orange-handled scissors, and he was gripping them like a knife.

She wrenched them from his tight grip. "Give me those!"

"Hey!"

"Why were you carrying it like that?"

He finally looked away from the boys, down at his feet. "It just makes me feel better to have them," he said.

She switched the wagon handle to her other hand. "This Chris Stewart thing has you freaked out, huh?"

"That's not... Never mind. Let's go."

Sammy started walking in the direction of home. As Crystal followed, she slipped the scissors into her back pocket and wondered what Sammy had been about to say.

ELEVEN

One week missing

DALE SAT IN his car, staring at the small patch of grass on the corner of Tenth and Hillcrest. The last of the night-time gloom shrouded the street in an eerie white gauze. He'd been there for an hour, just sitting. Watching.

No bundles of newspapers had been dropped off at the corner today. No kid to roll them.

A boy crossed on foot in front of the car, walking closely with an adult male—a father, most likely. They chatted back and forth. The boy wore a shiny silver whistle around his neck, and the man carried a flash-light. Dale had seen this several times in the last hour—paperboys walking with an adult or older sibling, cars and trucks slowly driving kids along their routes as they threw the papers from an open window. The carriers who hadn't quit altogether in the last week, that is.

After one week the investigation was no further than it had been when the call came in. Nothing on vehicles. Nothing from the canvasses and grid searches. Nothing on the composite sketch Dale had created of a man sup-posedly seen chatting with Chris as he rolled papers.

And then Marilyn Klein at the fair last night.

Dale couldn't get the sound of her voice out of his head. The things she'd said, all of it true. How he'd treated her two years ago. Like a hysterical housewife.

He had no explanation for his failure of imagination back then. He of all people.

He picked up the thick Sunday-edition newspaper lying in the passenger seat and read an interview with Marilyn and Lyle on page two. Marilyn renewed her theory about a well-organized child prostitution sex ring operating in the Midwest that their private investigator had discovered. She pleaded with parents to talk to their kids about strangers, to be more vigilant, watch them carefully, and trust no one.

Dale had never worked on any child sex ring cases, but that didn't mean Marilyn was wrong, or that they didn't exist. Still, his gut told him it wasn't someone from a child sex ring who had taken Matt or Chris. Just yesterday, Dale had been in a conversation with Agent Miller about the FBI expert from DC who'd built them a profile of the suspect they should be looking for: white male, age thirty to thirty-five, middle class, employed, clean-cut. A lone hunter, hiding in plain sight. Charming, friendly, well liked, and a *pedophile*—an adult sexually attracted to young children. There was an actual name for it. Dale had not heard that word until yesterday, but he hadn't needed to. He'd already known it existed.

The rising sun slid behind a cloud, casting a shadow over Dale's face. He laid the paper down and leaned his head back against the headrest with his eyes closed. He hadn't slept at all last night. Hadn't taken his medication, eaten, or showered in over twenty-four hours.

Dale lifted his head and cranked the handle of his window to let in a little fresh air. He opened his sketchbook and checked his notes. Next name on the list: *Sebastian Kovacs, Southlawn Drive*. The Cox kid's tutor. The guy with the accent who walked every morning.

Dale started the car and pulled onto Tenth. He wanted to catch Kovacs at home, early, maybe right after one of his "bird-watching" excursions.

One block later, Dale parked in front of the house, grabbed his sketchbook, and got out. No car in the carport, but a lamp burned in the front window. After he rang the bell three times, the interior door finally unlocked and opened. Kovacs's face appeared in the gap.

"Yes?" he said.

"Mr. Kovacs, I'm Sergeant Goodkind. We met at the Coxes' the other day."

"Oh, yes."

"Can I speak with you for a moment?"

"I don't know anything about that missing boy," Kovacs said, shaking his head.

"I won't take up much of your time. Could I come inside?"

"I didn't see anything."

Dale planted a fist on his hip. The guy was already nervous. He had to maneuver carefully. "I understand. It's just our standard questions for everyone in the neighborhood." He gestured for Kovacs to open the door. "This won't take long."

"Oh-*key*," Kovacs said quietly. He unlatched the chain and opened the door. As Dale entered, he noticed small beads of perspiration dotting Kovacs's brow and upper lip. He wore a plain dark-gray polo shirt, black slacks, and sneakers. He could've passed for a harmless tourist.

"Were you walking this morning?" Dale asked.

"Yes."

"Where do you usually go?"

Kovacs switched off the lamp atop a piano in front of the window. "Just around the neighborhood. Different places." The only other furniture in the living room was a pale-blue velour couch situated by the fireplace and a cuckoo clock ticking from the mantel.

"We can go into the kitchen to talk," Kovacs said, moving to the next room.

The kitchen was as sparse as the living room. Just a small beat-up wooden table and two mismatched chairs. Bare counters and walls except for a Special Olympics calendar hanging next to a yellow rotary phone.

"Would you like some tea? I'm making some for myself." Kovacs held up an ornate teapot from the stove. The fat porcelain belly was painted with cobalt-blue-and-gold flowers and swirls.

Dale shook his head. "No, thank you."

While Kovacs filled the pot beneath the sink tap, Dale discreetly read the small handwriting filling the blocks of the calendar.

Monday: Sammy C. 8:00 a.m.–9:00 a.m. (summer only)
Monday, Wednesday, Friday: Jeffrey F. 4:30 p.m.–5:30 p.m.
Tuesday: Jessica T. 10:30 a.m.–11:30 a.m. (summer only)
*Tuesday, Thursday: David M. 3:00 p.m.–4:00 p.m. Piano *mother paid through October*
Saturday: Daniel D. 9:00 a.m.–12:00 p.m. (ACT Prep)
Wednesday: Aaron B. 1:00 p.m.–3:00 p.m. Piano

His tutoring and piano lesson schedule. Mostly boys, Dale noted. He tapped the calendar with his fingertip and said, "What subjects do you teach?"

Kovacs moved the kettle to the stove and lit a burner. "Just math. And a few piano." He gestured for Dale to sit on a stool, while he remained standing on the opposite side.

Dale sat. He opened his sketchbook and clicked his pen. "How many kids?"

"Six right now."

"That doesn't seem like very many. Is that typical?"

"Sometimes more during the school year."

"How long have you tutored Sammy Cox?"

"Eight months."

As if he'd been coached by a lawyer, Kovacs offered only exact answers related to the question and nothing more.

The teakettle whistled, and Kovacs moved it to another burner. He retrieved a mug from the drying rack in the sink and balanced a small strainer across the top. From a copper tea tin, he filled the strainer with leaves and carefully poured the hot kettle water over it. The fussy process momentarily distracted Dale.

"Do you own a vehicle, Mr. Kovacs?"

"No."

"You've never owned a vehicle?"

Kovacs stirred the tea with a tiny spoon. "A few years ago, I had a car. But I sold it. Too expensive."

"What kind of car?"

Kovacs shrugged. "I don't remember."

Of course he didn't. Dale made a note to check with the DOT and county treasurer. "So, you take walks every morning around the neighborhood? Around sunrise?"

"Yes." When Kovacs lifted the steaming mug, his hands trembled.

Dale stopped writing and leaned on his elbow. "Do you know Christopher Stewart in any capacity?"

Kovacs set the mug down without taking a drink and wiped his hands on the front of his pants. Sweaty palms.

"No. I don't know him."

"Ever seen him on his paper route? During your walks?"

The clock in the living room sounded. Seven loud *dings* and *cuckoos*. Kovacs waited until the clock finished before answering.

"Yes. A few times."

"Did you see him last Sunday? The morning of August twelfth?"

A slight hesitation. A quick sideways glance. "No," he said. His top lip glistened with perspiration again.

Sunlight streamed through the small window over the sink, illuminating the starkness of the room. On the ledge of the window, Dale noticed a small toy. He stood and picked it up.

A model car.

"Is this from one of those kits you glue together?" he asked.

"Yes, I believe so," Kovacs answered.

He turned the car over his hand. A Corvette. He'd seen the Cox boy playing with a model car the day he interviewed him.

"Where did you get it?"

"A student gave it to me. As a thank-you gift."

"A student," Dale repeated, narrowing his eyes. "Which student?"

Kovacs matched Dale's stare for a moment. "I don't remember," he finally said.

"You don't remember."

"Many students, many thank-you gifts."

Dale replaced the car on the windowsill. "Mind if I look around a little?"

Kovacs's expression remained neutral, controlled. "Yes, of course," he answered.

He'd dealt with authorities before, Dale could tell. The man calculated every word, gesture, and expression for minimum impact, maximum deflection.

Dale looked out the uncovered sliding-glass doors. Small yard, rusty chain-link fence, no outbuildings, no garage.

"Just you here?" he asked. "No wife, no roommate?"

"Yes," Kovacs said. "I am not married."

Kovacs waited in the kitchen as Dale moved on.

In the hall, he opened the first door. Coat closet. Next door, a cramped bathroom that smelled of mildew. Two small bedrooms directly across from each other—one with only a double bed and mismatched bureau, the other completely empty.

The house was eerily familiar. Post–World War II cracker boxes, his father used to call them. Same basic layout wherever you went.

Somewhere was a basement door.

Dale returned to the kitchen. He peered around the other side of the refrigerator. A door.

He pointed. "Where's that go?"

Kovacs glanced over his shoulder. "The basement."

Dale crossed the room. He tried the white porcelain knob. Locked.

"It's just the hot water heater and furnace down there," Kovacs said. "And many spiders." He attempted his first smile since Dale arrived.

"Do you have a key?"

"Somewhere. I'd have to find it."

Dale bent over and peered through the skeleton hole

but couldn't see anything. As he straightened, tiny pins pricked the back of his neck. The style of the house, the layout of the interior, and now the basement door next to the fridge, locked by an old skeleton key.

He'd been inside a house nearly identical to this before.

Another house, from another life.

He brushed his fingertips over the cool, smooth knob.

The sound of the metal key sliding into the hole, the firm click releasing the lock, the squeal of the turning knob, the long creak as the door opened. *Reeeeek*. The voice, behind him. *You first, big guy*.

Dale swayed, dizzy, and pressed a hand against the wall for balance. His face tingled.

"Mr. Goodkind?"

The lines of the room became wavy. Sweat slicked his back and under his arms.

Kovacs stepped toward him. "Are you okay?"

Dale blinked. Backed away from the door.

"You're pale. Do you need some water?"

An expression of concern spread across Kovacs's face.

Dale straightened the knot of his tie and cleared his throat. "I'm fine," he murmured.

Kovacs lifted his wrist and made a show of checking his watch. "I'm sorry, but I need to be somewhere soon. Can we continue this another time?"

Dale crossed his arms over his chest to slow his breathing. "Sure."

"Very good, then," Kovacs said, and led Dale to the door.

Once outside on the stoop, Dale gulped a mouthful of cool morning air.

Kovacs closed and locked the door behind him.

DALE GLANCED IN his rearview mirror at the shrinking neighborhood, but Kovacs's house still loomed from the corner. He pulled into a Sinclair station and stopped.

His heart wouldn't stop pounding. He laid his index and middle fingers on the inside of his opposite wrist to take his pulse, just like Dr. Smith had shown him. He counted for sixty seconds. One hundred and fifteen beats per minute. He closed his eyes and tried to take several deep breaths.

He hadn't had an episode that bad since last Christmas. Maybe it was the increased Ludiomil dosage. Dr. Smith had warned him there would be an adjustment period and possible side effects. Plus, he'd missed a dose yesterday.

Or maybe it was Kovacs's house. The unnerving similarity.

Side effects or not, he should've told Kovacs to unlock the door so he could search the basement, but he'd blown it. It wasn't likely that Kovacs would let him in a second time to finish the search. Now he'd need a warrant, and he didn't have enough probable cause for a warrant.

Dale exited the car and went inside the station to use the pay phone to call Dr. Smith. Her answering service picked up on the second ring. He asked for her next available appointment. She had a cancellation at two o'clock tomorrow afternoon, and Dale took it. He'd tell the lieutenant he was following up on a lead and would be out of the office for several hours.

He slammed the receiver on the hook, and the pay phone dinged in protest. The attendant glanced at him.

He'd made it eight months without an incident. Eight

months, down the drain. He was right back where he started.

Dale returned to his car and started driving toward home again. His mind finally cleared enough to consider damage control. His slip at Kovacs's house wasn't catastrophic. He would do a full background check on Kovacs as soon as he got to the office in the morning. Run his driver's license and social security number. Put a call in with the Immigration and Naturalization Service and the DOT. Before he left for the appointment in Ames, he would talk to the area elementary schools about the tutoring, get names of families and interview them. If even the smallest blip turned up, he'd go for a warrant.

Feeling calmer, Dale stopped at Hy-Vee to buy some doughnuts. It was just after seven thirty, and if he hurried, he could have breakfast with Curtis and Connie. He'd barely seen them in the last three days.

He would get glazed twists, Connie's favorite. She was still furious with him after discovering what he'd done with his last paycheck and being forced to dip into their small savings account to pay bills. And when he couldn't explain why he'd given the check away, it had only angered her further. She was on hour twenty-seven of her ice-out. Maybe doughnuts would start a thaw. He was willing to try anything.

Dale knew he'd put Connie through a lot in the last two years, since Matt Klein's disappearance. He'd promised her he wouldn't spiral over a case like that again. Until a week ago, that is, when he'd had the unbelievably bad luck of catching yet another missing-kid case. Now he was working around the clock. Filling more notebooks with obsessive notes. Not sleeping. Acting irritable. Spiraling.

But maybe it wasn't bad luck. Maybe it was fate. Maybe he was meant to catch these cases, because he was going to solve them. It was a classic glass-half-full/glass-half-empty conundrum, depending on how one chose to look at it.

Dale parked at the far end of the Hy-Vee parking lot and checked his wallet for cash. Three bucks. Just enough for a bag of doughnuts. As he was about to exit the car, he opened his sketchbook to a clean page to jot down a new list before he forgot it. While sitting at the corner this morning, he'd considered how a perpetrator could've gotten Chris into a car so fast without a single witness seeing or hearing anything. No scream. No cry. Nothing.

He cracked his knuckles and made a list of scenarios. The guy could've pulled a gun on him and forced him inside the car. Knocked him out and dragged him unconscious. Tased him. Lured him with a lie: asking for directions, an offer of candy.

His hand froze. *Hey, big guy, do you like chocolate bars?* The voice was still so clear after all this time.

He pictured Kovacs on his morning walks, "birdwatching."

Do you like birds?

Have you ever used binoculars before?

Would you like to take a look?

It was possible.

But did kids fall for those tricks anymore? And wouldn't Chris have at least tried to run at the sight of a weapon? Fight? Yell and scream? He'd asked the exact same questions about Matt Klein.

Predators. Another word the FBI expert from DC had used. "They choose their victims because the kids are trusting," she'd said. "Or they've earned their trust somehow, through positions of authority, favors, or treats."

Tutors were trustworthy.

Dale slapped the notebook closed and rubbed his face. The Cutlass motor coughed, and he tapped the gas pedal with his foot to keep it from dying. Just a few yards away, Dale noticed a young boy, a paperboy, resting on the street corner at the edge of the parking lot. He was leaning against a light pole with his empty canvas bag slung over one shoulder, flipping through a comic book and paying no attention to anyone or anything around him.

He was alone.

Dale backed out of the parking spot and rolled to the curb in front of the boy and stopped. He looked to be about Curtis's age, eleven or twelve, and wore the same shaggy haircut popular with prepubescent boys.

Dale leaned across the seat and rolled down the window.

"Hey, son," he called.

The boy looked up from his comic book.

"What are you doing?"

"Reading," he said. He flicked his head to get his long hair out of his eyes. He didn't appear guarded or cautious about Dale's presence.

As Dale was about to scold him for hanging around a street corner alone and give some version of a cop's lecture on safety, he stopped. He was curious to see how far he could push before the kid sensed danger.

"Do you need a ride somewhere?" Dale tried to

sound friendly. "I'm on my way to church. Which way you headed? I can give you a lift."

The boy closed the comic. "I live on Bundy." He pointed south. "That way."

"That's right where I'm going! Get in. Take a load off."

Without hesitation, the boy got inside the car.

Unbelievable. Dale's smile faltered. Only a week after Chris's abduction just blocks away, Dale was able to lure a kid into a strange car with a strange man, no questions asked, just by being normal looking and friendly.

"You a paper carrier?" he asked, nodding at the canvas bag.

"Yeah," the boy said. "Just finished my route. I'm tired. This neighborhood is hilly."

"I bet," Dale said. "What's your name?"

"Jason."

"Cool. That's my nephew's name." He nudged the boy more. "How about I blow off church and we hit the Hardee's drive-through and get you a Coke, Jason?"

Surely this would trip his alarm bells.

"Okay!" Jason's face actually brightened.

Dale was dumbfounded.

The idling car motor chugged as Dale hesitated. He shouldn't take it any further. He was due home an hour ago. Connie and Curtis would be waiting to eat breakfast with him. Not to mention that the lieutenant would rain hell down on his head if he found out about this little informal experiment.

But Dale had to know how far someone could get with kids despite everything in the news. The consequences were worth the answer.

He pulled onto Fleur Drive and started driving.

Several minutes later, he bought Jason a Coke at the Hardee's drive-though. When Dale passed the boy's neighborhood, suggesting they cruise around for a while, the kid didn't utter a peep of concern.

After thirty minutes of driving around the South Side, making it as far as the city limits, Dale finally took the boy home. He walked Jason to the front door of his modest blue house on Bundy and knocked, waiting with his badge in hand to have a stern and, frankly, frightening discussion with Jason's mother.

TWELVE

Three weeks, two days, four hours missing

SAMMY ENTERED MISS WARE'S seventh-grade science class just as the last tardy bell rang. She shot him a stern look. She'd written him four tardy slips already, and they were barely one week into the new school year.

He sat at his desk at the back of the room and crossed his arms on top of his red Trapper Keeper. He laid his head down, thinking about the new request.

That's what they were called now, *requests*. But from the beginning, there had been rules.

The Model Car Club was a secret.

Only special boys were invited to join the Model Car Club.

Members of the Model Car Club got perks, like extra model parts, deluxe tubes of paint and brushes, and all the candy and soda they wanted.

But if a member ever told anyone that the club existed, they'd be kicked out forever.

What happened during Model Car Club meetings was secret and never to be talked about with anyone, not even each other. That's how all secret clubs worked.

Sammy knew the rules, and he'd agreed to them because the Model Car Club was fun. At first.

But then, the rules changed.

More rules were added, and each rule was worse

than the last. And once he joined the Model Car Club, he had to do whatever he was asked to do. No refusing.

If he ever talked about the Model Car Club to any-one, he'd have to pay for every perk he'd ever been given, and it would be hundreds of dollars that would take him years to pay back. He would be punished, and the punishments would be terrible.

The first time he'd tattled about the club, he'd been caught and punished. And he'd been told that if he ever tattled again, his mother and his sister would be killed, and their house set on fire.

He'd heard the threats dozens of times. And even though he'd agreed to them, he'd tattled one more time without getting caught. But still, no one had helped him.

So, he had to just keep doing as he was told.

That meant no refusing.

He rubbed an itch out of his nose. Miss Ware's room smelled like gas from the Bunsen burners, and she never opened the windows, even when it was hot and stuffy, like today.

Miss Ware started attendance. "Cox, Samuel?"

First on the list. When Sammy raised his hand, his sweaty skin stuck to the plastic of his Trapper Keeper.

"Fatty Cox," someone snickered behind him. Sammy didn't turn around.

Miss Ware continued. "Davidson, Joshua."

A hand in front of Sammy popped up.

Sammy stared at the back of Josh's curly head of hair. Josh Davidson used to be Sammy's best friend. They'd been friends since first grade, but they'd drifted apart last year, after Sammy joined the secret Model Car Club and Josh got into sports. Josh was now friends with boys who played football and baseball and already had dark hair on their legs. Boys who teased Sammy about his weight and gave him wedgies in PE and made his life miserable. Sammy didn't play any school sports, and didn't have any hair on his legs, and once upon a time he would've liked to try junior high baseball. He'd had a pretty good throw before he got too heavy and winded easily.

But he hated baseball now.

He hated math and school and teachers and the paper route.

Josh and his desk mate rolled spit balls and shot them through disassembled pen cases at Tammy Larson, the most popular girl in their grade. It looked fun. No one ever asked Sammy to shoot spit balls with them. Instead, they shot spit balls *at* him. In science class, he didn't have a desk mate. No one had chosen to sit next to him at the beginning of the year.

The secret Model Car Club had ruined everything.

Sammy straightened and raised his hand again as soon as Miss Ware finished roll call. He asked if he could use the restroom.

Miss Ware removed the bathroom pass from a hook on the wall and held it out. "Make it quick, Samuel," she said.

Sammy took the pass—a laminated four-by-six index card that said *Miss Ware's Science Class Pass* on one side and *If you sprinkle when you tinkle, be a sweetie, wipe the seatie!* on the other—and strolled down the empty hall in no hurry. As he walked, he brushed his fingertips over the rough, brown brick walls.

He was relieved to find the boys' room empty and the only stall with a door available. He locked himself inside, his gut already cramping. His stomach hurt all the time now, and teachers like Miss Ware were annoyed with his constant bathroom requests. They assumed he was screwing around.

He sat on the toilet just in time. He leaned on his elbows. He might be here a while.

Someone had scratched *bag yer face* onto the metal door. Sammy reached out and traced the rough letters with his fingertip.

He felt like crying. It was only Tuesday and he was already having a terrible week.

Everything had started going wrong yesterday. It had been Labor Day and no school, so he'd ridden Chrissie's bike to South Town Park by the library. The weather had been warm and sunny, and he'd felt better than he had in ages. Chrissie was helping him every Sunday morning with his paper route, so Sundays weren't so bad anymore. Now that school had started, math tutoring and the baseball rec league were over. And, he'd decided, he was done with the Model Car Club for good. He just stopped going.

He started to feel safe, and it made him stupid.

At the park, he pumped higher and higher on a swing until the chains slackened and his stomach flipped. He felt light and free, the wind lifting his hair and the last of the summer sun on his face.

But no.

He wasn't free.

You haven't been to a club meeting for a while.

The voice. He dug his toes into the powdery dirt, stopping so abruptly it hurt his ankles.

I feel like you're avoiding me.

He'd been found again. He couldn't go anywhere.

I've been waiting to give this to you, but you're never alone anymore.

The too-small Smokey the Bear T-Shirt he'd dropped at the fair weeks ago.

Once upon a time, Sammy had liked the attention. He'd *craved* the attention. At home, there was never enough to go around. Chrissie tried to look after him, but she was always busy doing schoolwork and typing on her typewriter. And his mother was always at one of her jobs or doing laundry or sleeping or just too tired. She was a just-a-minute mom. *I'll help you in just minute, I'll look at it in just a minute, I'll play with you in just a minute,* but she didn't tell time like other mothers. A minute could mean an hour, or tomorrow, or never, and Sammy would get tired of waiting. Eventually, he stopped asking.

So, he'd liked the attention. He'd been happy to join the club, and it had been so much fun at first.

Until it wasn't.

Come sit with me on the bench so we can talk. I have a request.

Sammy hated that word now. *Request.* It only meant bad things.

No refusing.

He'd gotten off the swing and sat on the bench, clutching the T-shirt that he knew he would never wear as long as he lived.

In the bathroom, Sammy finished his business and left the stall. While he washed his hands at the sink, another seventh-grader entered and hurried to the urinal, unzipping his fly with panicked urgency, like he was about to pee his pants.

Sammy watched the boy in the mirror. He was new

this year. He was small and pale and seemed nervous, scurrying from place to place as if constantly late. They were in the same lower-level math class together, but until that moment Sammy hadn't paid much attention to him.

The boy zipped, then darted from the urinal to the sink and started washing his hands. When he pumped the soap dispenser and nothing came out, he clucked his tongue, helplessly looking around.

We need a new club member. I want you to find us one.

Sammy switched off the faucet and moved out of the way. "This one has soap."

"Thanks," the boy said.

Sammy dried his hands on the cloth-towel dispenser. *Find someone who could use a friend.*

"You're in seventh grade, right?" Sammy asked.

The boy dried his hands on the front of his I-Cubs shirt. "Yeah." The hems of his jeans were about an inch too short and exposed his white sweat socks.

"We have math resource together," Sammy said.

"Yeah."

"I hate math."

The boy smiled. "Me too."

Find something he likes. Something to talk about.

"You like baseball?" Sammy asked.

"Yeah!" the boy said brightly. "I went to a I-Cubs game this summer for my birthday and caught a foul ball."

"Awesome. I love…baseball too." The grossness of the lie clogged his throat. He hesitated, starting to chicken out.

No refusing. You know what happens when you refuse.

Sammy swallowed hard. "What's your name?"

The boy looked up at the ceiling as if trying to recall his own name, creating a strange pause.

"Curtis Fuller," he finally said in a quick breath. "You're Sammy. I know your name already."

"Cool. I'll look for you at lunch today."

Curtis's face bloomed with pleasure. "Okay. See you later."

He darted out the door and was gone.

Sammy started to follow but realized he'd left Miss Ware's hall pass on top of the toilet paper holder in the stall. He retrieved the laminated slip, and as he walked by the sinks, he caught a glimpse of himself in the mirror.

He had a small chocolate-milk stain in the center of his shirt again.

Sammy leaned closer to the glass, unblinking, daring the reflection to a stare-down.

He thought about the final warning at the park yesterday.

That Stewart kid is dead, you know. Just like the Klein kid. They didn't know how to keep a secret. That's what happens when you don't keep a secret. You disappear forever.

It wasn't a warning anymore. It was proof of what would happen to him if he disobeyed, or ever tried to tell again.

Sammy pinched his cheek, hard, between his thumb and index finger, squeezing until his eyes watered.

The reflection blinked first.

THIRTEEN

One month, twelve days, five hours missing

EVERYONE IN CRYSTAL'S journalism class was talking about a new trivia show that had debuted a few weeks ago and was trying out the reversed-answer-and-question format.

"This legendary Benedictine monk invented a bubbly beverage…"

"Who is Dom Pérignon?"

"This is another word for lexicon…"

"What is a dictionary!"

Kevin Jackson slid a cassette tape into Mr. Hollister's player and blared a Prince song from the crackly speaker.

Crystal paid little attention to the frenzied hum around her. Mr. Hollister was a lax teacher and frequently left the room to sneak a cigarette in the teachers' lounge, so it was usually up to Crystal as managing editor to keep everyone on task. But today, she was too distracted.

She should've been editing Kevin's article on the Lincoln High volleyball game last night, or proofreading an op-ed about the first woman vice presidential nominee, but instead she was poring over an article in the *Register*.

Mystery Man and Car Continues to Elude
       Police After Six Weeks
A dark-haired mystery man seen walking
near paperboy Chris Stewart before the
youngster vanished on the morning of
August 12 continues to elude police,
as well as a silver Camaro seen driving through the neighborhood around
the same time.

Crystal removed her magnifying glass from her pencil bag.

On Wednesday, police released a composite drawing of a dark-haired man
seen walking near the corner of Tenth
and Hillcrest… The unidentified man is
described by witnesses as white, approximately 30-35 years old, around 6
feet tall, and has short light-colored
straight hair parted in the middle.
Also being sought is a late '70s silver or gray Camaro. Police, however,
are unsure if the mystery man and car
are in any way connected.

Crystal sat back, tapping the end of her magnifying
glass against the paper. Early-seventies Camaro Z/28.
She jotted the information down in her spiral notebook.
Her friend Somphone shook a piece of paper in her
face. "Done," she said.
Crystal scanned the paper—a review of the soon-to-
be-released movie *Country*, about an Iowa family fight-

ing to save their farm. Somphone had scored a special invite for National Honor Society students to a sneak preview over the weekend.

"Thanks," Crystal said, and filed it in her journalism class folder to proofread later, though it probably didn't need it. Somphone's work was always near-perfect.

Somphone had moved from Laos to the United States and started at Wright Elementary in first grade, but she and Crystal didn't become friends until fourth grade when a few kids in their class started making fun of Somphone's eyes, pulling the edges of their own toward their temples and chanting, "Me Chinese!" Crystal, too, was teased about her eyes, and the girls eventually forged a friendship through their shared outcast status.

"What are you working on?" Somphone asked.

Crystal laid her forearm across the notebook. "Nothing. Just playing around with some ideas for another article."

"You should write about that teacher-in-space thing. I heard one of the third-grade teachers from Wright is applying. You could interview her."

"Maybe."

A teacher in space? Snooze. Nothing exciting would ever come of it.

Mr. Hollister finally returned, smelling like a dirty ashtray. He told Kevin to turn off the music and everyone else to shut up and get busy.

Somphone opened her physics book and started working through a set of problems.

Kevin sat at the desk next to Crystal and nudged her elbow. "When's the next meeting about the yearbook cover designs?"

Crystal flipped through the pages of her datebook. "Next Tuesday."

Kevin nodded and gleeked on the boy next to him, spraying a mist of saliva across the desk.

Disgusting. It was hard to believe she'd gone to homecoming with him last year and let him clumsily feel her up in the back seat of his dad's Oldsmobile.

Crystal returned to her work. She outlined another essay idea about Satanic cults and rituals spreading through the Midwest and a possible connection to the paperboy cases, but she eventually gave up and scratched it. The more she wrote about it, the dumber it sounded. Satanic worship seemed like something parents and politicians made up to blame for every teenage infraction. Listening to headbanger music? Satanic cults. Wearing black T-shirts and studded leather belts? Satanic cults. Smashing pumpkins on the driveways of despised teachers? Satanic cults.

The notion was so stupid she couldn't bring herself to write about it. Back to square one.

She picked up the newspaper again with Herb Almeida's front-page article. It reported that the reward was now $93,000 for any information leading to Chris Stewart's recovery. Crystal tried to imagine that much money. Lately she'd started to childishly daydream about solving the case and collecting the reward. All her college tuition problems would be solved. Her mother could quit her second job. Crystal would be a hero. She'd probably get her name and face in the paper. Maybe Herb Almeida himself would interview her.

But she couldn't waste her time on childish fantasies. She needed to focus on the essay for the scholarship, which was her best chance. And so far, her best topic idea was still the missing-paperboy stories.

She should check the library for any books about child abductions. Sammy would be there anyway, since Tina had signed him up for another "stranger danger" after-school program.

Last week, it had been a presentation for latchkey kids called "On Your Own," teaching safety tips and good practices. *Don't ever answer the door if it's a stranger. Don't ever tell a stranger on the telephone you're home alone. Never talk to strangers or get into a strange car. Post all emergency numbers next to the telephone. Always use the buddy system.* It must have scared the shit out of Sammy. He asked her to walk with him everywhere now.

Crystal leaned over. "Somphone," she whispered. "Can you give me and my little brother a ride to the library after school? I don't want to walk in the rain."

"Sure," Somphone answered.

Crystal turned to the *Register* page with the composite sketch of the mystery man in Christopher's case. She held the paper closer, studying the shape of the man's eyes, mouth, and hair. She read the description of the car once more.

Something niggled at the back of her mind.

Kenny Harris.

She'd seen a silver muscle car in his garage. She didn't know much about cars, but it could've quite possibly been a Camaro.

And Kenny lived in the same neighborhood as Christopher.

Interesting.

She flipped to a clean page of her notebook and started writing.

September 24, 1984
Herb Almeida DM Reg article mentions silver or gray Camaro being sought in case.
    K. H.? Southlawn Dr.
    Confirm make and model of car inside his garage.

She underlined the last notation three times.

AT THE LIBRARY, Sammy went straight to the meeting room for the presentation, and Crystal and Somphone claimed their usual table next to a window and near the newspaper racks. Somphone immediately got out her calculus book and started working through the assigned problems for tomorrow. Crystal did a quick drive-by of the study rooms—sometimes Sebastian tutored students there—but they were empty today. Next, she scanned the card catalog for books on child abductions. Disappointment all around.

She returned to the table and jotted down more ideas for her essay.

The High Price of Abduction: What It Costs to Search for a Missing Child
Mystery in Iowa: The Missing Paperboys of Des Moines
The High Price of Keeping Kids Safe

She made a giant *X* over the page. Crap ideas, all of them.

"Are you working on your American history paper?" Somphone asked.

Crystal removed her heavy glasses and rubbed the indentations behind her ears. "Not yet."

"What are you writing about?" Somphone fiddled with the fringe ends of her long, black braid draped over her shoulder.

Crystal slapped the cover closed, embarrassed. "Oh, it's just a little… I'm working on an essay for that journalism scholarship I told you about."

"What's your topic?"

Crystal hesitated, preparing to lie, but reconsidered. She trusted Somphone not to laugh at her idea. "It's about the missing paperboys. I just can't find the right angle."

Somphone stared at Crystal, her face blank. Her silence made Crystal nervous.

"I think those boys were kidnapped by a pedophile," Somphone finally said.

Crystal cocked her head. "What's a pedophile?"

"It's an adult who is sexually attracted to young children."

"You're making this up."

"It's true. Look it up in the dictionary."

Crystal didn't need to. She knew her friend had probably recited the definition word for word.

"How do you know about this?"

"I read an article about pedophilia in a medical journal when I was studying for the ACTs." She brushed the ends of her hair across her lips. "I bet Chris and Matt were snatched by someone who wanted them for *sexual gratification* reasons."

"That's disgusting."

"But it's a real thing." She sat up straighter. "There are also these types of pedophiles who go after kids they kind of already know, and they, like, gain their trust even more by being nice and buying presents and stuff."

"Like bribing them?"

"Mmm, more like…*charming* them into thinking they're friends. And parents, too. Like, they make people not suspect them because they're so nice and helpful with other things." Somphone dropped her braid and picked up her pencil. "Those pedophiles have a whole MO."

"MO?"

She sighed, exasperated. "Modus operandi?"

Crystal helplessly shrugged. "Some of us aren't walking dictionaries."

"It's Latin for *mode of operating*. It's a particular way or method of doing something, especially one that is characteristic or well established."

As Somphone spoke, Crystal hastily reopened her notebook and started writing everything down. She should've mentioned this to Somphone weeks ago.

"There are lots of famous missing-kid cases in the United States, if you're looking for more," Somphone continued. "A few years ago, there were those cases in Chicago and Oakland. And then all those kids in Atlanta."

Crystal's eyes widened. "What kids in Atlanta?"

"A bunch of black kids were kidnapped and killed in the late seventies, early eighties, I think. The Atlanta Child Murders. That's what they were called."

"Why haven't I ever heard of these cases? I read *The New York Times* in the school library every single day."

Somphone looked at Crystal like she was stupid. "Because the kids were black."

Crystal's cheeks grew hot at her ignorance. "I should go downtown to the Central Library and look some of this up in the archives," she said.

"I can drive you down there if you want," Somphone said. "They have some anatomy books I need to study before I retake the ACTs. And I'll find that medical journal article for you."

"That would be great, thanks." Finally, Crystal was on to a big idea. There was still so much to learn, though.

Sammy approached their table carrying a thin coloring book from the program he'd just attended.

"How was the meeting?" Crystal asked, taking the booklet from him. The title on the front read *Say NO! To Strangers*.

She flipped through the pages. "Did you learn how to say no to strangers?" she joked, but Sammy didn't laugh.

"I'm not afraid of strangers," he said. He grabbed the booklet from her and tossed it into a nearby garbage can.

FOURTEEN

Two months missing

DALE AWOKE AT DAWN. He lay staring at the triangle of light across the bedroom ceiling from the streetlamp, listening to the rattle and whoosh of their old furnace as it cycled on and off. He hadn't had a good night's sleep in weeks. Maybe Dr. Smith would give him a prescription for sleeping pills at his next appointment.

He rose, careful not to disturb Connie, still sleeping tightly curled in a ball beneath the comforter, and went to the kitchen to make a pot of coffee.

The early-October days were getting shorter, cooler. He shivered despite his warm flannel pajama shirt and pants. Connie would soon bring out the electric blankets and plastic tubs of sweaters smelling like mothballs. In two weeks, they'd set the clocks back an hour, and he'd leave for work in the dark and come home in the dark.

As the coffee brewed, Dale wandered into the family room and switched on the console television. He cranked the noisy dial, but most of the local channels still displayed the off-air bull's-eye signal or crackled with static. Last night, he would've liked to watch that new show *Miami Vice* all the guys at the station kept talking about, but Connie wouldn't allow it after proclaiming it pornographic. She did that more and more lately—dictated what he could and couldn't watch. He kind of liked the grittier shows, but Connie hated them. They were too upsetting, she said. She preferred wholesome family programs, like *The Cosby Show*, nice stories portrayed by nice actors. So, that's what they watched.

Dale gave up and switched the television off. He shuffled back into the kitchen and poured himself a cup of coffee. Outside the kitchen window, brown and crimson leaves from the oak tree in the backyard swirled to the ground, littering the grass. He would need to rake soon.

Two whole months.

For weeks, Dale had been following up on hundreds of tips generated by the tip line. He and his team had dredged ponds, walked miles through woods and cornfields, dropped divers into dozens of wells and cisterns, searched the garden sheds and basements of every known criminal living in the South Side. They'd tracked down supposed Chris Stewart sightings across the Midwest: Omaha, Kansas City, St. Louis, Chicago. They'd even sent a couple of investigators to Puerto Vallarta after Chris's uncle swore he'd seen him there while on vacation. But it wasn't him.

The reward was now up to $121,000, and Dale had been sure that amount would stir up something new, but nothing. The case was cold, and Dale knew it.

In the meantime, new cases piled up on his desk. An attempted sexual assault of a jogger at Gray's Lake. A robbery at a parking garage downtown. A stabbing at a bar on the North Side. Criminals didn't politely stop so cops could focus on searching for one missing kid. Dale was forced to do more and more of his investigative work for Chris's case in his off hours at home.

He sat at the kitchen table, sipping his hot coffee, and

removed his old Matt Klein case file and notes from his workbag. Even though he knew every corner of the case by heart, he kept trying to read the pages as if for the first time, hoping something new would shimmer on the horizon like a mirage.

He opened Chris's case file and laid it next to Matt's. Clipped to the inside of each folder was an eight-by-ten—the boys' most recent school photos, the photos used in all the media coverage. Both boys were handsome, all-American, their youth frozen in time, their smiles oblivious to the fates that awaited them just months after the camera bulbs flashed. Both had the same straight, shiny hair, a little grown out, swept to the right side with a deep left part. To Dale's eyes, the boys could've visited the same barber. The DMPD had recently formed a Profile Unit and evaluated the two cases for points of similarity. A solid benchmark was five points. The Klein-Stewart comparisons had eleven.

Agent Miller had also brought in several resources through the newly formed NCAVC, the National Center for the Analysis of Violent Crime, and their office generated a daily avalanche of material for Dale to read through. Crime-scene profiles. Victimology profiles. Criminal profiles. He picked up the latest report.

Common Characteristics of a Pedophile
Perpetrators are often male, over thirty years of
age, single or with few friends. Employment may
put them in contact with children...show prefer-
ence for child activities...hobbies are child-like
such as collecting popular or expensive toys...
...seek out shy, withdrawn, or vulnerable chil-

dren, may develop a close relationship with a single parent...

...often keep large collections of pornography somewhere in the home...

Show preference for certain physical characteristics in victims, such as body type, facial features, hair color or style...

As a child, grown-ups had frequently complimented Dale's hair—dark and thick, with natural waves.

He slapped the report facedown on the table and bumped his coffee mug, sloshing liquid over the sides and splashing the papers.

"God—" He clamped his mouth shut, catching the swear on the tip of his tongue. He rarely used profanity. But lately it was like trying to hold in a sneeze; the urge was overpowering.

"Dammit," he muttered under his breath.

Dale stood and ripped a paper towel from the rack next to the sink. He dabbed the papers and mopped the side of the mug.

He turned the FBI profile back over. The damp paper was stained and rippled, but the ink was still readable.

Employment may put them in contact with children.

Like tutoring.

Dale had tracked down every kid Sebastian Kovacs had tutored in the last year and spoken with them and their parents. Even though they'd all admitted to paying him under the table, no one had reported any concerns. He'd run Kovacs's driver's license, but not so much as a parking ticket had turned up. A check with the county treasurer had found one car registered to Kovacs two years ago, a two-door Ford, which was the same make of a car spotted in the Klein case, but Kovacs's registered vehicle was a red 1980 Granada, wrong model and color. Dale was still waiting on INS to get back to him.

Not enough to get him a search warrant for Kovacs's house.

He yawned and rubbed his face. It was Friday, and lately he'd come to dread Fridays.

For the past five weeks, Dale had kept a standing meeting with Bud Stewart after work at the food court in Southridge Mall. Dale would update Bud as much as he could on any new information about the case, and Bud would bring Dale any and every lead he came across. No matter how farfetched it sounded, Dale listened, took notes, and promised to follow up. So different from how he'd treated Marilyn Klein.

Every time they met, Bud looked haggard and wore a thin veil of desperation over his face. He talked about how he and Cindy's little corner store was struggling under the weight of Chris's case, and how the family was stretched thin financially. Donations and volunteers were drying up. People grew tired of being concerned and helpful and eventually returned to their own lives.

At some point during their meetings, Bud would inevitably stare off into space, his eyes growing shiny with tears. *I just don't understand*, he would say, shaking his head, unconsciously picking at the edge of his Styrofoam cup. *I just don't understand how they got him. Chris is a smart boy. He would never get into a stranger's car without a fight.*

Chris *is*. Always present tense.

Dale had considered the mode of abduction as well. Of all the witness accounts taken, of all the people driving by or jogging within a block of Tenth and Hillcrest, of all the neighbors in the surrounding houses with occupants awake at that hour and with windows wide open, no one had heard a single sound. Not a scream, a cry, or even a yelp. No scuffle or commotion from a struggle, no excited voices, no slam of a car door, no squealing tires. It had been the same in Matt's case, and two other high-profile cases a year later in Nebraska.

In September and December of 1983, there had been two boys kidnapped and murdered in the suburbs of Omaha—a thirteen-year-old from Bellevue while delivering *Omaha World-Herald* Sunday papers, and a twelve-year-old from Papillion while walking to school. A man had approached each boy, pulled a knife, covered their mouths, and forced them into his car within seconds. Their bodies were recovered days later. A month after the second murder, a preschool teacher who lived in the area called the police to report that she had seen a young man in a tan sedan cruising the streets, loitering around the neighborhood. She'd gotten a description of the car, the driver, and a partial plate number. By January, the assailant had been caught and confessed. Some radar tech at Offutt Air Force Base, a Boy Scout assistant den leader, and a former decorated Boy Scout himself. He was white, middle-class, clean-cut, and nice looking. No one would've ever suspected him, and Omaha cops wouldn't have caught him without the descriptions from the preschool teacher.

But Dale and his team had no such leads. He kept running it over in his mind. How could a grown man get a thirteen-year-old boy into a car against the boy's will without anyone seeing or hearing a single thing? Had there been a weapon, as in the Omaha cases? Chloroform? Stun gun? Whatever method, the boys were overpowered in seconds.

Chris Stewart was small for his age, thin and slight. Five feet, and barely 105 pounds. About the size of Dale at that age, or of Curtis now. But even Curtis was getting harder to wrestle to the ground and pin when they horsed around. Were a stranger to grab Curtis's arm and pull him, or bear-hug him from behind and pick him up, Dale was sure Curtis would fight. Kick, scream, claw, dig in his heels, wrench his arm free, even if he had to dislocate his shoulder to do it. He just couldn't believe that Chris Stewart and Matt Klein went as silent as air.

In Matt's case, witnesses reported seeing a strange man asking for directions in the area that morning. It was possible the same MO was used on Chris. Dale pictured the scenario that Bud could not: a midwestern kid, drilled to be respectful and polite and helpful, responding to a friendly stranger with little hesitation. *Hey, son, can you help me? I'm lost.* The boy, approaching the car. *Sure. Where're you going?*

Midwestern kids were taught God and manners, that such and such was *good* and such and such was *bad* and there was no in-between. They were hurried out of the room before serious adult discussions, shielded from words like *abuse*, *rape*, and *pedophile*. They remained safe and protected in the belief that the world was as happy as the inside of their own home. *Bad* was other places. Other cities. Places with more people than morals. *Good* was here, and people carried the belief in their back pocket with a sense of pride that bordered on stubborn smugness.

Dale knew this all too well.

He'd been one of those well-mannered midwestern kids who said *please* and *thank you* and *yes, sir* and *no, ma'am* and did what adults told him to. He'd never talked back; he'd never questioned.

He'd gone inside the house, willingly. Refusing would've been rude.

"You're up early."

Dale startled. Connie stood in the doorway of the kitchen, her flannel robe zipped to her chin.

"You scared me," Dale said.

"Sorry." She shivered and rubbed the sides of her arms. Her brown hair was rolled in small dark curlers held in place with pink plastic pins. One of the curlers at the nape of her neck was falling out.

"What are you doing?" she asked.

"I couldn't sleep. Thought I'd get a little work done."

Connie sat in the chair next to him. She picked up the files with the photos of Chris and Matt clipped to the inside covers.

"I never told you this," she said, "but until the Stewart boy went missing, in my heart I always thought Matt Klein ran away, or that his parents did something to him."

"Why would you think that?"

"I don't know. The mother is so…different." Her face was placid as she studied the photos.

"What do you mean? Different how?"

She waggled her head. "On television, her hair and makeup are too perfect and she hardly ever cries. She just doesn't seem sad enough."

The corners of Dale's mouth twitched with annoyance as his mind flashed to the scene at the fair. Marilyn's distraught behavior and *unperfect* hair and makeup would've surely satisfied Connie.

"Well, he didn't run away, and Marilyn and Lyle had

nothing to do with it," he said. "He was abducted and probably raped and murdered by a pedophile."

Connie flinched. She closed the file and delicately crossed her hands over the top. "You don't have to talk like that," she said. "Forget I said anything."

"What?"

"You're fishing for a fight."

"I'm not."

"You are. You know I don't like that kind of talk." She drummed her fingers and looked away. "Anyway. I pray for the families every night." Connie stood and carried his coffee mug to refill it from the pot on the counter. She started humming softly to herself. The conversation was over.

A heavy sadness settled onto Dale's shoulders, pressing down on him. Once, Dr. Smith had asked Dale if he'd ever tried talking about the pressure of his job with his wife, and he'd told her no, Connie found those kinds of conversations distasteful.

"And how does that make you feel?" Dr. Smith asked.

"Alone," Dale had answered.

Dale so badly wanted to tell Connie that lately he'd started to lose his faith in prayer. That when he prayed, it felt passive, like an excuse for not *doing* something. He no longer believed prayers would help find Chris. They hadn't found Matt. The burden of finding Chris was in Dale's work, and prayer wasn't going to help him.

Connie returned with the warm mug and handed it to Dale. He thanked her.

"I have faith you'll catch the animal who did this." She dryly pecked his cheek and set a frying pan on the stove to make him some eggs.

He looked back at the FBI reports before him, and

the sharp teeth of annoyance sank into his skin once more. Connie made criminals into *animals* and *monsters* because those terms were easier to digest than the fact that criminals—all criminals, no matter the crime—were just people. People who did horrible, heinous things. They were bankers, lawyers, and car mechanics; they were spouses and siblings and parents. They were military men and assistant den leaders for the Boy Scouts. Sometimes they lived just four houses away. They could be in Connie's Bible study group, and she'd never know it because it wouldn't occur to her that it was even a possibility. She was shunting the burden of truth to the Dales of the world, and that's what made him feel so alone.

Dale watched his wife move around the kitchen, the hem of her robe brushing the brown checkered linoleum. There was so much he kept from Connie. He never talked much about his work. He hadn't told her about the daily friction with Bradley, or the test on the paperboy and its resulting thirty-day probation, or the appointments with Dr. Smith and the medications.

He'd never told her about the years he'd lived in Hampton when he was a boy, before his family moved to the South Side. He'd never told anyone about Hampton. Not even Dr. Smith.

Connie cracked an egg into the skillet and resumed humming. The humming made Dale want to throw his mug against the wall.

He took a deep breath and counted, five seconds in, five seconds out.

Change the subject.

"Has Curtis made any friends at the new school yet?" he asked.

Connie stopped humming. "He made one," she said cheerfully. "A boy in his math class. They eat lunch together and talk about baseball. The boy gave him a walkie-talkie, and they chat at night. It's really cute." She tapped a spatula against her chin, thinking. "His name is totally slipping my mind, though."

Dale's own anxiety level lowered. "A friend is good. A good sign."

"I think so, too," she said. "That reminds me. Can you pick Curtis up from school today? I'm helping my sister wallpaper her bathroom, and it'll probably take all afternoon."

"Sure."

Connie slid the egg onto a plate and set it in front of him. "Don't be late. You know how he gets when you're late."

She ran her fingers through his hair, massaging his scalp. He closed his eyes.

"Your hair is long," she said. "You should go to the mall and get a haircut soon."

THAT AFTERNOON, despite his wife's warning, Dale left the station fifteen minutes late. Plenty of things made Curtis anxious—thunderstorms, fire alarms, the dark— but the tardiness of his father had to top the list.

He hurried across the parking lot and slid the key into the driver's side door.

"Will you find this boy?" A soft voice behind him. He turned around, his keys dangling in the lock.

It was Marilyn Klein, wearing slacks and a long wool coat, standing next to a station wagon parked one space away. She must've been waiting for him.

"Hello, Marilyn," he said.

She approached him slowly, hugging herself, as if chilly. "Are you going to actually *find* this boy?" she asked again.

Her beautiful blonde hair was curled and styled as usual, not a strand out of place, and bright-red lipstick outlined her mouth. "You wasted so much time…" She turned her head to the side. When she finally spoke again, her voice was barely audible. "Telling us Matty had run away. Telling us we were overreacting." She laid her palm over her heart. "You called me hysterical."

Dale slid his heavy workbag off his shoulder and let it fall to the ground. He took a step closer to her.

"Marilyn, I'm so sorry. If I could go back and change everything about how I first handled Matt's case, I would, but back then we didn't know—"

"All this time," she interrupted, "I've been saying it could happen again, it *would* happen again, and now it has."

Dale closed his mouth. Excuses were just that: excuses. They wouldn't bring her son home.

The last time he'd gone to the Kleins' house for a meeting—many months ago now, when he'd still been WDMPD—the front porch light was still burning brightly, as it had since the morning Matt disappeared, because Marilyn said she wouldn't turn it off until he came home.

She clenched her fists at her sides. "You let that monster who took Matty get away."

For a moment, Dale thought she might try to hit him.

But she turned back to her car. "Now he's followed you *here*," she said, opening the door. "Isn't that interesting."

DALE SCREECHED TO a stop in front of Brody Middle School twenty-five minutes late. Curtis paced back and forth beneath the front entrance overhang. He was overdressed for cool-but-not-cold weather in a knit hat, mittens, and a heavy jacket, the top and bottom snaps misaligned. As soon as he spotted his father's Cutlass, Curtis broke into a sprint, the straps of his overloaded backpack straining against his slight shoulders. Dale removed his .38 from his holster and tucked it beneath the front seat. Curtis hated guns, and just the sight of one made him more anxious than he already was.

Curtis got into the car and slammed the door, his cheeks bright pink.

"Where were you?" he cried.

"I'm sorry, little man," Dale said. "I got hung up at the office."

"I thought you forgot about me," he said. "I saw this van, a funny-looking white van, and it drove by twice, and it was going real slow, and I got so scared it was a kidnapper that I hid behind the wall until it was gone."

"Curtis, calm down. I'm so sorry." Dale stroked the back of his son's head, feeling his small body tremble. "Did anyone from the van approach you or try to talk to you?"

"Well, no." He twisted the dangling straps of his backpack.

"I'm sure it's nothing to worry about. But it's good that you're being so careful."

Curtis wiped his eyes.

"We could stop for some ice cream," Dale said. "How does that sound?"

"No, thank you. I need to go to the library. My books are due today." He stiffened with fresh anxiety. "I have to turn in my books or they'll be late and I'll get a fine, and I have another book on hold. It's the new *Garfield* book, and I need to get it before they take it off the shelf and let someone else have it, and then I need to find a book about frogs because I have a report to write for science about frogs, but I don't know anything about frogs!"

"Okay, okay," Dale said. "We'll go now. It's fine. Not a big deal."

Curtis finally removed his bag and tucked it between his feet. He settled back into the seat, his little body rigid in a forever uncomfortable-looking posture. Dale slid the console gearshift into drive and steered onto the street.

The parking lot of the South Side Library was nearly empty except for a couple of vehicles, unusual for this time on a weekday. Dale parked between two spaces near the back of the lot and kept the motor idling. A cop's habit—to sit, stand, or park with the best vantage point of all surroundings and exits.

"I'll wait here," Dale said.

"Okay." Curtis exited the car and trotted across the lot, his small stack of books clutched to his chest.

Dale rubbed a patch of rough stubble on his cheek. He'd forgotten to shave this morning.

He grabbed his workbag from the back seat and rifled through the increasingly disorganized contents until he found and removed a file folder of new reports Lieutenant Duff had given him before he left for the day. He licked his index finger and thumbed through the pages, scanning for anything that might be promising.

A report dated Sunday, August 19, caught his attention. One week after Chris's abduction, filed by Bradley. Dale didn't recall seeing Bradley patrolling the neighborhood that morning.

Bradley's report detailed a run-in with two kids standing at a corner talking to a man.

Sammy Cox, age twelve; Crystal Cox, age eighteen; and Sebastian Kovacs, age twenty-four, of Southlawn Drive.

Dale sat up straighter.

Stopped minor female and male after observing adult male carrying large black backpack talking to minors at street corner and minor male appeared distressed. Upon questioning, kids repeatedly stated they knew adult male personally.

Adult male not forthcoming and appeared nervous at this officer's presence. Questioning ended without further incident.

Bradley's time stamp was nearly twenty minutes before Dale had gone to Kovacs's house. And during their interview in the house, Kovacs had made no mention that he'd just seen and talked to Sammy and Crystal on the street, or to another cop.

And he'd been carrying a large backpack when Bradley stopped him, yet Bradley hadn't asked Kovacs what was in it.

Dale glanced at the library entrance, but Curtis still hadn't emerged. He leaned his head back against the seat and closed his eyes. In an hour, he was supposed to meet Bud Stewart at the mall, and he was already exhausted.

In his session with Dr. Smith earlier that morning, he'd told her he actually agreed with what Marilyn had said. "It is curious that yet another boy in my new jurisdiction went missing." He'd thought about his next comment carefully. "Maybe I'm cursed. Maybe things from my past are somehow attracting the same type of things in my present."

"Define these *things* in your present," she said.

He shrugged. "Things with my cases. But you know I can't talk about them specifically."

She stared at him for a long moment. Behind her, in a fish tank on the shelf, red and blue betta fish swam circles around a pink castle and bubbling treasure chest.

"Okay, then let's talk about these *things* from your past," she said. "We've been skirting this topic for some time now. In one of our first sessions you mentioned that your father moved the family from Des Moines to Hampton when you were ten for a job with a fertilizer company, and moved the family back to Des Moines when you were twelve, after the fertilizer company closed."

"Yes."

"And you said that you hated the two years you lived in Hampton. Can you tell me why?"

The treasure chest yawned open and closed. The betta kept swimming.

Mr. Parkhill.

We both have names that are compound words, he'd said. *Isn't that special?*

"I don't want to talk about Hampton," Dale answered. He'd left the session before his time was up.

In the car, Dale opened his eyes. He cranked the driver's side window down to let in some fresh air.

Dr. Smith's questions had ruffled the ashes.

He flipped through the sketchbook and his pages of notes, stopping on a list of scenarios he'd previously jotted down: *forced at gun or knifepoint, unconscious*

by blunt force, taser or stun gun, lured with a lie or
promise of something...

He glanced at the library entrance again. Still no
Curtis.

Back to his sketchbook. Timing was everything in
crimes. It was all about opportunity. The perfect circumstances. Dale knew this fact beyond his job experience. He knew it personally.

He pictured Chris Stewart at the corner of Tenth and
Hillcrest that August morning. Sitting on the ground,
rolling his papers. A car slows to a stop next to the curb.
I'm lost. I'm looking for my dog. Can you help me... The
ways to lure are infinite. Whatever the excuse, Chris
approaches the car, and as he leans down into the open
window, the man reaches out and grabs the back of
Chris's shirt. In one fluid motion, he pulls the slight
boy completely through the window and puts a knife
to Chris's throat. One spurt of adrenalized strength and
he has Chris in the car, pinned down on the front seat,
and immobilized without a flicker of resistance. Chris
lies stunned, unmoving, staring at the man, eyes wide,
too terrified to cry.

It could've happened without a single sound.

A car horn beeped and Dale jerked awake, disoriented. He hadn't realized he'd closed his eyes again. He
checked his watch. Only a minute had passed, but it felt
like an hour. He sat up and finally saw Curtis exit the
library, walking up the ramp. He ambled now, unhur-
ried, examining a new book in his hands. Paying no
attention to his surroundings.

A breeze picked up, sending swirls of dry leaves
skittering across the pavement, clicking like typewriter

keys. Clouds gathered in the west, preparing to bring gray, autumn rain.

A man exited the library and hurried up the ramp, following Curtis. Dale's jaw muscles tightened. The man called something out to Curtis, but the boy didn't hear, still too engrossed in his book. The man jogged a few steps, caught up, and grabbed Curtis's shoulder.

Dale reached beneath the driver's seat and retrieved his .38. With his badge in one hand and the gun concealed at the side of his thigh in the other, he exited his car and ran across the parking lot.

"Hey!" he shouted.

Curtis and the man turned to him.

"Police! Get away from that boy!" He thrust his badge in front of him.

The man's hands shot into the air.

"Dad?" Curtis's face twisted in confusion.

Dale slowed as he neared them. "I said get away from him," he said.

Curtis's eyes pinballed from the badge to the gun to the man and finally landed on his father's face. "Dad! What are you doing?" he cried.

"I—I'm a librarian," the man said, his voice shaking. "He left his library card on the counter."

Curtis held up a small white rectangle with his name printed on the front.

Dale then saw a name tag pinned to the man's green polo shirt.

Des Moines Public Library
FRANK
Senior Librarian

His arm slumped and he nearly dropped his badge. He holstered his gun.

"I'm sorry," Dale said. His breaths were so shallow he could barely get enough air to push the words out. "I thought… I thought you were…after him."

Frank slowly lowered his own hands. "Jesus Christ," he said. "What the hell is wrong with you?"

Dale covered his face. "The paperboy…thing…" He couldn't breathe. His heart slammed against his ribs. "I'm sorry."

Frank took a few steps backward, eyeing Dale, seemingly unsure how to respond. "Forget about it," he finally said, though his tone was anything but magnanimous. He turned and hurried down the ramp, back into the building.

"Why did you do that?" Tears welled in Curtis's eyes.

Dale still couldn't breathe, couldn't stop shaking. "Curtis, I…" He choked on the words.

"What's wrong with you?"

"I'm sorry," Dale whispered. "I'm sorry. I'm sorry. I'm sorry." They were the only words he could speak, like a prayer, an incantation. He reached out to touch Curtis, but Curtis recoiled and scurried to the car.

Dale followed, his feet leaden. Once inside the car, he gulped down more breaths. Raindrops began to patter against the roof and smear the windshield. Curtis was crying, making small mewling noises.

Dale reached out to straighten his coat, which had become bunched up around his waist, and fixed the mismatched snaps with clumsy fingers.

"It's okay, little man. I'm okay."

But Curtis continued to cry. Dale couldn't bring himself to look at the pain on his son's face.

His unfocused gaze tracked across the empty parking lot, past the library, and to the hill directly behind the building. There, a figure sat beneath a pine tree.

He squinted, the figure coming into focus. Familiar dark hair, dark complexion. Two round lenses of a pair of binoculars. The straps of a black backpack.

Dale squeezed his eyes closed. Opened them.

Not a hallucination.

Sebastian Kovacs stood and ran into the park behind the library.

He'd been watching the entire time.

FIFTEEN

Two months, ten hours missing

CRYSTAL SAT AT the kitchen table debating which pose to submit for her yearbook photo. Chin on her fist and smiling, or back to the camera and looking over her shoulder unsmiling?

She held up a sheet of wallets and scrutinized the looking-over-the-shoulder pose further. It was a good picture. She'd worn a blue sweater with a white ruffled-collar blouse underneath. Tasteful and mature. Tina had helped feather her bangs that morning, and applied some makeup—blue eye shadow to match the sweater and a touch of lip gloss. Crystal had removed her glasses for the picture, and without them she looked older. She wasn't JCPenney-model pretty like her mother or the popular girls at school, but she looked *smart* in the picture, and that was still something at least.

The police scanner chattered in the background, and she paused to listen. "Ten-fifty, accident on Army Post Road."

"Ten—fifty-one, tow truck needed." Nothing of interest today.

Crystal returned to the pictures and wished she had more poses to choose from, but two were all that came in the Sears discount package, the only one Tina had been able to afford. Crystal's senior picture had to be just right. There were so few opportunities for her to appear in the yearbook besides the journalism class and National Honor Society group photos. She wasn't in any sports or clubs, and no one ever thought to take candid shots of her bent over a dissected frog or cheering during a pep assembly. This year, she vowed to ask one of the yearbook staff members to snap a picture of her and Somphone in their caps and gowns. She'd personally make sure it was included on the graduation page.

Every now and then, her college and career ambitions made her feel like she'd missed out on typical teenage fun, but at the same time, she didn't feel like a typical teenager. Once, when she'd told Sebastian that she sometimes had trouble fitting in with kids her own age, he'd said it was because she had an "old soul," and it made her feel like he was the only person in the world who truly understood her.

Crystal decided to definitely go with back to the camera and unsmiling. She looked better in profile.

She also decided the wallets might look snappier with a fancy border, so she retrieved her mother's pinking shears from the junk drawer and started cutting apart the rows of pictures. On the blank side of each, in her best cursive handwriting, she wrote *Crystal M. Cox, Class of '85*, and made a neat stack with their pointed edges perfectly aligned.

The television clicked off in the next room, and Sammy wandered into the kitchen. He dropped onto a chair and jostled the table, making her mess up a *C* on the back of one picture. Crystal shot him a look.

"Will you play Chutes and Ladders with me?" Sammy asked.

"I'm busy." She signed another picture.

"Just one game? Please?"

Crystal snipped a crooked edge with the shears. "That's a kid game. Why would you want to play that?"

Sammy swiveled the chair back and forth. "I dunno. I just do. You used to play games with me all the time."

"When we were little." She switched to the pen. "Ask Mom when she gets home."

Sammy stood and bumped the table again. "Never mind." He trudged back into the living room and flopped onto the couch.

Crystal stopped writing and watched him. It was true, they used to play board games together all the time when they were children. Candy Land, Sorry, and Crystal's favorite, the Game of Life. She'd loved spinning the wheel and waiting with anticipation to find out her next adult milestone. Marriage? Career? Number of children? But she and Sammy hadn't played those games in years. It was weird that he'd asked after all this time.

Crystal started to say something to him but was interrupted by a knock at the door. She answered and was deeply pleased to find Sebastian standing on the stoop.

"Hello, Crystal," he said.

Cree-*stahl*. Her cheeks burned as she opened the door for him to enter.

"What are you doing here?" She saw him less now that he wasn't tutoring Sammy every week.

"I was just at the library," he said. "Thought I'd drop in and say hello." He was breathing heavily and perspiring, as if he'd been running. Damp hairs curled around his face. His binoculars hung around his neck, and he wore the black backpack again.

"What were you doing at the library?"

He kept glancing out the screen door at the street. "What? Sorry."

"I asked what you were doing at the library."

"Oh, um, bird-watching." He held up the binoculars.

"I thought you only did that in the morning."

"Yes, right." He touched his forehead. "Sometimes I go in the evening. But it started to rain, so I left."

"Would you like to sit down?" She was suddenly self-conscious about being home on a Friday night in sweat pants, listening to a police scanner. She must look like a loser with nowhere to go and nothing else to do.

"How about something to drink?"

"Something to drink would be nice. I'm quite thirsty." He peered into the living room. "Hello, Samuel. How are you?"

Sammy ignored him, rolled onto his stomach, and buried his face between the cushions.

"He's pouting," Crystal said in a low voice, "because I wouldn't play a game with him."

Sebastian nodded but made no further comment.

Crystal switched off the scanner and opened the refrigerator to hunt for a suitable beverage. It occurred to her that she couldn't think of a single time Sebastian had stopped by their house for a social visit outside of tutoring. And here he was, stopping by to see *her*. A smile crept across her lips.

She finally selected cranberry juice and poured two glasses. Sebastian sat in the chair Crystal had just vacated. He picked up a sheet of uncut photos and leaned closer. Crystal's skin flushed again. She touched her neck. It was probably getting splotchy.

"My senior pictures," she said, setting a glass in front of him. "They're terrible. I'm not very photogenic."

Sebastian ignored the glass and continued to study the pictures. "Not terrible at all," he said softly. "Quite pretty, in fact." He picked up the second sheet of pictures she'd rejected for the yearbook, the pose with her chin on her fist. "You should use this one. Your eyes look magical."

A wave of warm pleasure spread so intensely through Crystal's body that she had to sit down and take a big gulp of her juice.

Sebastian finally looked up from the pictures and clasped his hands in his lap. "How is school?"

"Good." She turned the glass between her fingers. He still hadn't touched his yet. Maybe he didn't like cranberry juice. She should've brewed some coffee. Juice was for kids.

"Have you applied to any colleges yet?"

Crystal ticked a list off on her fingers. "Iowa State, the University of Iowa, and Miami University. But Miami is my first choice."

"That's a fine school. Good journalism program. How is the article for that scholarship going? What's the name again?"

"The Young Journalists Writing Award."

"Right. You were trying to find an angle for the paperboy stories?"

"Yeah." She leaned her elbows on the table. "I'm still struggling. I've started a dozen different drafts but haven't settled on anything."

The television switched back on and blared the theme song of *The A-Team*.

"I've done some interviews and tons of research. I'm kind of interested in how the press covers missing-children cases nationwide, but I don't know."

Outside, rain began to pound the roof, and sheets of water ran down the windowpanes. The room darkened, and Crystal leaned over to switch on a light.

"Who have you interviewed?"

"Oh, like people at the mall, parents, you know, and their feelings or thoughts about the cases, the safety of kids. I also talked to a deputy about the 'stranger danger' program at the library Sammy went to."

Sebastian leaned forward. Their fingertips were mere inches apart. "A police officer?"

"Well, kind of. He was from the sheriff's department."

"Not the Des Moines detective working on the Stewart case?"

"He wouldn't be able to talk to me about it since it's an open case."

"I see." Sebastian shifted his weight in the chair. "Has he ever come back to talk to Sammy about the paper route?"

"No. Why?"

He ran his fingertip along the points of Crystal's pictures, then watched the rain patter against the window, his expression pensive.

She inched her hand closer to his, but Sebastian leaned back against the chair.

"No reason," he finally said. "It's not important." He finally picked up the glass and drained the juice in two gulps. "Would you like me to read the essay draft you're working on?"

"Really? That would be great. I'll go get it." Crystal left the kitchen and bounded up the stairs two at a time; the flutter in her stomach returned. As she searched her desk for the most current draft, she heard Sammy's walkie-talkie crackle loudly from his bedroom. A boy's voice cut through the static and echoed across the hall.

"Tubbs, this is Crockett. I just got home. Over."

She couldn't remember where she'd put her latest draft. She opened her schoolbag and searched the pockets.

"Tubbs, over. Do you hear me? The eagle has landed. I repeat, the eagle has landed."

The essay wasn't there. Crystal sat back on her heels and slapped the tops of her thighs, frustrated.

The walkie-talkie emitted an ear-piercing squeal and Crystal huffed, annoyed the volume was turned up so loud. She searched her desk again and finally found the typed draft stuck between the pages of her red notebook.

As she left her room, the boy's voice blared again, so she stepped into Sammy's room to turn the radio off.

"Sammy? I hope this thing is working." The boy sniffled and his voice cracked. "Can I tell you something? I hate my dad so mu—"

She switched off the power and hurried down the stairs. At the bottom step, Sammy's and Sebastian's hushed voices carried from the living room.

She peeked around the corner. They sat close together on the couch, in deep discussion. Sammy scowled, his brow furrowed into angry wrinkles and his mouth set in a stern pout. Crystal pressed herself to the wall, straining to hear what they were saying, but all she gleaned was random words from Sebastian. *Angry... I'm sorry... made this for you...*

This was beyond a disagreement about math. Confused, Crystal adjusted her glasses, as if the action might bring the scene into perfect focus and help her understand it.

Sebastian pressed something small and brown into Sammy's hand, and Sammy vacantly stared down at it. Sebastian then wrapped an arm around his shoulders and whispered into his ear, but Sammy shook his head and recoiled.

Crystal, too, shrank away, suddenly uncomfortable. Squeamish, even, about their interactions.

She silently slipped into the kitchen.

She immediately regretted spying on them. It probably wasn't anything. Sammy was crabby all the time these days, and like Crystal and her mother, Sebastian had to deal with the mood swings.

And yet...

She wanted to know what Sebastian had given Sammy.

On the chair where he'd been sitting, she noticed Sebastian's partially opened backpack. The same backpack he carried on his walks. She glanced toward the living room and, still hearing the hushed voices, lowered the rest of the zipper slowly so as not to make any noise.

She peered inside, expecting to find bird identification books of some kind or writing journals, but instead, the first thing she saw was dozens of cassette tapes. She walked her fingers down the spines, counting: ten copies each of two different Duran Duran albums, ten copies of the new Culture Club album, and an eye-popping twenty copies of Michael Jackson's *Thriller*. There were also several Atari games still in packages, and, in the very bottom of the bag, a fat roll of one-hundred-dollar bills secured with a rubber band.

Crystal picked up the roll and turned it between her fingers. There had to be several hundred dollars in it. She bit her bottom lip, trying to figure out why he'd be carrying so much cash. Her mother always wrote him a check for the tutoring sessions, and other families likely wouldn't pay him in hundred-dollar bills.

She replaced the money and told herself it was probably a bank deposit or something. A perfectly reasonable explanation.

She finished searching, but found nothing resembling the small brown item Sebastian had handed Sammy.

Someone moved off the couch in the living room. Crystal hurriedly rezipped the bag and sat. She ran her damp palms down her thighs and tried to quell the nervous knot in her stomach. Why was she so nervous? It was all innocently explainable, she reminded herself.

Sammy ran up the stairs in a blur, and Sebastian entered the kitchen. His gaze skipped to the bag, and for a brief, heart-stopping second, Crystal was sure she'd been busted for snooping.

"Here," she said quickly, holding out the typed pages, hoping to divert his attention.

Sebastian moved the bag to the floor and sat next to her. She exhaled a small, relieved breath and passed him the newly typed draft.

"'Have You Seen Me? How the Press Covers Missing Children in America,'" he read aloud, and nodded in approval.

He seemed fine, Crystal reassured herself. Like his normal self. Another sign that the discussion in the living room and items in his bag amounted to a whole lot of nothing.

Sebastian picked up one of her pictures from a pile. The picture he'd said made her eyes look magical.

"May I have one?" he asked.

A big, dippy grin spread across Crystal's face. "I don't care," she said, trying to play it off with nonchalance and failing miserably.

Sebastian carefully set the picture on top of his binoculars. As he settled deeper into the chair and started reading her essay, Crystal waited in silence, every cell in her body tingling.

Despite her pleasure, though, she couldn't stop glancing at the black bag on the floor.

Later, after Sebastian left, her picture tucked into the front pocket of the backpack, Crystal asked Sammy what he and Mr. K had been talking about, what Mr. K had handed him. She fully expected to hear any one of the reasonable explanations she'd already worked out in her mind.

But Sammy only stared blankly at her for a long moment, then said, "I have no idea what you're talking about."

SIXTEEN

Two months, two weeks, fourteen hours missing

ANOTHER FRIDAY EVENING, and Dale sat in the Southridge Mall food court alone, waiting.

Not for a meeting with Bud Stewart, but for a sighting of Sebastian Kovacs.

He sat at a table next to the carousel, where he could watch one of the main entrances, and sipped a cup of cold coffee. He'd been there for hours, but it wasn't like he had anywhere else to be.

Dale was halfway through a thirty-day unpaid suspension from the force—his punishment for the incident at the library after the branch manager called the station and reported it—and had been barred from doing any official work on the Stewart case until he was reinstated in mid-November. He'd already been on thin ice with the earlier probation. If he didn't get it together, he could lose his promotion or even be fired.

The fallout from the library incident hadn't been restricted to his job, though. When Connie found out what had happened, she'd snapped and told him to leave the house, find somewhere else to sleep. She didn't care where, just not in their house. He was out of control again, and this time he'd traumatized their son.

Dale had moved into a cheap motel by the airport the next day, and Connie said he couldn't see Curtis until he got himself straightened out. There was no end in sight to his exile.

So, he spent all of his time surveilling Kovacs, *unofficially*, until his suspension was up.

In the last two weeks, Dale had followed Kovacs to his tutoring jobs, the library, the grocery store, the bank. He sat in his car watching Kovacs's house, sometimes for hours at a time. He could picture every inch of the exterior. Every roof shingle, every gutter, every window outline, every shrub. He'd learned intimate details of Kovacs's life. He tutored students in their homes every Monday through Friday between three and five pm, though it appeared he was no longer tutoring Sammy Cox, something Dale would look further into. On Saturdays, Kovacs gave piano lessons in his house starting at nine am and ending at three pm. He still walked to South Town Park every morning at sunrise with his binoculars and black backpack, but changed his route daily. Yet no matter which route he took, he ended up deep in the park where Dale would inevitably lose him.

However, Dale had trailed Kovacs to Southridge Mall two Friday evenings in a row, where he'd observed him make a number of perplexing purchases. A pair of designer Calvin Klein blue jeans from County Seat. A half-dozen cassette tapes from Sam Goody. A pair of Nike sneakers from Foot Locker. A Walkman from Radio Shack.

Gifts, from what Dale could tell, that would appeal to prepubescent boys.

After two and a half hours of waiting, it was clear Kovacs wasn't coming this week. Dale dumped his coffee in the trash and started walking. He hated the mall, but he couldn't bear to go back to his depressing motel room that smelled like greasy takeout. He stopped in Kay-Bee Toys thinking he might buy an early Christmas present for Curtis.

Dale started in the Legos section. He picked up a space set but put it back, realizing he had no idea if Curtis still played with Legos anymore. He checked out a diesel freight train set, four hundred and twenty-five pieces. He would've loved it as a kid. When he was twelve, he'd developed an obsession with trains, especially electric train kits. He'd even started a little snow-shoveling business in his neighborhood, trying to save up enough money to buy an Allstate Military Train with Rocket Launcher kit.

So, you like toy trains? I have a really nice train set in my basement. You should come see it sometime.

That's how it had started. With his love of trains.

Dale shoved the box back onto the shelf, knocking the other boxes down in the row.

He moved on to the next aisle. Model kits.

He scanned the dozens of boxes. There were so many to choose from. Airplanes, helicopters, military ships, pirate ships, trucks, and cars. So many cars.

Dale picked up a box for a 1969 Chevelle SS 396.

A muscle car. Like the one in Kovacs's kitchen. Like the one Sammy Cox had been playing with.

He replaced the box and hurried out of the store with a new idea. Across from Kay-Bee Toys was Haircrafters Salon. He touched the shaggy hair at the nape of his neck that Connie had gotten on him weeks ago about getting trimmed. He walked over to the salon window and peered inside.

She was there, washing a woman's hair in a basin.

He went inside.

A young woman behind the desk greeted him.

"I want a haircut," he said.

"Do you have an appointment?"

"No. I want Tina Cox to cut it."

"Oh, well, let me see." The woman ran her finger down the page of a large appointment book open on the desk. "She's with a client right now, but…" She clicked her tongue. "Just a cut, right?"

"Yes."

"Hmm. She could possibly squeeze you in a quick trim if you don't mind waiting—"

"That's fine," Dale said. He gave her his name and sat in the small waiting area.

Thirty-five minutes later, Tina stood before him.

"It *is* you," she said, smiling.

"It's me."

She fluffed her bangs off her forehead. "It's nice to see you again," she said. "You're here for a haircut?"

"I am. I hope you can help this mess. I'm a little overdo for a trim."

"I see that." She led him to a styling chair, where she draped a black plastic cape around his neck.

"Thanks for fitting me in," he said.

"Lucky for you, I have a few minutes before my next appointment." As she burrowed her fingers deep into his hair, her perfume enveloped him. Something sweet and powdery.

"What do you normally get?" she asked.

He watched her in the mirror. "Uh, a buzz cut, I guess. I'm not very trendy."

"No perm?" Tina laughed, and her large, black hoop earrings swayed like tire swings, brushing the tops of her shoulders. "A buzz cut it is."

She misted his hair with a water bottle and combed it out. Dale's neck and shoulders relaxed beneath her touch.

"How's Sammy?" he asked. "Still delivering papers?"

"He's good. Yep, still doing the route. Crystal goes with him since the...you know. The Stewart kid."

Tension crept back into Dale's neck at the mere mention of the case. He changed the subject.

"Is Sammy still tutoring with Mr. Kovacs?" he asked, even though he already knew the answer.

"No," she said. "Not since school started." She lowered her voice. "Plus, I just couldn't afford him anymore with the holidays coming up."

Dale was ready to push harder. "You liked Mr. Kovacs, though?"

"Yeah, he's a really nice guy. Sammy probably would've flunked sixth grade without him."

"You trusted him to be alone with Sammy in the house?"

She scoffed. "Of course! I trust my kids with him more than with my ex."

Dale tried another approach. "How did you find him? For the tutoring, I mean."

"My friend Kathy recommended him. She used to work here at the salon and talked about how patient he was with her son Corey, and how affordable his rates were."

This was good. Exactly what he'd hoped for. Dale mentally started a new file. "What's your friend's last name?"

"Collier." Tina flipped on electric clippers and started shaving his neckline. "Her husband died and mine wasn't around, so we used to talk about how, you know, it's good for boys to have a male presence around as much as possible."

Dale ignored the pang of shame about his own situation. "Where does your ex-husband live?"

"Miami." Tina exhaled, and her warm breath grazed his ear. "It's hard being a single parent," she said. "Chrissie's a great help, don't get me wrong, but Randy, that's my ex, is such a deadbeat. He's always behind on his child support payments, hardly sees the kids, blah, blah, blah. You know how it goes."

"Yeah," Dale said.

"And now"—she brushed a hair sliver off his cheek with her fingertip—"he just sprang the news on me that he's getting married and his fiancée is pregnant. Her name is Candy. They'll be Randy and Candy Cox." She laughed with a small snort.

"Oh, that's bad."

"Exactly! But I haven't figured out how to tell the kids yet. I'm putting it off, I suppose. I don't know how they'll take it. Especially Sammy. The divorce was really hard on him." Tina turned off the clippers and switched back to the scissors. "It's not that I miss *him*, but I do miss having someone to come home to every night, you know?" She gently pushed his head down to cut the back of his hair. "It gets lonely. Since Randy and I split up, I've only dated a couple of guys. One was really nice and so good with Sammy, but…" She rubbed her lips together. "There just wasn't any spark."

Tina moved in front of him and leaned over to trim along his brow. "I don't know why I'm telling you all of this. I'm babbling. I shouldn't complain. I have a lot to be thankful for." The neckline of her blouse gaped open and Dale couldn't help but glance at her cleavage.

"You're not babbling," he said, forcing his gaze away. "I like your honesty."

"I'm sure it's way harder being a parent and a cop with all the horrible stuff you see," she said. "Doesn't it ever get to you? Like when that Marilyn Klein made such a scene at the fair? Ugh." She clicked her tongue. "I felt so bad for you."

He shifted his weight, and the plastic cape rustled. Tina's comments had caught him off guard, and he suddenly felt exposed in a way he wasn't used to, not outside Dr. Smith's office, anyway. Connie never said things like that to him, or asked how he felt about his work, and he certainly never talked to other guys on the force about it.

"You get used to it, I guess," he finally said.

"Still," Tina continued, "it has to be hard carrying around all the sad and depressing things you see."

There was something warm and comforting about Tina. Disarming, even. She was surprisingly easy to talk to in a way Connie wasn't. He didn't think Connie was that way on purpose; it was just another complicated part of being married to a cop.

"It is hard to talk about the things I see," he said quietly. "It's hard on my wife. We have...struggles."

Their eyes met. "I'm sorry to hear that," she said.

Tina straightened and squeezed a small dollop of foamy mousse into her palm and rubbed it through his hair.

"All done," she said, spinning the chair to face the mirror.

He turned his head from side to side. "Looks good. Thank you."

Tina removed the cape and brushed his neck and face clean with a dry towel.

"Very handsome," she said. She rested her hands on the tops of his shoulders, and their eyes met once more in the mirror reflection. "You can come back to me anytime."

SEVENTEEN

Two months, two weeks, four days, thirteen hours missing

"SAMUEL, TURN THAT OFF!" his mother called.

Sammy sat on the floor in front of the console television transfixed by the news footage of starving people in Ethiopia. Children with swollen, empty bellies, too weak to even cry. Men and women with every rib showing, every bump of their spines dotting their backs. The children looked like they were going to die at any moment, right before his very eyes. He leaned closer to the screen and touched the face of an infant tearlessly crying. He wondered if it was painful to die of starvation, and how long it would take.

His mother stepped in front of the screen and pushed off the power button. "You shouldn't watch this," she said.

"Why not?"

"It's disturbing. It's not appropriate for children." She dried her hands on a towel. "Come eat your dinner."

Sammy rose and followed her into the kitchen. She set a plate in front of him, Double cheeseburgers, tater tots, and pickles on the side. To drink: Tab soda. Her answer to putting him on a diet.

He thought about what his mother had said, that starving kids on television were too disturbing, and he nearly laughed. He wanted to ask his mother if she was joking. He propped his head in his hand and blew billowing steam off the tater tots. Sammy loved his mother, but sometimes he hated her, too.

Crystal slumped into the chair across the table from him and kicked his feet out of the way.

Sammy leaned closer to his plate and caught a tangy whiff of the pickles. He picked up one perfectly golden potato and popped it into his mouth. Then another. And another. He squeezed a glob of ketchup onto the center of his plate and dunked the burger. Dunked more potatoes. He ate the pickles, one after another without stopping. When all the food was gone, he licked the last streaks of ketchup off his empty plate.

Sammy eyed his mother at the stove, grilling two more burgers for herself and Crystal. He was still hungry. He thought of the starving people on the television and felt bad.

"Are you sure you don't want to trick-or-treat tonight, Sammy?" Tina asked. She flipped one of the burgers, and grease splattered the wall behind the stove.

"I already told you," he said, "I don't want to."

It was October thirtieth, Beggars' Night for the city of Des Moines, and his mother wouldn't stop pestering him about trick-or-treating no matter how many times he gave the same answer.

Tina set a plate down in front of Crystal. "I just hate for you to miss out on all the fun. I loved Halloween and dressing up when I was a kid. I was sad when I got too old to do it."

"If you love it so much," Crystal asked, cutting her burger in half with a knife, "then why do you turn off our porch light to keep trick-or-treaters from stopping at our house?" She handed Sammy her pickle. He greed-ily ate it in less than three bites.

Tina pointed the spatula at Crystal. "Because bags of candy are expensive."

Sammy moved his plate aside and laid his head on the table in the crook of his arm. Last year, he'd dressed up as Yoda with a plastic mask and an old white bath-robe of his father's that he'd found in a closet. He'd carried an empty plastic ice cream bucket and told the same joke at every house for his "trick." *Why did the ghost go trick-or-treating on the top floor? Because he was in high spirits!*

Mr. Tibbs meowed beneath the table and rubbed against Sammy's leg. Sammy nudged him away with his foot.

The ghost joke was stupid. All jokes were stupid.

Sammy got up to look for something else to eat from the fridge. He opened the door and studied the shelves. Dried-out leftover meatloaf, a package of bologna, milk, and condiments. His mother hadn't bought groceries in over a week. He grabbed the Anderson Erickson milk carton. When he set it on the counter, he noticed two printed photos on the back, one on top of the other.

Matt Klein and Chris Stewart.

HAVE YOU SEEN EITHER OF THESE YOUNG MEN?

Their pictures were everywhere: on milk cartons, paper bags at the Hy-Vee grocery, bulletin boards in the post offices and banks, on the nightly news, and in the papers.

Sammy tipped the carton and stared into the boys' eyes. *They didn't know how to keep a secret. That's what happens when you don't keep a secret. You disappear forever.*

A cramp rippled through his stomach.

Sammy replaced the milk carton in the refrigerator door without pouring himself a glass. His stomach hurt too much to eat anything else. He sat back down at the table.

Tina slid a burger from the skillet and onto a bun for herself before taking a seat at the table next to Sammy.

"I've never understood this Beggars' Night," she said. "It's so weird. In Florida, we just trick-or-treated *on* Halloween night like everyone else. I don't get why they do it on a different night here."

"I know why," Crystal said. "I read about it in the paper." She balled up her napkin. "It was started in 1938 during World War II by the Des Moines Playground Commission, or what we now call Parks and Recreation. And they started it because Halloween night had become a problem with vandalism and destructive behaviors like setting fires and breaking windows." She leaned forward for effect. "Just real hooliganism, as they called it back then."

On the table next to Crystal's plate lay a steak knife. Sammy reached out and traced the black handle with his fingertip. He wanted to take it to replace the scissors, or any one of the knives from the knife rack, but his mother would notice. She'd ask questions. Throw a fit. Turn the house upside-down looking for it. She paid close attention to very particular things: her cigarettes, money in her wallet, rolls of tape, and *anything* from the kitchen.

"Here's another interesting fact," Crystal continued. "The commission started a campaign to encourage less-

violent forms of Halloween fun and declared Beggars'
Night to henceforth be October thirtieth between the
hours of six to eight in the evening. And they further
required that children only receive their treat after *earn-
ing* it by performing a trick or telling a riddle. It was
also their way of encouraging children to aid in the
war effort by working for their candy and not disturbing the sleep of war workers late at night." She closed
her mouth and finally shut up.

Sammy laid his head back down. He didn't care how
Beggars' Night had started.

"That's interesting," Tina said, but her tone sounded
forced. She took a large bite of her burger.

Sammy sat up. "It's fucking stupid!" he blurted.

Crystal's mouth fell open, and Tina stopped chewing. Sammy had never used a swear word in front of
their mother before.

Tina swallowed. "Sammy!" she said. "Watch your
mouth!"

But Sammy didn't care. Beggars' Night *was* f-word
stupid. Everything had become f-word stupid, and he
was tired of pretending like it wasn't.

He stormed out of the kitchen and flopped onto the
couch in the living room.

Outside, trick-or-treaters streamed along the sidewalk in front of their house. A scarecrow. A gremlin.
A little girl in a homemade Rainbow Brite costume
with a wig made out of bright-yellow yarn that she
kept scratching. Four Ghostbusters. The one dressed
as Venkman had been a friend of Sammy's until sixth
grade, when everyone declared Sammy was too fat to
play with anymore.

Tina sat next to him. She smelled like cigarette smoke and burger grease.

She handed him a red Tootsie Pop, his favorite. The wrapper had the picture of a Native American Indian aiming a bow and arrow at a star that could be turned in to stores for a free sucker.

"What's wrong with you lately?" she asked.

He kept staring out the window.

"Why don't you go with your new friend? The one you talk to on your radio all the time?"

Sammy knew she couldn't remember his name, and he couldn't bear to say it out loud. "His mom won't let him go. She doesn't allow him to have candy."

Tina reached out to push his hair off his forehead. "Well, that's no fun."

Sammy jerked his head away from her.

"Why are you so crabby lately?"

He buried his face in the cushion. "I don't know." The house was chilly, and he shivered, but his mother refused to run the furnace until November to save on their electric bill, no matter how cold it got.

"I'm sorry. I'm just tired."

Tina patted his knee. "Go to bed early tonight, okay?" She stood. "I'm going upstairs to take a bath."

"Okay," Sammy said, but he didn't look at her.

Crystal entered the room and sat cross-legged on the floor. She pulled on the knob of the console television and turned the dial to channel five. The screen crackled to life. *Family Feud* with Richard Dawson.

Sammy closed his eyes. He'd told Curtis Fuller the ghost joke today at school, and Curtis had laughed at it. It cheered him up, he said. He needed cheering up since his dad moved out. Curtis said Sammy was his special friend—his *secret* friend—and that he didn't want his dad ruining it with all his strict rules.

That word was everywhere, *secret*. It made Sammy's skin crawl. He never wanted to hear it again. Once upon a time, secrets had meant something fun, or something to keep him out of trouble. Now, secrets were ugly and scary and rotted his insides.

Curtis already trusted Sammy, he could tell. Sammy acted interested in his baseball cards and sneaked him pieces of bubble gum. He'd told Curtis that his dad had moved out, too, and that he understood what it was like to live with just a mom.

It had been that easy.

Sammy had been that easy, too, when a grown-up started being extra nice to him. Spending special time with him, listening, being interested in the things Sammy liked.

Mr. Tibbs jumped onto the couch and burrowed his head against Sammy's leg. Sammy scratched between his ears, gently at first, then with a little more pressure, until Mr. Tibbs's head was pressed to the cushion and the cat meowed.

"Hey!" Crystal yelled, and Sammy jerked his hand away as if he'd been bitten. The cat darted from the room.

Sammy wrapped his arms around himself and pinched his fat belly as hard as he could. He'd never hurt his cat before. He didn't know why he had just now. He was so mixed up, it made him want to cry.

"Why were you doing that?" Crystal's face scrunched in anger.

"I was just playing." He got off the couch and started for the stairs.

In his room, he lay down on his bed and switched on his walkie-talkie.

"Crockett, this is Tubbs. Are you there?"

Within a few seconds, his speaker crackled.

"This is Crockett, over!" Curtis was always excited to use the walkie-talkie Sammy had given him.

"Is your mom close by?"

"Negative, over."

"What did you eat for dinner?"

"Fried chicken and dumplings, over. Very delicious, over. How about you?"

"Burgers and tater tots," Sammy replied. "They were okay."

"Hey, Sammy, I mean, Tubbs, I have good news."

"What is it?"

"My mom finally agreed to let me have a sleepover, and she's not going to tell my dad so he won't make a big deal out of it. This Friday night. She's going to call your mom. Please confirm, over."

Crystal pushed his door open. "Who are you talking to?"

Sammy leaped off his bed. "No one! Stop eavesdropping!" He slammed the door in her face and lay back down.

"Crockett?" he said quietly. "Are you still there?"

"Affirmative," Curtis answered. "So, how about the sleepover? This Friday. That's three days from now. Can you come?"

Sammy stared up at the water spots on his bedroom ceiling. He was out of time. If he didn't deliver a new boy now, he'd end up just like Matt and Chris. *Disappeared.*

He didn't need to ask his mother. He already knew she'd say yes.

"Affirmative," Sammy said.

Curtis clicked the radio three times, their code for *that is awesome*.

Sammy knew what he had to do next.

"Crockett?"

"Yeah?"

"Does you mom have a Polaroid camera?"

"Affirmative!"

Sammy clicked the button three times.

No refusing.

EIGHTEEN

Two months, three weeks, ten hours missing

MISSING IN AMERICA: A DARK THREAT OF TERROR
By Crystal M. Cox

In an August 15th, 1984, editorial, <u>Des Moines Register</u> editor James P. Gannon proclaimed that our capital city has a dark threat of terror walking the streets. It took Matthew Klein from the West Des Moines suburb in 1982, and it took Christopher Stewart two years later on the South Side. "A sinister shadow," Mr. Gannon called it, darkening our doorways and our lives.

Marilyn Klein, Matt's mother and now missing-child activist, has been vocal about her beliefs that Matt was taken by an organized national child sex ring.

With high profile cases like the Atlanta Child Murders, the murdered paperboys in Omaha, Nebraska, and the high number of abductions in Chicago, Illinois, and Oakland, California, cit-

izens are on high alert for people
acting strange or suspicious, for anyone who remotely resembles a sinister
shadow. Satanic cult activity, rampant
drug abuse, burglary and

CRYSTAL STOPPED AND stared at the words she'd just typed, chewing on the side of her thumbnail. She yanked the paper from the carriage, crumpled it, and tossed it onto the floor with the growing pile of discarded false starts. Every topic she'd tried just wasn't right. Too general. Too unfocused. Too bland. And she had only a couple of months left until the scholarship deadline.

She opened the top drawer of her desk and removed the letter, hidden inside a copy of her dictionary, and unfolded it to read once more.

Dear Crystal Cox,

Congratulations! We are pleased to offer you admissions to the University of Miami School of Communication in Journalism, beginning Fall term of 1985.

We are very enthusiastic about offering you a spot in our program and hope that you will accept this invitation to join the other talented men and women in our school.

We're further pleased to inform you that your combined high school academic record and ACT

test score qualify you for a merit scholarship val-
ued at $4,000 ($1,000 annually).

A final commitment must be made by April 15,
1985, to ensure your spot in the program and to
reserve student housing if needed.

Again, congratulations, and go Hurricanes!

She traced her fingers over the words. The letter
had arrived that morning. She'd locked herself in the
bathroom, sat on the toilet lid, and unfolded the paper
with trembling hands. Then that first word, *Congratu-*
lations. She'd leaped to her feet and mimed a spastic
dance of joy.

But now, reality.

Crystal had done the math a dozen times. Private,
out-of-state tuition at MU was nearly $5,000. Even with
the yearly merit scholarship, she would still owe nearly
four grand. Her mother's annual earnings at the salon
and restaurant barely cleared $10,000. Crystal knew this
as fact, since she'd peeked at Tina's tax returns while
filling out student loan applications last month.

If she won the YJWA, that would give her another
two thousand annually, and she could cover the rest
with student loans, especially if she lived off campus
with her father, got a job within walking distance that
could accommodate her limited eyesight, and ate nothing but canned soup.

She switched off the typewriter. Icy rain tapped
against her bedroom window.

She *had* to win the award. There was no plan B.

Crystal opened her notebook and faced another blank page with no new ideas.

"Chrissie!" Tina hollered from her bedroom. "Come help me!"

Crystal closed her notebook and slipped it into her school backpack. She trudged to her mother's room.

"What?"

Tina stood before piles of clothes littering the top of her water bed. She wore a white, poufy-sleeved uniform blouse with embroidered edges and black slacks. A heaping basket sat on the floor next to her.

"Can you help me finish this?" Tina asked. "I'm going to be late for my shift at the restaurant." She took a drag from a cigarette and set it in an ashtray atop the headboard.

"Where's Sammy?"

"Staying over at a friend's house."

Crystal crouched on the floor and sorted through the clothes in the basket, creating three separate piles.

"This is good, right? That he's finally got a friend his age?" Tina rolled a pair of tube socks. "He's doing better, don't you think?"

Crystal looked up at Tina. Her expression was hopeful, pleading, almost.

"Yeah," Crystal said. "Sure." She said it even as she thought of the bed-wetting and his bizarre outburst at Halloween. She said it because she didn't want to crap all over her mother's optimism and put her in a bad mood. She needed to soften her mother up if she was going to have any hope of broaching the topic of college again.

This was how Crystal would forever think of her mother: frosted blonde hair curled and teased and sprayed into an airy white cloud, and that pretty face at any age with a perpetually tired but hopeful expression. Crystal hadn't inherited her unwavering optimism, and her father had once told her that was a good thing. Sometimes, he said, her mother needed to take the rose-colored glasses off and see things for how they really were.

Tina hurriedly loaded Sammy's clothes into a round basket and held it out to Crystal. "Can you put these away?"

Crystal took the basket and crossed the hall. She opened the door and was greeted by a wall of boy smell: dirty feet, hormonal fart-y funk, and noxious model paint and glue fumes. She unloaded clothes in the dresser first, then moved on to hang up shirts in the closet.

She opened the bifold doors and found Sammy's usual chaos. Boxes of spilled puzzles, board games with crushed and flattened lids, Masters of the Universe and G.I. Joe action figures mixed and mingled with Hot Wheels cars. She moved the toys aside with her foot and started hanging his shirts on hangers.

Finished, she was about to close the doors when she glimpsed the corner of a small cardboard box on the shelf above the clothing rod. A pair of blue jeans was oddly draped over it. She pulled the jeans off, exposing red letters on the side of the cardboard. She tilted her head and read: *HVAC*.

Crystal slid the box down and sat on a rumpled sleeping bag on the floor. She pulled the flaps apart and peered inside.

On top were dozens of candy bars and more empty wrappers. She dug through Kit Kats and Whatchamacallits, Jolly Ranchers and Starburst, wondering where he'd gotten the money to buy so much candy. Their mother kept all his paper route earnings in a mason jar in the kitchen to help him save up for an Atari, but the last time Crystal checked, the jar had been at nearly $85, so he clearly hadn't been spending it.

She popped a watermelon Jolly Rancher into her mouth and kept looking. Mixed in with the candy bars was a brown cloth pouch. She pulled apart the drawstrings and dumped the contents into her palm. Hard white chips that smelled like garlic. She put the pouch back together and set it aside.

Crystal rummaged deeper into the box and, beneath the layers of candy and wrappers, found a magazine, facedown. She turned it over and was shocked to find a half-naked woman on the cover. "Playmate of the Year." Curious, she looked inside. Page after page of fully naked women. Beautiful women with long legs and full, round breasts. She leaned closer to one picture, trying to understand the appeal to men, wondering if Sebastian liked this type of woman. Surely not. He was sophisticated and intellectual. He appreciated deeper things in a woman, she was sure.

She shut the pages, surprised Sammy was already into this stuff. He'd never seemed the least bit interested in girls.

Crystal stood, preparing to rat him out to their mother about the magazine, when a picture slipped from the pages onto the floor. She picked it up. Another Polaroid of a shirtless boy, this time one she didn't recognize. He had shiny red hair and a mass of freckles over his nose and cheeks. His arms were crossed over his bare chest and his smile was relaxed. The picture cut off at his waist, barely catching the elastic band of white underwear.

She squinted, scrutinizing the background. Same plain wooden studs and plywood walls. She leaned closer. Just behind the boy's shoulder, the corner of what looked like a striped mattress.

Crystal crawled over to Sammy's bed and lay on her belly, reaching beneath, pushing the junk and garbage aside. It was still there. The first Polaroid of a young Corey Collier. She sat up and held the two pictures side by side. The background was the same.

Two pictures of shirtless boys no longer felt like harmless fun, like adolescent kids goofing off with their mother's camera. It now felt...troubling, though she couldn't pinpoint why.

Her mouth turned dry, the sliver of candy stuck to the roof. She picked it off with her fingernail and spat it back into the wrapper.

Where was Sammy getting all this stuff? Maybe the Polaroids and magazines had come from the same place. Crystal checked the cover of the magazine in the box, but the address label had been peeled off. This was snitch-worthy stuff, but Crystal still wasn't exactly sure what she would be snitching about, and she didn't want to get her brother in hot water over nothing.

"Chrissie!" Tina shouted. "I have another basket for you to put away!"

Crystal tucked the Polaroids into the back pocket of her jeans, replaced everything in the box, closed the flaps, and shoved it back onto the top shelf. She arranged the jeans as she'd found them and closed the doors.

When she returned to her mother's bedroom, Tina

was folding a basket of sheets. Crystal grabbed a crumpled pillowcase and helped. The Polaroids crinkled in her back pocket every time she moved.

The dirty magazine wasn't a big deal, but the Polaroids...

She needed to get to the bottom of what they were about before deciding whether or not to rat on Sammy. She would start with the one boy in the pictures she recognized, Corey, and figure out where he and his mother had moved, and when.

"Whatever happened to Corey Collier and his mom?" she asked.

"Kathy?" Tina struggled to fold a fitted sheet.

"Yeah."

Tina gave up and bunched it into a messy ball. "She moved to Grimes like a year, year and a half ago. I can't remember exactly when. I haven't seen her in ages." Tina pointed to another pillowcase. "Hand me that one, will you?"

Crystal tossed it across the bed. "Why did she move?"

"She'd just gone through a bad breakup with a boyfriend, and her kid was still having all kinds of problems. I guess she just wanted a fresh start."

"Who was the boyfriend?"

"Kenny Harris, if you can believe it."

Crystal stopped folding and limply held a sheet in her hand. "Kathy Collier dated Kenny Harris?"

"Yeah, I thought you knew that. That's how I met him. Why do you ask?"

"No reason. Just...randomly wondered about them."

"Must be something in the air," Tina said. "That cop who interviewed Sammy, he was in the salon the other day and asked about Kathy. Weird. I haven't thought about her in so long."

"Sergeant Goodkind was asking about the Colliers?"

"Well, not them specifically. Their names just came up in the conversation." Tina checked her watch. "Oh my god, I have to go. Can you finish this?"

Crystal nodded.

"Thank you!" She kissed the top of Crystal's head and left.

As her mother's car coughed to life outside, Crystal went into her bedroom. She pulled her red notebook out of her backpack and paper-clipped the two Polaroids to the back cover. Then she flipped to a clean page and started writing down every single detail she knew about Kenny Harris.

NINETEEN

Two months, three weeks, two days, three hours missing

SAMMY ENTERED THE DARK, quiet house and wiped his wet shoes on the welcome mat. He dropped his newspaper bag from his shoulder, leaned his head against the door, and started to cry.

Crystal had a cold and had been too sick to go with him this morning, so he'd gone alone for the first time since August. But it was okay, because he'd put the new pictures he'd taken on Friday night in an envelope and carried them in his newspaper bag to deliver while on his route.

He was sure he'd be praised. Instead, he'd been punished. It wasn't fair.

He hadn't been prepared to run for the church, and he hadn't brought the scissors.

The grip on his forearm. The hiss in his ear.

You took too long. You've been avoiding me.

Mr. Tibbs wandered into the kitchen and rubbed against Sammy's leg. Sammy wiped his nose on the sleeve of his coat and wanted to kick Tibbs as hard as he could, to send the cat spinning across the floor in a gray blur. But he didn't, and the old cat just kept meowing for his breakfast.

He was taking too long to get Curtis to a club meeting. It didn't matter how much he explained that he'd already picked the boy and made friends with him, that he'd gotten Curtis interested in building models, that he now had the Polaroids.

It didn't matter.

I'm done waiting. It's time for you to deliver him. Next week. At the club meeting on Monday.

Sammy covered his face with his hands and cried harder. He was in so much pain today. It had been extra rough, mean. He sobbed until he choked, dry-heaving.

After a few minutes, he calmed down. Dried his face again and blew his nose into a dish towel. He shed his shoes and coat in a wet pile in front of the door and went into the living room. Multicolored twinkle lights blinked from a white artificial tree in front of the window. His mother had already put their Christmas decorations up, even though Thanksgiving was still over two weeks away. Christmas was her favorite holiday, and she would've decorated before Halloween if she'd had the time.

Sammy approached the tree and pinched one of the small, red lights between his fingers. His father had always said the red bulbs looked pink when the lights were on. The smooth glass warmed his fingertips, and when it blinked, his fingers glowed from the inside.

Sammy carefully lowered himself onto the telephone bench and laid his head down on the tabletop.

He couldn't take it anymore.

Sammy lifted his face, the dark-green phone inches from his nose. He picked up the receiver and put his finger in the hole to turn the rotary dial through the series of numbers written on a small slip of paper taped to the side of the phone base. Long-distance calls were expensive and his mother would be angry at him when she saw the phone bill, but he didn't care.

The crackling line buzzed, ringing on the other end. It was later in Florida because of the time difference, so maybe his father would be awake already. Sammy was desperate to hear his voice.

He would tell him. He would just say it.

He'd told the story of what was happening to him before. He could do it again. And if his father knew, he'd come get Sammy. Take him back to Florida to live with him.

Someone picked up the other end mid-buzz. The sound of brief jostling.

"Hello?"

Candy. His father's girlfriend.

"Hello?" she repeated, annoyed.

"Hi," Sammy said, quietly. "Is my dad there?"

"Oh, hi, Sammy," Candy said, softening her voice. "He's on a fishing trip with some friends. He won't be back until tomorrow morning."

Sammy laid his forehead down against the cool wood, disappointed. He hadn't met Candy yet, but his father had sent a picture of them recently, standing on his boat with dark tans and matching shell necklaces. She was young and had a nice-looking face. His father said she was a schoolteacher and loved kids.

"Do you want me to give him a message?" Candy asked.

Sammy's throat tightened with the threat of tears. "Yes, please," he croaked. "Can you tell him to call me as soon as he can?"

"Sure."

He wanted to say it. He needed to say it. Even if it

was to Candy. She was probably a good listener. She could tell his father everything he said.

"I—"

"Okay. 'Bye now."

Click. Then, the steady *mee, mee* disconnection signal.

"I need to tell you something," Sammy whispered to the beeping signal. "I need you to tell my dad that someone has been hurting me." The signal sped up. *Me, me.* "Please tell my dad that I'm scared and I need his help." He was crying again now, teardrops splashing on the table in a small pool. "When it first happened, I tried to tell Mom. I said that he did something to me I didn't like." His voice was husky. "But she said I misunderstood. That he's a good person and everyone likes him and I shouldn't make up stories like that." *Me, me, me, me.* "So, I told someone else, but no one helped me. I need someone to help me make it stop."

He sobbed loudly. The hyper beeping stopped and the line went silent.

Sammy sat up. "Please give my dad that message," he finished, and gently replaced the receiver.

The Christmas lights blinked a pattern. Slow, fast-fast, slow, fast-fast, slow.

Sammy picked up the receiver again and dialed the Dial-A-Story number at the South Side Library to listen to the three-minute recording of a librarian reading a children's book. He was too old for Dial-A-Story, but the librarian had a nice voice and sometimes did accents. The recording started. *Clifford's Kitten.* He'd already heard it a few days ago. He hung up.

A gust of wind whistled through the leaky front window, rippling the sheers.

Sammy stood and trudged up the stairs. In his room, he went inside the closet and removed his box from the shelf. He opened the lid and pawed through the candy, searching for the last Hershey chocolate bar he knew was in there. He found it and tore the wrapper open. As he took a bite of the wafer and chewed, he removed the magazine with all the naked girls in it, flipping through the pages to the back where he'd stuck a Polaroid of the boy with the red hair. Sammy didn't know his name or who he was, but he liked the boy's freckles. It's why he'd chosen that one.

Sammy reached the back page, but there was no picture. He turned every page again, slowly this time, but the picture was gone. Maybe it had fallen out in the box. He dumped the contents onto the floor. Nothing.

He stood, worried his mother had found the pictures and confiscated them. He could come up with a lie for her, no problem, but he'd be in so much trouble at the next club meeting for losing them. They had been loaned to him only. He had been given strict orders to keep them secret, and to return them.

He crouched on his hands and knees to look under his bed, shoving toys and dirty clothes aside, flinging them over his shoulder. Sometimes he looked at the pictures in bed and fell asleep, dropping them onto the floor.

Panic crawled up his throat. He rifled through every desk and bureau drawer, looked under the rest of the furniture, and searched the closet again. Not one but two pictures were gone. Someone had to have taken them.

Only one person in his family was known to snoop around in everyone else's business.

Sammy crept across the hall to Crystal's bedroom,

dimly lit with early-morning light. She lay on her back, rasping through her slack mouth. The smell of her grape-scented hair spray mingled with Vicks VapoRub.

He quietly looked through the papers and folders on top of her desk, searched the tidy drawers, and thumbed through the small collection of books on her shelf, but no pictures. He carefully opened her bifold closet doors and felt around the modest piles of sweaters and jeans, but nothing.

When he lowered to his hands and knees to peek under her bed, Crystal broke into a fit of hacking coughs and he froze. Once she settled back down and rolled over to her opposite side, he noticed her school backpack on the floor next to her desk. He grabbed it and carried it into his bedroom.

There, he pulled open the zipper of the first compartment. Textbooks, a set of gym clothes, a plastic pencil bag. In the second zippered pouch, folders and notebooks, including the red spiral notebook she was always writing in. He pulled it out and started flipping through the pages.

Most of the pages contained newspaper articles she'd cut out and glued down, but other pages were covered in her tight, cursive handwriting. Notes about the Matt Klein and Chris Stewart cases. Things she'd written down, then crossed out. Random descriptions of cars and houses, a hand-sketched map of their neighborhood, and other pages of diary-like entries.

A chunk of entries at the back of the notebook caught Sammy's attention.

K. H... . Southlawn Drive...
silver or gray—possible Camaro

...heating and cooling...
Kathy C. from salon (82–83?)
...pedophile: an adult who is sexually attracted
to kids.

Sammy's breath grew shallow. Slowly, hands shaking, he turned the last page. Paper-clipped to the cardboard back cover were the two Polaroids. He pulled them free and stared at the faces of Corey Collier and the redheaded boy with the freckles.

Keep them safe. They're for you to enjoy.

Sammy clenched his eyes shut, shivering violently now.

All boys should have a little fun. The private kind.

Crystal had been inside his secret box. She'd seen the magazine, the pictures.

Sammy opened his eyes and crushed the pictures in his hands. He ripped dozens of pages out of the back of the notebook, then yanked the box from the top shelf and dumped out the contents. He stomped all the candy bars beneath his feet. He tore apart the magazine, shredding the naked, dirty girls with his bare hands. He gathered the carnage in his arms, put it back inside the box, and quietly carried it downstairs. There, he stuffed it into the kitchen trash can with wet coffee grounds, rotten potato peels, and empty cartons leaking sour milk. He bundled and tightly knotted the garbage bag, pulled it free from the can, and carried it outside, walking across the wet pavement in only his socks.

Under the carport, he hurled the sack over his shoulder as hard as he could into the large outdoor can, knocking it sideways and sending it spinning across the driveway.

Sammy clenched his fists, panting, his breaths forming puffs in front of his face. He swallowed back a scream so violent it threatened to rip his throat in half.

An airplane roared overhead, taking off from the nearby airport.

Had Crystal told their mother about the box or the Polaroids? He didn't think so. Otherwise Tina would've jumped all over him about it. What did it mean that Crystal hadn't tattled on him yet, or even asked him about the secret box? He kept turning everything over in his mind, like a Magic 8 Ball giving him different answers with each try.

Slowly, he uncurled his fingers. Snow began to mix with the light rain.

The pictures were gone now, so if Crystal did say something, it was just her word against his. His breathing returned to normal.

He set the can upright. Tiny flakes collected in his hair and clung to his eyelashes.

Inside, Sammy returned to Crystal's bedroom and replaced the notebook in her backpack. As he was about to zip the pouch closed, something shiny in the bottom caught his eye.

It was a small, blue metal oval with the letters *DMPD* printed in gold on the side. The pocketknife from the cop at the fair.

Sammy opened the blade and ran his finger along the smooth, sharp edge.

An idea.

He finished repacking her bag and leaned it back against the desk the way he'd found it. He closed the door behind him.

In the hall, Sammy studied the blade again, wondering how sharp it was, how well it could cut. He glanced around, looking for something to test.

Mr. Tibbs darted through his mother's ajar bedroom door and down the stairs. Sammy entered and paused, waiting for his eyes to adjust to the gloom. His mother lay curled in a ball on the far side of the water bed.

When he was younger, Sammy used to have bad dreams and would wriggle himself between his mother and father in bed. His mother would wrap him up in her arms, whispering that he was safe now; it was only a dream and he'd forget about it by morning. He'd slowly drift back into a pleasant, sweaty sleep.

He gently pushed on the mattress, sloshing the water and creating a tiny ripple.

But Sammy knew that safe wasn't real. Forgetting wasn't real.

He carefully lifted the edge of the sheet, exposing the brown water mattress beneath. He pressed the blade to the skinlike bladder and pushed the tip through. It easily slit the rubber and created a satisfactory gash. Water immediately seeped through the hole. The blade was surprisingly sharp and strong.

The idea opened further, blooming into a plan.

He had one week.

For the first time in a long time, hope sparked in his chest.

"Bag yer face," he whispered.

Sammy retracted the blade and slipped the knife into his pocket. He pulled the sheet back over the corner of the mattress and quietly left the room.

TWENTY

Two months, four weeks, two days, eight hours missing

CRYSTAL AND SOMPHONE entered the large rotunda of the Des Moines Central Library and brushed fat snowflakes from their hair. The stained-glass skylight dulled beneath the snow cover, but the mosaic lighted floor glowed beneath their feet.

Crystal pulled off her fingerless gloves and tucked them into her pocket. She flexed and unflexed her fingers, the tips numb. It had been snowing on and off for over a week.

Somphone switched her bulging backpack from one shoulder to the other. "I'm heading to the stacks room to look up some books for my English paper."

Crystal unbuttoned her long wool coat. "I'll be in the reference section."

Somphone handed her a slip of paper. "This is the name of that article and journal I told you about."

"Oh, yeah. Thanks."

"See you in a few hours." Somphone slipped on the headphones of her Walkman and crossed the rotunda.

Crystal entered the reference room, busy for a snowy Sunday afternoon, and settled her belongings at an empty table. She had only three hours before the library closed, so she'd have to work quickly.

She located the journal Somphone had written down,

then moved to the index files to look up every article written about the Klein case since 1982. She scribbled a list on a fresh page of her red notebook, then cast her net wider for cases around the country, using the *New York Times*. A six-year-old boy from New York City who went missing in '79; the Oakland County child murders from '76 to '77; the Atlanta child murders from '79 to '81; the murdered Florida boy in '81; and the two paperboys in Omaha last year. She pulled the microfilms from her list, switched on a reader, and wound the first reel through the machine. Crystal crowded the screen, reading intently and taking notes.

As she worked her way through the stack of reels, she noticed that not one news article mentioned the word *pedophile* in any of the cases. Before Somphone had said the word, Crystal had never even considered such a thing, let alone known a *name* for it. She'd heard people called perverts, peeping toms, and flashers—names that sounded vaguely offensive—but mostly harmless labels.

But that word, *pedophile*, sounded so foreign and dangerous. It sounded like a person who lived in *other* places, *other* cities, big cities with high crime rates. Not here. Not in Des Moines. With the Klein and Stewart cases, though, she couldn't brush it away anymore with "not in our neighborhood, not in our city."

Crystal took a break and stretched her arms over her head, cracking bones between her shoulder blades.

She loaded another reel and advanced to an interview Marilyn Klein had done with the *New York Times* in 1983, on the one-year anniversary of Matt's disappearance. In an accompanying photo, Marilyn clutched the last school picture taken of Matt. Her dark, half-mooned eyes sunk into her skull, and deep lines cupped the corners of her mouth.

Her words were prophetic, haunting.

I feel like Matty's kidnapper could be anyone. Every person who crosses my path is a suspect. Teachers, bus drivers, my friends, my neighbors. I could go crazy just thinking about it, all the places he could be. Is he in another state? Another country? Or, if he was being held in a house on the next block, how would we ever know? How well do we ever really know what goes on inside our neighbors' houses?

Crystal chewed on the eraser of her pencil, considering what Marilyn had said back then.

How well do we ever really know what goes on inside our neighbors' houses?

She slowly laid down her pencil. After months of searching for the right topic and angle, after so many false starts and tossed drafts, *this* was what Crystal wanted to write about in her essay.

That criminals, pedophiles, *bad people* could live anywhere, even next door. That no city, no neighborhood was immune, and to believe otherwise only helped pedophiles hide in plain sight.

This was the topic. What she *needed* to write about, she now knew with certainty.

After a couple of hours of taking notes and sketching a new outline, she shut the film reader off and returned the last boxes of reels to the metal filing cabinets. She squinted at the clock ticking on the wall. The library would close in less than thirty minutes.

From the newspaper rack, she grabbed the Friday edition of the *Register*, since her mother got only the weekend editions. Back at her table, she opened the medical journal, found the article Somphone had so accurately quoted, and started reading. It was mostly dry psychobabble, until she reached a section labeled "Typography." There, her attention spiked.

```
Preferential child molesters engage
children in sexual activities by "seduc-
ing" them—courting them with attention,
affection, and gifts. The pedophile se-
duces children over a period of time
by gradually lowering their sexual in-
hibitions. Many of these offenders are
simultaneously involved with multiple
victims, operating what has come to be
called a "child sex ring." This may in-
clude a group of children in the same
class at school, the same church, the
same extra-curricular activities, or
the same neighborhood.
```

Crystal stopped reading. An MO. *Modus operandi.* Her stomach turned greasy, nauseous. She forced herself to continue.

```
 Pedophiles know how to identify with
and talk to children, but more im-
portantly how to listen to them. They
like child-like activities and hobbies,
often working or volunteering in a po-
sition that involves regular contact
```

with children. They frequently target
children who are shy or withdrawn, or
who come from troubled or underprivi-
leged homes, especially single parent
homes where offenders can insert them-
selves into the family by being helpful
to the single parent and have ample opportunities to be alone with the child.

One particularly difficult offender
to catch is the morally indiscriminate
preferential child molester, who has no
conscience, and therefore no limit on
whom he victimizes. Such an offender
is more likely to abduct, hold prisoner, or murder children.

Crystal stared so hard at the words she could've
burned a hole through the paper.

Likely to abduct. Like Matt and Chris.

"Ladies and gentlemen," the librarian called, "the
library will be closing in fifteen minutes."

Crystal muttered under her breath. She still hadn't
checked the *Register*. She quickly skimmed the head-
lines for Chris's name. There were fewer and fewer articles being written about him, so it was unlikely she'd
find anything new, but she checked anyway.

To her surprise, she found an ad with Chris's picture on page six.

FROM THE PARENTS OF
CHRISTOPHER THOMAS STEWART, MISSING CHILD
Bud and Cindy Stewart are asking for
any information on the whereabouts of

their son, Christopher "Chris" Stewart, or about a late 1970s silver or
gray Chevy Camaro seen in the vicinity
of Tenth and Hillcrest on the morning
of August 12, 1984, between the hours
of 6 a.m. and 7 a.m.

Chris was last seen at the corner
of S.W. Tenth and Hillcrest Drive between 5:15 and 6:00 a.m. Chris is 13
years old and his birthdate is 4/9/71.
He has dark brown hair, brown eyes, is
5'1" and 105 lbs. He has a small scar
above his right eyebrow and talks with
a slight lisp.

IF YOU HAVE ANY INFORMATION RELATED
TO CHRIS'S DISAPPEARANCE, PLEASE CALL
287-9009. Please contact us day or
night. Callers can remain anonymous
and all information will be kept confidential.

Another mention of that silver or gray Camaro. A
muscle car. She was so close to something, but she just
didn't know what.

Crystal spread the articles, newspapers, and medical
journal out in front of her, using the entire real estate
of the table. She chewed the pencil eraser once more,
her heart thumping loudly in her ears. Everything she
knew and had learned flashed through her mind like
a badly spliced movie, flickering and jumping around.
It was hard to make sense of all the puzzle pieces scattered in front of her.

The journal article.

...children in the same class at school, the same church, the same extra-curricular activities, or the same neighborhood.

The Polaroids of Corey Collier and the redheaded boy. Marilyn's words from the interview.

...if he was being held in a house on the next block, how would we ever know? How well do we ever really know what goes on inside our neighbors' houses?

The conversation with her mother just last week.

Kenny Harris, if you can believe it.

Then her brain stopped on the picture of Kenny standing in his garage, a silver muscle car parked behind him.

Southlawn Drive.

Crystal leaped to her feet and approached the reference desk.

"Excuse me," she said, but the librarian was busy checking out someone's books and didn't hear her.

She glanced at the clock again. Five minutes now.

"Excuse me!" she said loudly.

The librarian looked sharply at her. He finished stamping a book and slid it across the counter.

"Yes?" He took the card of the next patron in line.

"Can I see the telephone book from 1982, please?"

The librarian pointed to a row of shelves close to where Crystal had been sitting.

"There," he said. "Third shelf down."

"Thank you." Crystal hurried to the aisle the librarian had pointed to.

Four minutes left.

She scanned the shelves until she found the row of fat yellow books, then ran her fingertip over the wrinkled spines to 1982.

She jerked the book free and kneeled on the floor.

Cole... Coleson... Collie... Collier.

Finally: *Collier, Katherine A. 1301 SE Southlawn Drive.*

She roughly turned the thin pages and accidentally tore one.

Hammes... Harmes... Harkness... Harris.

Harris, Kenneth J. 1223 SE Southlawn Drive.

She unfolded a printed city map from the back of the phone book and plotted the addresses. The map quivered in her trembling hands.

Her finger traced the streets to Southlawn Drive.

Two years ago, Corey Collier had lived just seven houses away from Kenny Harris.

She slid her finger west, to the corner of Tenth and Hillcrest. Barely two blocks from where Chris Stewart was abducted.

What was it Marilyn Klein had said?

Every person who crosses my path is a suspect. Teachers, bus drivers, my friends, my neighbors.

Crystal shoved the phone book back onto the shelf and jogged to her table. She opened her red notebook to copy down the addresses but stopped, realizing the notebook felt thin beneath her hand. Several pages were missing. She frowned. She flipped to the cardboard back cover.

The paper clip was empty. The Polaroids, gone.

Someone had deliberately ripped out the notes referring to Kenny Harris, and had taken the pictures.

A shiver rippled down her spine. She knew who.

Sammy.

Crystal slumped back into her chair. The world instantly morphed into something unrecognizable. It became grossly tilted and distorted, untrustworthy. Crystal woozily tilted with it.

She cradled her head in her hands, trying to stop the swirling questions in her head. If Sammy was involved in this mess, was he in danger, too? She rewound her memory back all the way to that first morning in August, when Chris went missing and she'd found Sammy running down the street.

"Are you ready to go?" Somphone loomed over her, buttoning her fleece-lined jean jacket. "The library's closing."

Crystal looked up at her friend, dazed.

"Are you okay?" Somphone asked. "You look weird."

Crystal cleared her clogged throat. "I'm fine. Just... tired." She slid her notebook and papers into her backpack, her muscles stiff and mechanical. She started to fold the *Register*, but stopped at the Stewarts' ad.

"Do you want to get a burger at A&W?" Somphone asked.

Crystal grabbed a pen and scrawled the phone number onto her palm.

"I can't," she said. She zipped her bag. "I need to get home."

"What's wrong?" Somphone asked. "Why are you in such a hurry?"

Crystal shoved her arms into the sleeves of her coat. "I need to find my brother."

TWENTY-ONE

Two months, four weeks, two days, eleven hours missing

AT HOME, Crystal flung the back door open and bumped the overflowing trash can, knocking an empty milk carton onto the floor. She stepped over it and shed her coat and shoes.

"How was the library?" Tina called from the living room.

Crystal followed her voice to where Tina sat in the middle of the floor, painting her toenails.

"Why aren't you at work?" Crystal asked.

"The restaurant didn't need me today, so for once I'm enjoying a day off." She hunched over her feet with a fuchsia-colored bottle in one hand, the brush in the other. "Did you get your homework done at the library?"

The television blared a *Hogan's Heroes* rerun.

Crystal cleared her throat and answered in a scratchy voice. "Yeah. Hey, where's Sammy?" She didn't want to waste another minute.

"His room." Tina dunked the brush and laughed at something on the television.

Crystal hurriedly climbed the stairs. She opened Sammy's door without knocking and closed it behind her.

"What the frick, Chrissie. Knock first." Sammy sat on the floor assembling another car model.

She shakily pushed her glasses up the bridge of her sweaty nose. Fear nearly choked off her voice. If she started this line of questioning, she had to be prepared for the places it could take her. And she wasn't sure she could handle any of those places.

"What did you do to my notebook?" she asked.

Sammy set down a black rubber wheel and looked at her. "What notebook?"

"My red notebook," she said. "You know which one."

"I didn't do anything to it."

"Sammy, I know it was you who ripped out those pages."

"I don't know what you're talking about." His face remained blank, his voice unnervingly calm.

Crystal darted to the open closet and yanked the folded blue jeans from the top shelf. Sammy didn't move from his spot on the floor.

The box was gone.

She ran her palm across the empty shelf. "Where is it?" she said.

"Where is what?"

"The box!"

He folded his hands in his lap in a maddeningly serene gesture. "Chrissie, I don't know what you're talking about."

"The box! The box!" she stupidly repeated, then lowered her voice so their mother wouldn't hear. "The one with all the candy and the dirty magazine in it."

Sammy stared at her, his eyes tiny, dark pinpoints.

Crystal dropped her hands to her sides. She moved closer to him. "Tell me about the pictures. Who took them? Where did you get them?"

Sammy looked away, out his bedroom window that

faced the street, and sighed as if she were a mere irritation. Pesky.

"I don't know what you're talking about," he said again.

She clamped her arms over her chest. "You do know. The *Polaroids*, Sammy. Of those boys."

"I don't." Sammy picked the car back up and resumed gluing the wheel.

"I'm telling Mom what I saw," she said, but immediately regretted it. She'd reached for a threat too soon. It could shut him down.

He slid his gaze to her then and lifted one shoulder in a small shrug. "Go ahead. But you don't have any proof. It's your word against mine."

They locked eyes for a long moment, and Sammy's icy stare gave her chills. Crystal blinked first.

She dialed herself back and tried for a caring, older-sister approach. "Just tell me where you got those pictures," she finally said. "If you're in some kind of trouble, I can help you."

He huffed. "I told you. I don't know what you're talking about."

"Did Corey Collier give you those pictures?"

"I don't know who he is," Sammy said. He picked up another wheel and delicately dabbed a dot of glue on the silver hub.

"Sammy. Look at me."

He ignored her. Crystal swallowed down a scream. She'd never seen him behave this way before. He'd turned into a stranger right before her very eyes.

"Sammy!" she hissed. "Do you know something about Kenny Harris? Is he involved with Chris Stewart's disappearance? Are you in danger?"

Sammy set the car down and tilted his head, his expression almost amused. "That's crazy. How would I know what happened to Chris Stewart? You're losing your mind."

Crystal sagged against the headboard of Sammy's bed and blinked back hot tears. Everything around her continued to warp in dizzying directions. Even her own brother was unrecognizable now.

"Why won't you talk to me?" she whispered.

Sammy adjusted his legs, wrinkling the newspaper beneath him. He finished gluing another part onto the car.

"Don't worry, Chrissie," he said. "Everything's going to be okay."

CRYSTAL WALKED BACK DOWNSTAIRS, her legs heavy. She sank into the recliner as her mother now painted her fingernails the same color.

Sammy hadn't reacted at all the way she'd thought he would. As Somphone drove her home, she'd pictured him becoming upset once she confronted him. She'd thought he'd break down and tell her everything, whatever "everything" was. Instead, he'd stonewalled her. Clammed up.

Ever since their father moved, Sammy and Crystal had been close. She was often left to babysit him while their mother worked, and she'd become something like another mother to him. He'd never kept secrets from her before. The idea of him keeping one now hurt her deeply.

Crystal laid her hands on top of her thighs. Her palms were white, her skin cold and clammy. Maybe Sammy didn't know anything. He'd been so adamant just now.

He hadn't budged an inch no matter what she'd said. Maybe the box and the pictures were something totally innocent. Maybe he'd come into possession of them by accident and hadn't even realized it.

No.

She turned her hands over and dug her fingers into her knees. His denials were lies. She'd seen it in his face and knew it in her heart. He was hiding something.

Tina screwed the nail brush back onto the bottle and moved to the recliner next to Crystal. She gingerly picked up her lighter and lit a cigarette.

"You look pale," she said. "Are you sick again?"

Crystal rubbed the center of her forehead. "No," she said. A budding headache pricked behind her eyes.

"Do you want me to do your nails?" Tina offered.

"No, thanks," Crystal said. She leaned back in the chair. She wasn't ready to let her brother off the hook that easy.

"Do you think something's going on with Sammy?" she asked.

"What do you mean?"

"I don't know." Crystal had to approach this cautiously. If she set her mother off, it could make Sammy clam up more and the situation worse. She decided to inch her way into it, reveal only a single piece of her information.

"The other day I saw a *Playboy* magazine in his room. It's gone now, but when I asked him about it he wouldn't tell me where he got it."

Tina half blew, half laughed on her wet nails. "A *nudie* magazine?" She clicked her tongue. "God, I was hoping those wouldn't start showing up for at least another year."

"You're not mad?"

"No. It's a pretty normal thing for pubescent boys to have."

"Where did he get it, then?"

"Who knows," Tina said, and took a drag of her cigarette. "Maybe that new little buddy he's been hanging out with. It's *good* that he has a friend." She splayed her fingers and held them out in front of her. "Isn't this a pretty color? I can't remember the last time I painted my nails."

Crystal sank deeper into the chair. Her mom looked relaxed, untroubled. Happy, even. And if she pushed this further by mentioning the Polaroids, Sammy would only deny it, just like he'd said.

Tina stood and hobbled to the stairs with her toes stretched apart. "I'm gonna take a bath as soon as these dry. Will you please thaw out some hamburger for sloppy joes tonight?"

"Sure," Crystal said. *Hogan's Heroes* ended. She watched the credits roll, feeling defeated.

There had to be something she could do. This couldn't be the end of it. She wasn't ready to let it go.

Crystal stubbed out the cigarette her mother had left smoldering in the ashtray and moved to the telephone table, where she lifted the receiver. If her mother wasn't going to be any help, then she would call her father and talk to him. The line rang five, six, seven times. She drummed her fingers. Ten, eleven, twelve rings. She dropped the receiver hard onto the base, frustrated.

For so long she'd fancied herself this promising future reporter, yet she couldn't even get to the bottom of what was going on with her own brother.

Crystal heaved herself up from the chair and approached the Christmas tree. It looked like how she felt. Fake and stupid. She didn't know what else to do.

In the kitchen, she took a pound of plastic-wrapped hamburger from the freezer and set it in the sink to thaw. As she filled the other basin with warm water, she switched on the police scanner.

A stray dog running around on Ingersoll, a tow truck needed for a stalled car blocking traffic on Park Avenue.

The scanner.

Where it all started, the morning Chris went missing. When Crystal went searching for Sammy. Had Chris not gone missing, she wouldn't have gone out that morning, or seen Sammy running down the street with the scissors, or searched his delivery bag and found the first Polaroid.

She leaned against the counter and rubbed her throbbing temples. She couldn't get the image of the red-haired boy out of her mind. The sliver of underwear band. The corner of a mattress behind him. Or the picture of a shirtless Corey Collier.

She couldn't stop thinking about Kenny's house, just seven houses away from where Corey used to live, blocks from where Chris had disappeared.

And she couldn't stop thinking about Sammy. Her little brother who'd innocently asked her where pickles came from.

She'd been so focused on her own problems the past few months that she'd blinded herself to everyone and everything else around her. And worse, she'd only thought about how the missing-paperboy crimes could help *her*. All while possibly overlooking crimes in her own backyard. Maybe in her own house.

Everything seemed to be leading her to one of two

awful truths: either Kenny was somehow involved in the paperboy disappearances, or he was a pedophile targeting her own brother. She selfishly prayed that the former would be true.

And deeper still, in the darkest corner of her mind, lurked a series of images she couldn't shake. Sebastian on the couch with Sammy, the night he came to their house from the library, sweaty and breathless. The small object he'd pressed into Sammy's hand. The odd items and roll of money in his backpack.

No. She refused to believe Sebastian was a possible third awful truth.

But how could she prove any of this? She wasn't a real reporter yet, or a cop, or anyone with actual authority. Despite her efforts to prove herself an adult to everyone around her, she was still just a kid. She'd never be taken seriously. She kept reaching a dead end.

The wall phone rang, and she snatched up the receiver before a second ring, irrationally hoping it was her father calling back. But it was only Peg, Tina's boss from the salon, asking for Tina to cover an evening shift tomorrow night. Tina was in the bath, Crystal said. She'd give her mother the message.

She hung up and searched for a pen and paper in the junk drawer to write a note.

After she jotted down Peg's number, she turned her hand over and opened her fingers. There, on her palm, was the Stewarts' phone number from the ad in the paper, begging anyone with information to call them. She recalled the last line of the ad: *Callers can remain anonymous and all information will be kept confidential.*

Anonymous. Finally, an opening out of the dead end.

Crystal picked the receiver back up and dialed the numbers she'd scribbled onto her palm. A woman answered after several rings.

"This is the Stewart residence."

Crystal licked her lips, her mouth dry. "May I please speak to Bud or Cindy Stewart?"

"This is Cindy Stewart."

She cupped her hand around the mouthpiece and kept her voice low. "I have some information that may be related to Chris's case. About a couple of boys and some pictures someone took of them. In their underwear." She took a deep breath. "I can't tell you how I know about the pictures or how I saw them, but one of the boys' names is Corey Collier, and he used to live on Southlawn Drive not far from where Chris was kidnapped."

Crystal paused. Silence filled the line. Doubt seized her throat.

She'd sounded ridiculous. Crazy, even. She held the receiver out from her ear a few inches, ready to hang up.

"Please, go on," Mrs. Stewart finally said. "I'm listening."

Crystal closed her eyes and exhaled, encouraged. "There's a man who lives on Southlawn Drive, just a few blocks from Corey Collier's old house," she said, her courage gaining strength. "His name is Kenny Harris and he drives a silver muscle car."

TWENTY-TWO

Three months, one hour missing

DALE AWOKE IN the uncomfortable motel bed, shivering and stiff. It was early, still dark outside, and cold. The thin, cheap bedspread wasn't enough to keep him warm, and the wall radiator seemed to have only two settings: off and sauna.

He rose and rolled his neck, his joints crackling like snapping twigs. He shuffled into the bathroom and washed his face. A fresh sports coat, slacks, shirt, and tie hung from the shower curtain rod. His thirty-day suspension was up. Today he went back to work.

He squeezed a mound of shaving cream into his palm and slathered it along his jaw. Connie bought his shaving cream for him. She liked the subtle scent of this brand.

At home, their bathroom vanity was crowded with her makeup and toiletry bottles of he didn't know what. Once, he'd unscrewed the lid from a small jar of her face cream and held it to his nose. It smelled sweet, like flowers of some kind. At night she dabbed it under her eyes with her ring finger. She wore Enjoli perfume and he'd liked that commercial from a few years ago—*I can bring home the bacon...fry it up in a pan*—and used to playfully sing it to her in the kitchen and make her laugh whenever she cooked actual bacon. He couldn't remember the last time he'd made her laugh. Before the Stewart case, for sure. Maybe even before the move.

He dragged the razor over the side of his cheek.

Their problems were his fault. He was difficult to live with, prone to dark moods and irritability. When she'd ask what was bothering him, he'd brush her off. He never talked to her about things because it was too hard to articulate what he held inside him. He feared that if he released it, like letting water over a dam, it could drown everything in its path. It would have been easier if he'd just been a drunk and could blame his problems on the bottom of a bottle.

Why do you withhold so much from your wife?

Dr. Smith at his recent appointment.

What do you think I'm withholding?

Stress from your work, anxieties, fears. She'd listed them on her fingers. *These therapy appointments, the medication. You keep a lot of secrets from her. But the biggest secret you've been keeping is what happened when you were a boy.*

He hadn't answered, so she'd continued. *Can we talk about what happened when you lived in Hampton as a boy?*

Dale wiped his face clean and brushed his hair. Today would be a fresh start. He'd get back to work, back on the Stewart case, and, God willing, back home.

He ate a doughnut saved from yesterday, locked his room, and hurried across the parking lot to his snow-covered car. He started the ignition and let the motor warm up for a few minutes as the heater defrosted the windshield.

Hampton doesn't matter, so why talk about it? He'd been a kid. It was a lifetime ago.

But Dr. Smith never let him off easy. *Because it does matter. It's a big part of the reason you take these paperboy cases so hard. It's a big part of why you're so vigilant with your own son.*

Dale flicked the wipers and pushed the melting snow off the windshield.

Curtis. His own son was afraid of him now. He'd worked so hard to protect him from bad people, and now Curtis thought he was one of them after what he'd seen his father do at the library.

Dale thought about how the boy sweated so profusely in his sleep. When he was a toddler, he used to crawl into bed between Dale and Connie without disturbing them and would sweat so heavily Dale would wake up thinking he'd peed the bed himself.

He worried that Curtis had inherited the pervasive fears and anxieties he'd carried inside since he was a boy. Curtis had inherited his father's distinctive square chin, after all, and his hair color and allergy to shellfish. Maybe Dale had also somehow passed along his mental afflictions.

Or maybe he was the cause of them.

Dale had everything, and yet he was slowly grinding it down to nothing with the heel of his own boot.

What happened in Hampton, Dale?

I went down the stairs to the basement and I never came back up.

Dale shivered and rubbed his hands together to warm his fingertips.

Hampton didn't matter. That was in the past. He had to focus on the present. On getting his family and job back on track.

He had to focus on the case again. He was so close.

Kovacs was within his reach. He just needed to close his fingers around the man and squeeze.

THE QUIET NEIGHBORHOOD streets glistened with undisturbed snow. Dale stopped in his usual spot on Southlawn Drive and watched the little white house on the corner. The lamp glowed in the window. The sidewalk had already been shoveled.

Right on time, Kovacs came into view, striding down the Tenth Street sidewalk, wearing a black parka jacket, a dark knit cap, the binoculars, and the backpack, which appeared empty.

Dale leveled his stare at the man. Kovacs crossed the street into his yard and fished his keys from his coat pocket. As he inserted the key into the knob, Kovacs turned around to where Dale's car was parked, several feet away. Kovacs raised the binoculars to his eyes and pointed them directly at Dale.

Dale lifted his hand and formed his thumb and index finger into the barrel of gun, sighted right at Kovacs's forehead.

He lowered his thumb and mouthed, *Bang*.

Kovacs dropped the binoculars and hurried into the house.

THE STATION WAS quiet at this hour. Dale settled at his desk and faced a daunting pile of paperwork to get through. Overdue reports, forms, and messages he needed to return. Paperwork was the hidden lifeblood of the law enforcement world. Pretty much everything Dale did as an officer was reflected in some kind of paperwork. Get good at your paperwork, love your paperwork, they taught in the academy. Paperwork was the only constant in their unpredictable profession. And, as annoying as the piles, reams, and stacks of paperwork were, they covered cops' asses and helped put the bad guys in jail.

In the mess of his desk, someone had knocked over a brass-framed picture of Connie, Curtis, and him—an Olan Mills family photo, their last, taken at the church for the directory several years ago. He set it back up and buffed the glass with the cuff of his coat. They looked like a happy, normal family in the picture. They had been happy, once, hadn't they? Before the Matt Klein case landed on his desk two years ago. But maybe he'd never truly been happy. He wasn't sure anymore.

Dale turned his attention back to work and started with a file of tips and letters that had come in on the Stewart case in his absence. The majority were from cranks and nuts, or spurned lovers with an ax to grind, but he still had to read through each and every one to determine whether follow-up was needed. He started at the bottom and worked his way up.

The first tip was from a man calling himself "Howard X, former CIA operative," who claimed to know who had abducted both Klein and Stewart and demanded detective pay to help work on the cases. Another was from a Council Bluffs man who said the team should investigate the full-moon cycles because "full moons cause some people to lose their minds," and both Klein and Stewart had disappeared within days of a full moon. Another letter writer complained at length about all the "anonymous tips" mucking up the newspaper stories, even though he'd sent his letter anonymously. A letter dated last week had been sent by a man who'd spent time in prison and had a foolproof idea for how to solve the mystery of the missing paperboys: infiltrate sex cults in the community and get intel on who might be responsible for the possible sex-related abductions by setting up a massage parlor—paid for by the DMPD, of course—which he would "generously operate."

Hours passed, and at noon, Dale stopped to stretch his arms over his head, leaning back in his squeaky chair. The office was humming now with ringing phones and clacking typewriters, loud conversations and the echo of doors opening and closing all around the station. None of his fellow officers, Dale realized, had welcomed him back or asked how he was doing. It didn't seem possible for him to get less popular.

He swiveled his chair around and studied a centuries-old city map of Des Moines that hung next to the state flag, and at the top of the map someone had long ago penciled the word *respect*. Dale's father had once told him that in the late 1880s, the southern half of the Des Moines settlement was originally named *Sevastopol*, after a Russian fortress, and was an ancient Greek form of the word *sebastos*, meaning *venerable*, or *commanding respect*. And that was the South Side. The City of Respect. Just for everyone but him.

Dale defiantly reminded himself that he belonged here. This was his home, and he was good at his job. The time off from the suspension had done him good, renewed his energy and commitment to solving the Stewart case, even if it had further alienated him from the other officers.

He returned to the stack of tips with just a few left to read. The next slip was recent, dated just last night. He picked it up and started reading.

Message for: Sgt Goodkind

Date: Sun 11/11/84
Time: 1900
From: Cindy Stewart, 1905 Sheridan Ave.

Cindy Stewart reported that she received a tele-
phone call on their home phone tip line from a
female (possibly teenaged?) who refused to give
her name. Female stated that she recently saw 2
Polaroid photos of two different males approxi-
mately 12–13 yrs old "posing for the camera in
their underwear." Caller recognized only one boy
in pictures as male juvenile named Corey Collier.

Says he used to live on Southlawn Drive but
moved to Grimes a year ago. Caller identified
boy's mother as Kathy Collier.

Caller refused to say where she obtained photos.
Says she no longer has them in her possession
because they were destroyed by a third party.

Hung up before Stewart could ask more questions.
Cindy and Bud Stewart requesting follow-up and
call back from Sgt Goodkind. 287–7042

Dale turned the slip over and read the signature on
the back: *SPO Bradley.*

He shoved his chair back and stormed across the office. As he approached, Bradley was typing, his index
fingers hunting and pecking across the keys.

"Bradley," Dale said, "what is this?"

Bradley finished typing a line on a form, then turned
to Dale. "What." His expression showed annoyance.

Dale shoved the pink slip in Bradley's face. "You took this call from Cindy Stewart last night."

Bradley switched off the electric typewriter and snatched the slip from Dale's hand. He barely glanced at the writing. "Yeah? So?"

"Why didn't you bring it to my attention as soon as you got here this morning?"

Several cops nearby turned at the sound of Dale's loud voice.

"I put it on your desk just like every other tip that comes in," Bradley said, and handed the slip back. "What the hell else did you want me to do with it? Gift-wrap it with a pretty bow?"

Dale raked his hand through his hair. "A call comes in with info about potential kiddie porn with the name of a vic who also lives in the same neighborhood as an active missing-kid case, and you just stuck it in a folder between hundreds of other papers?"

Bradley stood and jabbed a finger in Dale's chest. "Don't put this shit on me, Goodkind. It's not my fault you've been benched for a month." He sneered. "If you weren't such a head case, maybe you would've found those kids by now."

Dale took a step toward Bradley, momentarily speechless. A mix of fury and embarrassment inflamed his cheeks.

"What did you just say?" he finally spit out.

Bradley crossed his arms over his chest and planted his feet wide. "You heard me. Those poor little bastards are dead and it's made you a head case, and everyone knows it."

Dale grabbed a fistful of Bradley's shirt and jerked him forward so they were nose to nose. "And how are you so sure those boys are dead, Bradley? You know something you're not telling me? Got another tip you haven't bothered to give me yet?"

"Screw you." Bradley wrenched Dale's hand from his chest and pushed him away. "You're out of control."

SPO Donovan stopped typing at his nearby desk and stood up. "Hey, guys. Take it easy."

Dale ignored him. "Screw me? Screw *me*?" His blood pumped furiously in his ears. "After the thousands of hours I've put in on these missing-kid cases, it's *screw me*? I'm the one out of control?"

Even though Bradley was right, he was overreacting about the tip, he couldn't stop. All the stress and anxiety he'd been carrying around for the last two years about the cases pushed to the surface, and he was tired of trying to hold them down.

"You were late for your shift the morning Chris Stewart disappeared," Dale finally said. "Isn't that a coincidence." He'd crossed the threshold from overreacting to irrational, but he didn't care. The release felt good.

Bradley snorted. "Are *you* accusing *me* of something? Are you out of control, or just crazy?"

Donovan inched around his desk and raised his hands. "Guys, just separate. Cool off."

Tiny shocks zapped Dale's brain, like it was short-circuiting. "I'm just saying that everyone is a suspect until they aren't."

"That's rich," Bradley said, "considering *you* lived in both jurisdictions at the time of each abduction. So, does that mean you're a suspect too? Until you aren't?" He laughed in Dale's face. "You know, the guys joke that you took those boys yourself and got 'em hidden in your basement somewhere. Soon you'll trot 'em like a goddamn hero so you can make lieutenant."

Dale cocked his arm back and threw a punch, landing his fist square with Bradley's nose. Bradley stumbled and cupped his face but recovered quickly, launching a hard return blow on Dale's left eye. White stars exploded, and his ears clanged like tolling church bells.

Donovan and another cop shouted and pulled Dale and Bradley apart. The men separated, panting, each clutching their face and grimacing in pain. Blood poured from Bradley's nostrils, dripping onto his gray shirt. He grabbed a handkerchief from his desk drawer and tipped his head back, pressing the material to his nose. Bright-crimson flowers bloomed across the white cotton.

Dale gently pressed two fingertips to the swelling tissue below his eye. He turned away and gathered his coat and keys. As he stumbled toward the door, still dizzy from the blow to the head, Bradley called after him.

"You're a real asshole, you know that, Goodkind?"

Dale ignored him and slammed the door. Bradley could file an assault complaint against him as far as Dale was concerned.

Screw you.

He couldn't lose any more time.

He had to get to Grimes as fast as possible to talk to Kathy and Corey Collier.

TWENTY-THREE

Three months, seven hours missing

THIS WAS THE break he'd been waiting for.

As Dale sped along Highway 44 toward Grimes, a small town about thirty minutes west of Des Moines, he couldn't stop thinking about the caller Cindy Stewart had described. This "possibly teenaged" female who clearly knew Corey Collier and his mother.

And knew something about Polaroids.

Kathy Collier had been polite but noticeably guarded when Dale called her from a pay phone and mentioned he needed to speak to both her and her son. While Dale hadn't told her any details about the reason for his visit, she'd still agreed to pull her son out of school to meet with him. At her home, though. She didn't want rumors to start flying.

In Grimes, he easily found their modest blue house on the east side of town. He parked in the driveway and checked his appearance in the rearview mirror. A dark half-moon had spread beneath his left eye.

A slight woman with tightly permed hair piled high on her head opened the front door of the house.

Dale exited his car. "Mrs. Collier?" he said.

"Yes," she answered, unsmiling. She held the metal screen door open for him.

Dale entered and offered his hand to her. "I'm Sergeant Goodkind," he said. "Thanks for agreeing to talk to me."

"Sure." She barely touched his hand. "Please take off your shoes."

Dale slipped off his black wing tips and followed her into a small, green kitchen. Everything was avocado green. Appliances, linoleum floor, curtains, even the plaid wallpaper. Dale hated avocado green. It reminded him of pea soup.

Mrs. Collier gestured to the table. "Have a seat." She pulled a white cardigan sweater tightly around her shoulders, stretching the fabric.

A teenage boy sat on the other side, the table rattling from his jiggling leg as he played a handheld video game. Space Invaders, Dale recognized. Curtis owned the same game.

Dale offered a greeting, but the boy ignored him and kept playing, his thumbs swiftly working two yellow buttons creating blips and beeps. Dale sat in a chair across from him.

"Corey," Mrs. Collier said gently. "Put the game down. This policeman needs to ask you a few questions."

Corey switched off the game. He dropped it with a clatter and stared glumly.

"Would you like some coffee?" she offered.

"No, thanks," Dale said. "I'm sorry to bother you, but like I said on the phone, I have some questions for both of you that may be related to the Christopher Stewart case."

Mrs. Collier sat.

"Corey," Dale said, "you're sixteen now, correct?"

The boy nodded and yawned.

"Driving?"

"Just a permit. Still need to take driver's ed." He leaned his head back against the chair and closed his eyes.

Dale turned to the mother. She was fiddling with the tasseled edge of a green place mat.

"When did your husband pass away, Mrs. Collier?"

"Call me Kathy," she said. "He died six years ago when Corey was still in elementary school. He had leukemia."

Dale opened his sketchbook and readied his pen. "Where do you work?"

"I do hair and nails at a salon here in town. Hair Apparent."

"And Corey is your only child, correct?"

"Yes."

"Before Grimes, you previously lived in Des Moines, on the South Side?"

"Yes." Her mouth set in a tense line.

"And you moved a little over two years ago?"

"Yes. Well, no. About a year and a half. Give or take."

"Can you tell me why?" he asked.

She glanced at Corey, but his eyes remained closed. Fake sleeping. Trying to show disinterest. Dale had seen it a hundred times during interviews.

"For a fresh start," Kathy said. "Smaller district, you know. Out of the city."

"Mm-hmm." Dale scribbled a note. "And why a fresh start?"

Corey lifted his head and glared at his mother.

Kathy's eyes skipped back and forth between Dale

and her son. Bright-pink patches spread through her pale cheeks.

"There was a…" She played with the tassel once more and swallowed hard. "Corey was having some problems. We both were."

"Okay." Dale waited for her to continue, but she clamped her mouth shut and stared at the place mat. She still hadn't asked what Corey might have to do with the Stewart case. "What kind of problems were you both having?"

She tucked a coil of hair behind her ear, her hand trembling. "Corey was getting into fights with other kids, skipping school, failing all his classes." She inhaled a shaky breath. "I—I was struggling as a single parent. I'd been dating someone, but we had a bad breakup." She glanced at Corey again. "It felt like a good time to start over somewhere new."

Failing all his classes. Dale's heart started beating a little faster.

"Did you ever send Corey to a tutor?"

"Yes." She tipped her head. "Why? I don't see what any of this has to do with that missing boy."

Dale leaned closer. "Kathy, this is very important. What was the tutor's name?"

"Sebastian Kovacs."

He sucked in a sharp breath that burned his lungs, like breathing frigid air. Every case had a moment when gut instinct became confirmation, and Dale always physically felt it in his chest.

Corey methodically popped every knuckle in both hands.

Dale steadied his voice. "How long did Mr. Kovacs tutor Corey?"

"Three, maybe four months. I can't remember for sure. Can you please tell me what these questions are about?"

Corey turned and looked out the sliding-glass doors that led to a small deck in the backyard. He blinked, slowly, his expression hard.

Dale discreetly studied the boy. Corey finger-combed his shaggy hair forward over his brow and into his eyes, as if trying to hide behind it. To disappear. He pushed up the sleeves of his black sweat shirt, revealing long, pale scars bisecting each wrist.

Suicide slashes.

Something stirred in Dale. Recognition.

The expression on the boy's face: anger, fear, defensiveness. Like a wounded animal. He remembered that feeling well.

He had to proceed carefully.

Dale set his pen down and wiped his palms on the tops of his thighs. "Your previous residence is only a few blocks away from the Stewart abduction site, and we recently received a tip on the Stewart case hotline involving Corey."

Corey's head snapped up. He spoke in a hoarse voice. "What tip?"

Dale hesitated. He didn't want to scare the boy off. As he opened his mouth to answer, the green telephone on the wall started to ring.

Mrs. Collier glanced over her shoulder at the clanging phone but didn't move to answer it. "What does Mr. Kovacs have to do with that missing paperboy?" Her brow wrinkled.

The loud ringing persisted.

"Oh, for crying out loud!" Kathy stood and crossed

the kitchen to answer it. "Hello? Yes, Mrs. Crowley. No, no, he's—yes, of course, I'll be there on time tomorrow. I promise."

"What tip?" Corey repeated.

"Corey," Dale said in a calm, low voice. "Did anyone ever take any Polaroid pictures of you?"

"What the hell, dude. Seriously?" Corey said.

"I'm here to help," Dale said. "Just tell me what happened. Was it Mr. Kovacs?" Dale knew this line of questions was all wrong, leading, but he needed to hear the kid say it. "Did he sexually abuse you?"

Corey slammed his hands down on the table. "Fuck this!"

Dale flinched.

"Corey!" Kathy cried. She hung up the phone and clamped her hands on Corey's forearm, but he jerked it free.

"Do you have kids?" Corey asked.

Mrs. Collier pawed at his back. "Stay calm, honey. Please, don't lose your temper again!"

"I have a twelve-year-old son," Dale said.

"Do you live on the South Side?"

"Yes. Why?"

The boy was so close to saying it, Dale could almost reach into his mouth and pluck out the words himself.

"Then I'd get my kid away from Southlawn Drive if I were you," Corey said.

He stood and shoved the chair away.

"Why?" Dale rose. "What do you mean—"

But Corey had already flung the deck door open and was running across the yard, his mother chasing after him.

TWENTY-FOUR

Three months, nine hours missing

1. Heath is making snowballs to build a fort in his front yard. Heath can build 15 snowballs in one hour, but 2 snowballs melt every 15 minutes. How long will it take him to make 210 snowballs?

SAMMY TAPPED THE eraser of his pencil against the math test. He tried to remember what Mr. K had taught him about word problems. *Underline the question. Put a box around key words. Circle important numbers. Solve by showing your work.*

He drew a crooked line under the question. He put a box around *how long* and *minutes*. He circled all the numbers.

But the blank answer space continued to glare at him. He still had no idea how to solve the problem. He moved on to the next question.

2. If there are 150 people born in the world every minute, how many people are born every hour? Day? Year?

Across the round table, Curtis hunched over his own paper, licking his lips as he wrote out his work in the margins. He gripped the pencil so tightly his fingertips turned white. The lead snapped, and he stopped to fish a new pencil out of his Trapper Keeper.

During their sleepover, while eating slices of pizza in Curtis's bedroom, Sammy had shown him the dark graphite scar in the palm of his left hand from the time he'd accidentally stabbed himself with a sharp pencil in fourth grade. The school nurse had put ointment on the wound, but when it healed, it had sealed in traces of graphite, creating a dark streak just beneath the surface of his skin.

Curtis had touched the mark with his finger, visibly impressed.

"Will it stay there forever?" he'd asked.

"I guess so," Sammy said.

"And it doesn't hurt?"

"No," Sammy answered. "It just looks weird."

"It looks cool." Curtis then offered Sammy the rest of his pizza. Sammy had accepted, even though he'd already eaten his share. Curtis would've given him the entire pizza and eaten none himself if Sammy had asked. He held that much power over him.

After finishing Curtis's slice, Sammy had taken a deep breath, knowing what he had to do next.

Do you want to join a secret club with me? We have a meeting next week.

Outside the classroom window, the sun reflected brightly off the snow. Sammy closed his eyes for a moment and a yellow orb burned behind his lids.

All new members have to take their picture, though. That's how it works. We can take them now, with your mom's camera if you like.

Sammy returned to his test. He couldn't remember

anything they'd studied in math so far this year. He skipped question 2 and moved on.

3. James and Frank deliver 100 newspapers every morning for a part-time job. James can deliver 19 newspapers in 1 hour, and Frank can deliver 27 newspapers in 1 hour. How long will it take each boy to deliver all their newspapers?

Newspaper delivery boys.

Just like Beggars' Night, math was f-word stupid. It was pointless. He'd said so to Mr. K during their final tutoring session last summer, but Mr. K hadn't scolded him for using a swear. He'd instead told Sammy to just focus on the system he'd taught him. *Underline, box, circle.* What did Mr. K know. He was f-word stupid, too.

Even thinking the full f-word felt good. Sammy wanted to shout it at every person who crossed his path, to see the shocked expressions on their faces and horrified reactions at what a monstrous kid he was.

Sammy leaned forward and scratched an answer in the blank space beneath question three: *James and Frank don't deliver newspapers anymore because they are dead.*

He didn't want to put this off any longer. He quietly tore a small corner off the back page of his test and wrote a single word: *bathroom*. He stood and laid his unfinished test facedown in the basket on Mrs. Kinkaid's desk.

"Can I go to the restroom?" he asked quietly.

Mrs. Kinkaid looked up from a worksheet she was grading and scowled. "Done already?"

He nodded.

She eyed him for a moment, then filled out a hall pass. The form kind, not like Miss Ware's fancy laminated pass that rhymed.

Sammy took the pass, and as he walked by Curtis, he dropped the small slip of paper on top of Curtis's test. He could've started this part of his plan after school, but he wanted to just get it over with, and math resource was the only class they had together.

In the bathroom, he locked himself in a stall. He leaned his head against the cold cinder block wall, slipped his hand into the front pocket of his jeans, and pulled out the blue pocketknife. The metal case felt warm against his palm from his body heat. He extracted the shiny blade and touched the tip once more.

On the metal wall of the stall he scratched a box around the words *bag yer face*. The blade satisfyingly scraped through the beige paint and penetrated the metal, creating tiny slivers that sprinkled onto the floor. Finished, he traced his finger over the lines and started to cry.

Sammy knocked his head hard against the wall with a thud and told himself to stop being such a crybaby. He had a plan that started now. Everything would be over soon.

The bathroom door squeaked open, and a small voice called out.

"Sammy?"

Curtis.

"Yeah," Sammy answered. Before he exited the stall, he stuck the knife blade down in his back pocket.

Curtis paced in front of the sinks. "I told Mrs. Kinkaid I had to go really bad so she'd give me a pass, and I told her that my test was done and that I think I did okay. Did you do okay? You finished fast. I had to hurry through the last problem to catch up with you."

Sammy turned on the water and slowly lathered his hands with soap. "I didn't even finish it."

Curtis stopped pacing and bugged out his eyes. "You didn't even finish?"

"Math is fucking stupid."

Curtis soaked in every word Sammy said.

"Yeah," Curtis breathed, "math is...effing stupid." His hesitation betrayed the newness of the swear on his tongue. He lightly kicked the trash can in a halfhearted attempt to show Sammy his own toughness.

"Is the secret meeting still on for today after school? Because my mom is going over to my aunt's to help her shampoo her living room carpet, and I told my mom that I was going to the library after school for a reading program with you and then your mom is picking us up and we're going over to your house to eat dinner and then she'll pick me up after dinner. That's a good story, right? My dad would never let me go, but it's just my mom and she doesn't tell my dad anything right now because she's so mad at him, and so I can go."

Sammy switched off the water. As Curtis talked, he danced around on his tiptoes. It was like he was so full of nervous energy that the heels of his feet defied gravity and he nearly levitated off the ground. Other kids found him annoying, but Sammy didn't mind his constant chatter. He liked how excited Curtis got over things and how he could talk for a long time without taking a breath.

Curtis pulled the hand towel down for Sammy. "So, is the meeting still on? I've never been a member of a secret club, and I've never lied to my mom before. I'm nervous, but I'm excited, too!"

As Sammy dried his hands, he had to turn his head away so Curtis wouldn't see new tears pooling in his eyes. Curtis was so excited about the club. During the sleepover, Sammy had talked up all the fun and exciting things they would do, and how even though it was a model car club, they would start trading baseball cards just for Curtis because that was what he was more interested in.

And now it was time for his plan. He was expected to deliver Curtis today, or face more consequences.

Curtis bounced around the sink, impatient for Sammy's confirmation. Sammy held his breath and slid his hand into his back pocket. He told himself to just get it over with quickly, before someone walked in, before he changed his mind.

He pulled the knife out and pointed it at Curtis's chest. Curtis froze.

"You're not in the club anymore," Sammy said, making his voice low, like a growl. "There's no club meeting after school, and don't ever ask me about it again."

Curtis's bottom lip quivered.

"We're not friends anymore, you and me," Sammy said. "Don't call me on the walkie-talkie anymore. Don't sit with me at lunch. Got it?"

A small squeak emitted from Curtis's throat.

"Got it?" Sammy raised his voice and jabbed the knife tip at him, pricking Curtis's shirt.

"Okay," Curtis whimpered.

"Don't ever tell anyone about the club, or I'll kill you."

"Okay." Fat tears leaked from his eyes and rolled down his cheeks.

Sammy took a step closer. "Stay away from me, and stay away from Southlawn Drive. If anyone else ever asks you to join a secret club again, don't."

Curtis whimpered.

"Say you understand. No more secret clubs."

"I understand. No more secret clubs."

"Now get out of here."

Curtis spun and fled the bathroom, crashing through the door and disappearing into the hall.

Sammy closed the blade and slipped the knife into the front pocket of his blue jeans. He returned to the bathroom stall, closed the door, sat on the toilet, and cried once more.

It was all part of his plan.

Everything would be over soon.

SAMMY'S MOTHER MARCHED him out of the main office of Brody Middle School, where he'd been sitting on the Brat Bench, as it was called by teachers and parents, waiting for her.

"What the hell has gotten into you?" She grimaced. "I can't keep taking off work to come get you."

Sammy crossed his arms over his chest. Most of the time when the school secretary called his mother at the salon, it was because Sammy was sick with another stomachache, or a teacher needed to talk to her about his grades. But not today. No stomachache, no bad grade. He was being suspended for the rest of the day for what he'd written on his test and for making Curtis cry in the bathroom, even though Curtis had refused to say what Sammy had done or said to him. In addition to the suspension today, Sammy would also have to serve detention every day after school for the rest of this week. But suspension was nothing. Detention was nothing. None of this affected the next step of his plan, which was all he really cared about.

When they got inside the car, his mother leaned over and rested her forehead against the steering wheel, her keys chiming in the ignition. "Sammy, Sammy, Sammy," she murmured. "What am I going to do with you."

He could see her shivering. She wore a short jean skirt even though it was winter, and her bare knees vibrated against each other.

"I'm sorry," Sammy said.

She lifted her head and looked at him. "Why did you act like that? Who was the boy you harassed in the bathroom? Principal Parsons wouldn't tell me."

Sammy had already prepared a lie for this question. "It's this kid from my class who picks on me about being fat, and the teachers never do anything. So, I lost my temper today. I stood up for myself. But Mr. Parsons and the teachers don't ever believe me that I get picked on all the time." He'd gotten so good at lying, it was practically effortless now.

Tina reached across the seat and smoothed his hair with her cold fingers. "You're not fat. You're perfect just the way you are." She sighed. "Well, I'm glad you defended yourself against that little asshole. What's his name? I'll call his mother."

"I took care of it, Mom. It was worth getting detention." That part was true.

She smiled weakly. "I hate that Principal Parsons," she said. "He's so smug."

"Yeah," Sammy said.

"All that 'children from broken homes' and 'living with a single mother' bullshit he gave me." Tina roughly turned the key, and the station wagon chugged several times before finally coughing to life. She revved the gas and flipped the heater on high, letting it warm up. She cupped her hands around her mouth and blew on them.

"God, I miss Florida," she said. "I miss the warm sun on my skin all winter. And the sound of waves, and salsa music playing from the Cuban stores." She closed her eyes. "What I wouldn't give for a plate of stone crabs and a slice of key lime pie."

"So why don't we just move there?" Sammy said. "We'd be closer to Dad and could see him more. I could learn how to deep-sea fish with him and help him with his business."

Tina's eyes peeled open, and she stared out the windshield across the parking lot. She spoke slowly. "Sammy, it's more complicated than that. Your dad and Candy…"

He waited for her to continue, but she didn't. "Dad and Candy what?"

"Nothing," she said. "I'll take you home first, but then I have to go back to work. My shift is until six."

"Okay," Sammy said, discreetly clenching his hand into a victorious fist. She'd bought his bullying story. No grounding. And he'd already known she had to work until six. He'd planned everything around it.

"Can I go to the library tonight?" he asked. Phase two of the plan.

"Um, sure. That would be okay, I guess."

Sammy relaxed back into the seat. It was all coming together.

TWENTY-FIVE

Three months, ten hours missing

CRYSTAL SAT AT her desk in her room and copied the words from a year-old *Newsweek* magazine article she'd checked out from the library yesterday. "Stolen Children: What Can Be Done About Child Abduction." She jotted down several good points she could incorporate into her essay—how kidnappings of children were easy to commit but difficult to solve, because it was often a friendly encounter that left behind little to no evidence and scant witnesses, if any.

The scratch of her pen across the paper and the neat strokes and curls of her cursive handwriting were a strange comfort. She wrote until her hand cramped and she was forced to stop and rub the throbbing muscles in the center of her palm.

She sat back and reviewed her notes. Her eyes kept drifting to one line.

...a familiar or trusted neighborhood figure talks a child into accompanying him with a believable excuse and without drawing the attention of anyone else nearby...
Someone the child knows and has reason to trust.

Crystal pulled a fleece sweat shirt over her head,

shivering in the chilly air despite a slick of perspiration between her shoulder blades. Her heart tapped an irregular beat in her chest.

She felt jittery, overstimulated, like she'd had too much caffeine. It had been nearly twenty-four hours since she'd made the anonymous call to the tip line, and the waiting was getting to her. She had no way of knowing what Cindy Stewart had done or would do with the information Crystal had given her. She hoped Cindy had passed everything on to the cops, and that the cops had immediately tracked down and talked to Corey. Maybe they'd even already talked to Kenny, searched his garage and gotten a closer look at the car parked inside. If that Sergeant Goodkind had gotten the tip, he'd be thorough, she was sure of it.

Then again, maybe nothing had happened. The Stewarts had probably gotten hundreds of crank calls since running the ad. Cindy could've just as easily hung up the phone and declared Crystal another crank caller.

There were still too many dots floating around in her head that she couldn't completely connect. Still too many missing pieces. And a good journalist never ran a story without all the facts.

Outside, falling snowflakes clung to her window, and her room grew dim. She pulled the cord on her banker's lamp, basking the pages of the magazine in harsh white light. The face of another missing boy dominated the cover. Kevin Collins, a ten-year-old who had vanished last year after basketball practice at his Catholic school in San Francisco. Marilyn Klein had been interviewed for the article and said she and her husband had received close to a thousand calls since their son disappeared over two years ago, all from people claiming to have information related to his disappearance.

Crystal's call to Cindy Stewart could be just one of *thousands*.

She laid the magazine down and rubbed the back of her neck. Even though she'd made the call anonymously, she still alerted to the sound of every passing car, fearing it might be the cops coming to talk to her after somehow discovering she was the tipster. She'd have to answer questions, explain everything to her mother, and Sammy would know she'd ratted him out behind his back.

The telephone rang, and Crystal yelped with a startle. She sprinted into her mother's room to grab the extension on her headboard.

"Hello," she answered breathlessly.

"Hey, Chrissie." Her father.

She exhaled, relieved. "Hi, Dad."

"Sorry I haven't called for a while. How are you?"

"I'm good." She tried to remember the last time they'd spoken. Early August? For her birthday? It seemed like years ago.

"How's the weather there?" he asked. "I saw on the news an early snowstorm is predicted to hit the Midwest tonight."

"Yeah, it already started snowing. And it's really cold."

An awkward silence filled the staticky line.

"Listen," he said, "I don't have much time. Is Sammy around? Candy said he called last Sunday and left a message. I haven't had time to call him back until now."

"He's not home from school yet."

"Oh, okay. Well, I'll try again later."

Crystal switched the receiver to her other ear. Even with the anxious distraction from calling the tip line, she hadn't stopped worrying about her college situation. She had to tell her father about the University of Miami and ask for his help. It was now or never. No telling when she'd get him on the phone again.

"Dad, wait. I need to talk to you about something."

She poured out everything about the acceptance letter, the cost of tuition, and her idea to live with him to establish in-state residency and reduce living expenses. She talked fast so he wouldn't have a chance to interrupt, and when she finished, she held her breath, waiting for his response.

He was quiet for a long time with only the sound of his breathing rustling over the mouthpiece.

"Oh, Chrissie," he finally said. "You know I can't help you out right now. Not with the wedding and new baby coming."

Crystal slumped into her mother's rickety papasan chair, the weight of the news dragging her down like there had been a dramatic increase in the earth's gravitational pull.

"No, I didn't know," she said.

Sadness spread through her chest as she realized that this new sibling effectively ended her last hope for Miami. And that everyone in her life, it seemed, was keeping secrets from her.

CRYSTAL WAS SITTING at the kitchen table alone in the waning light when her mother hurried inside the house with Sammy trailing after her.

"Hey," Tina said, short of breath. "Why are you sitting in the dark?" She flipped on the glaring fluorescent light, and Crystal squinted.

"Why are you here?" Crystal asked. "I thought you were at work."

"I had to pick Sammy up from school and have a meeting with the principal." Tina waved a hand. "Don't ask."

Sammy doffed his shoes and coat on the floor.

"Put that stuff away," Tina said sharply.

Without argument, Sammy carried the items to the hall closet and then belly flopped onto the couch. He was in trouble for something, Crystal could tell.

Tina heaved her purse onto the counter and started digging through it. She extracted her gold velveteen cigarette case and peered inside.

"Damn," she muttered. "I'm almost out of cigarettes." She glanced at the clock. "I don't have time to stop and get more. Chrissie, will you please go down to the corner store tonight and get me some? And a carton of milk, too. I'll leave some money and a note for you."

"Mom, I need to talk to you," Crystal said.

Tina scribbled on a scrap of paper and slapped a ten-dollar bill on top of it. She wiggled her finger in Crystal's direction. "And bring me change."

"Mom."

Tina snapped the cigarette case shut and stuffed it back into her purse. "What? Chrissie, I really have to go. I'm in so much shit with my boss for leaving in the middle of the day again."

"I talked to Dad. Just now. He called."

Tina stopped.

"Dad called?" Sammy said from the living room. He hurried back into the kitchen. "What did he say?"

Crystal stood and tucked her hands into the front pockets of her jeans. "He had a lot to say, it turns out." She looked directly at her mother.

Tina licked her lips and avoided Crystal's stare.

Crystal continued. "He told me that he and Candy are getting married Thanksgiving weekend. And they're having a baby in December."

Tina's cheeks flushed bright red, sharpening the foundation line along her jaw, but she still said nothing.

"Dad's having a baby?" Sammy asked.

Crystal nodded at her brother. "He thought we already knew."

Tina leaned against the counter and clamped her arms over her chest. "Damn you, Randy," she said quietly.

"She's due in four weeks!" Crystal shouted. "When were you going to freaking tell us?"

"Don't you raise your voice at me," Tina said. "I was trying to figure out the best time."

"He said he told you months ago. You've known about this for *months* and didn't tell us. That's so unfair!"

"Unfair to *you*?" Now Tina yelled back. "Your dad put it on *me* to deliver that news. He couldn't be bothered to tell you himself!"

"Chrissie, did Dad say he would call back?" Sammy asked.

She angrily put her hand up to shush him. "Why does it matter who told us? Just *someone* should have told us, for Christ's sake."

Tina yanked her purse straps over her shoulder. "I don't have to stand here and be judged by my eighteen-year-old *kid*." She sorted the keys on her ring and started for the door. As she reached for the knob, she stopped and turned back around. "Wait a minute. Why did he call today?" she asked. "He never calls during the week."

"I left him a message on Sunday," Sammy said. "Is he going to call back tonight?"

Tina narrowed her eyes at Crystal. "And why did the wedding and baby come up? What were you talking about?"

Crystal would have to tell her sometime; might as well be now. She reached into her back pocket, pulled out the folded U of M letter, and handed it to her mother.

"I applied to the University of Miami in September and got an early acceptance. I asked Dad if I could live with him to get in-state tuition."

Tina took the letter and read the wrinkled paper, her eyes skittering over the lines. When she finished, her expression was a mask of fury.

"You did this behind my back?"

"What was I supposed to do?" Crystal threw her hands in the air. "You didn't give me any choice." Her voice cracked.

Tina crumpled the letter and threw it on the floor. "You're not going. I don't care if *Harvard* wants you. You're not going!"

Crystal stared at the paper ball as if it were her own heart, ripped from her chest and lying at her feet.

"Out-of-state tuition?" Tina shouted. "Have you lost your mind? Where the hell do you think the money is going to come from, Crystal? We talked about this a million times. *I don't have it*. I can't even pay for fucking Christmas presents this year!" She held her arms out wide, fingers splayed.

Her mother rarely cursed, and the word pierced Crystal's eardrums. "I told you, I have a plan. With Dad," she said weakly.

Tina laughed ruefully. "A plan with your dad. And how's that 'plan' working out?" She made sharp, hateful air quotes with her fingers. "Let me guess, he said no."

Fat tears rolled down Crystal's cheeks. Everything she'd been carrying around for months—her anxieties over college, the scholarship essay, the troubles with Sammy—bubbled up the back of her throat, like hot lava pushing its way to the surface.

"I don't care if you and Dad are both irresponsible deadbeats!" Crystal screamed, the release of emotion so satisfying it made her dizzy. She snatched the paper from the floor and shook it in her mother's face. "I'm going! I'll find a way by myself!"

She moved to leave the room, but Tina blocked her path. She pointed a long fingernail under Crystal's nose. Her voice was low, almost a growl. "Don't you ever talk to me like that again. I'm warning you."

Crystal felt an unstoppable bile of words build in her throat. "You're just jealous!" she exploded. "Because I'm smart and I'm going to make something of myself instead of getting knocked up before my eighteenth birthday!"

Tina's hand shot out with a hard slap across Crystal's face, rocking her head to the side. Crystal gasped and cupped her stinging cheek. She turned back to Tina, incredulous. Her mother had never struck her before. Not even a spanking as a child.

Tina covered her mouth. She stared at Crystal with wild eyes.

Mr. Tibbs strolled into the room and lazily rubbed

against Crystal's leg. He meowed for his dinner, oblivious.

Tina wrenched the door open, slamming it against the trash can and knocking it over, and left. A moment later, her car revved and the tires crunch over the fresh snow on the driveway.

"Chrissie?" Sammy's voice was small. He stood in the threshold between the two rooms, tears dripping off the end of his nose. "Are you okay?"

Dazed and still cradling her face, Crystal drifted to the refrigerator. She found a bag of frozen peas in the freezer and gently pressed them to her throbbing cheek.

She closed her eyes. She couldn't think anymore. She hated this house. She hated her parents. She hated her life.

When she opened her eyes, she saw her mother's note on the counter.

Hi Judy,

Please sell Crystal one pack of my usual Capri 120's Super Slim Lights hardpack.

Thnx! T. C.

Just the sight of her mother's handwriting made her want to rip her own hair out in despair. This was her pathetic life. Stuck in her mother's house with no prospects, no future, no hope. All she was good for was fetching stupid cigarettes.

Crystal grabbed the note and money and flung the bag of peas onto the counter. She opened the hall closet and stuffed her feet into her winter boots.

"Where are you going?" Sammy asked.

"Anywhere but here!" Crystal cried, jamming her arms into her winter coat.

"When will you be back?" Sammy called after her. "I'm going—"

But Crystal slammed the door, cutting off his voice. Outside, her breaths exploded in angry white clouds amid the snow, which was falling heavier now. She started walking.

After several blocks, her fingertips and ears burned in the cold wind. She'd grabbed a scarf with her coat, but hadn't thought to get a hat or gloves. But she kept going, angrily kicking the accumulating snow out in front of her.

At the corner store, she bought the milk and her mother's Capris with the note for Judy, the owner, just as she had many times before. She stuffed the change into her coat pocket and stuck the receipt and her mother's note in the paper bag.

She started walking again, but now with no destination in mind. She just didn't want to go back home yet. Dusk was already descending with the shorter winter days. Crystal longed to talk to someone. To sit and empty her heart of all the worries and troubles she'd been trying to carry by herself. She could walk to Somphone's, just five blocks away, but quickly abandoned that idea. She and Somphone didn't have that kind of friendship. They didn't confide secrets or problems in each other, or stay up late giggling during sleepovers, or gossip for hours over the telephone. They sat next to each other in classes. They talked about homework and the school paper and college applications. They studied together at the library and sometimes got ice cream. But that was the extent of their socializing. Crystal could taste the loneliness on the back of her tongue.

By the time she turned onto Tenth Street, she had a destination.

WHEN SEBASTIAN OPENED the door, he took one look at her puffy eyes, the red mark on her cheek, and quickly ushered her inside. He took the grocery bag from her arms and helped her remove her boots and coat. In the living room, he wrapped a warm afghan around her shivering body and settled her onto his sofa. She accepted a cup of hot tea, that same sweet and spicy tea he'd made her once before, and she sipped it from a real hand-painted teacup and saucer.

He asked what had happened, and she broke down crying again, telling him the story about the fight with her mother and the shocking news about her father.

Sebastian lit a fire in the small fireplace. He let her cry, let the words tumble out, and just listened.

When she was finished, he put his arm around her shoulders and silently comforted her.

After a while, he gently said, "*Cree*-stahl, your mother does the best she can. She must feel tremendous stress raising children alone."

"I don't care. I hate her."

"You don't hate her."

Crystal took another sip of tea and sniffed. "I know. I'm just so angry right now." She was starting to feel calmer.

A log crackled and sparked in the hearth.

"I haven't seen my mother in years," Sebastian said. "I miss her very much. You should appreciate your time with your mother."

The room had grown warm, and Crystal shed the afghan. "I know that, but she doesn't have a clue how important college is to me. Or how hard I've been working on this essay for the scholarship to help *pay* for school. And worse, she doesn't care."

"She does care," Sebastian said.

Crystal set her empty teacup and saucer on the end table. "It doesn't matter anyway. I'll never have enough money to go. Forget about the scholarship. I'll never get the essay done."

"Why not?" he asked.

Crystal watched the snow fall through the front picture window and felt her heart rate slow, her blood pressure lower. Sebastian's house was cozy, calming in a way hers wasn't, because here she was understood and accepted, just the way she was. Here she was safe, protected from everything that was wrong.

"I just can't…pull all these ideas together," she answered. "About the paperboy cases. It was stupid of me to think I could make sense of it all."

"Make sense of what?"

She started at the beginning, on the morning of Chris Stewart's disappearance when she went looking for Sammy and found him running down the street with bruises on his arm. She recounted her interactions with Kenny, how she'd seen the car in his garage, and Sammy's strange behavior for months. Then she told him about the box and two Polaroids she'd found in Sammy's room, and how she'd called the Stewarts' tip line and given them Kenny's and Corey's names.

"Anyway," she finished, "it doesn't matter. Sammy got into my room and ripped a bunch of pages out of the notebook. The box and the pictures are gone. He denies he did anything, but I know he destroyed them."

"You gave them Corey's name?" Sebastian asked.

Crystal glanced at him, but he was fixated, unblinking, on the fire. The flames illuminated his dark eyes.

"Yeah. Why?"

"I knew Corey Collier," he said. His fingers tightened on her shoulder.

"You did?"

"He was my tutoring student a few years ago."

"Oh. I didn't know that."

Sebastian's expression grew distant, unreadable. "He was a…troubled boy."

His fingers gripped even tighter, scrunching the fabric of her sweat shirt. Fresh worry pricked at the back of Crystal's mind.

"Did I do something wrong?"

At last, Sebastian blinked and looked at her. He withdrew his arm. "Of course not," he said, but his tone was unconvincing.

"I feel like maybe I shouldn't have told them his name."

He forced a smile. "You're a conscientious young woman. You did what you thought was right."

He laid his hand over hers, and his touch sent a current of electricity through her chest, down her stomach, and deeper still.

Woman. Not girl.

She'd been right to come here.

Shadows danced around the room from the waffling flames. She'd been dreaming of this exact moment for so long.

"Sebastian," she whispered. She closed her eyes and

leaned toward him, pressing her lips to his. They were soft and warm and tasted sweet, like the tea. She pressed harder, opening her mouth, and raised her hands to his face. As her fingertips grazed the rough stubble of his cheeks, he captured them in his hands and pulled away.

"Crystal," he said quietly.

She blinked, confused.

"I'm sorry," he said. His beautiful face twisted with remorse.

She jerked her hands away. Her stupid, stupid hands.

"I didn't mean to mislead you."

She turned away, wishing she could die, right there.

"I care about you and your brother," he continued, "but I just bring you both pain."

Crystal abruptly stood. The afghan tumbled to the floor. She couldn't bear to hear another word. She wanted to leap into the fire and let the flames incinerate her humiliation.

"Please, wait." Sebastian laid his hand on her arm, but Crystal recoiled.

"Just...let me be." She hurried to the door and slipped her coat back on.

Sebastian's arms fell helplessly to his sides. "Please, don't go," he said. "I very much want to be your friend."

The final blow. That word, *friend*.

Crystal slid her feet into her boots, opened the door, and stumbled out into the snow.

TWENTY-SIX

Three months, eleven and a half hours missing

THE HEADLIGHTS OF Dale's car sliced through the driving lines of snow. The tires slipped on a curve and the back end fishtailed, but Dale pressed on.

He had to get to Southlawn Drive.

He switched off his police radio even though he was still on duty for a few more hours. He didn't want to get called away on another case. He was determined to close this one tonight.

It was Kovacs. Dale knew it with every molecule in his body.

Kovacs could've hidden Chris's body anywhere. One of the hundreds of abandoned wells or cisterns scattered around the South Side. An old farmstead just outside the city limits.

Or in his basement.

That basement with the skeleton key.

Without a warrant, Dale would have to somehow convince Kovacs to willingly take him down there. It would take a feat of verbal maneuvering like Dale had never done before, but Chris could still be alive. Being held prisoner. A small chance, but not implausible.

Nothing was implausible to Dale, because once, as a boy, he'd spent an entire night locked in a basement room.

He'd gone down the stairs because he'd been promised there was an electric train set, and he loved electric trains. But once he was inside the little room under the stairwell, he couldn't get out.

If you try to run, I'll make you sorry.

Corey's words clotted in his ears. *I'd get my kid away from Southlawn Drive if I were you.*

He squeezed the steering wheel harder and pressed down on the accelerator. Dale reached the South Side as darkness settled. The end of Chris's and maybe even Matt's cases were right at his fingertips.

Dale parked one street over from Southlawn and walked to Kovacs's house. The lamp glowed in the front picture window. Adrenaline coursed through his veins and pumped his heart. His swollen eye throbbed in time with his heartbeat, and his vision grew blurry.

Dale pounded on the door, rattling the small diamond-shaped window.

Movement inside. Hurried footsteps. Dale touched the butt of his pistol resting on his hip, then pulled his coat over it.

The door swung open. "I'm so glad you—" Kovacs said, but clamped his mouth shut as soon as he saw Dale on the stoop.

"Expecting someone?" Dale asked.

"No," Kovacs answered.

Dale stepped closer and put his arm across the door-frame so Kovacs couldn't close it. "I need to ask you some more questions."

"About?"

"The Stewart case."

"I already told you I don't know anything."

"I realize that, but I still need to speak with you again. About some new information."

Kovacs studied Dale for a long moment, his gaze lingering on the black eye. Finally, he opened the door wide, gesturing for Dale to enter.

The living room was warm from a fire dying in the hearth. He followed Kovacs into the kitchen without bothering to wipe his wet shoes on the mat. The men sat in the hard, wooden chairs across from each other, just as they had the first time Dale interviewed him.

Kovacs's brow glistened with perspiration. He sat stiffly with his hands tightly clasped in his lap. Dale leaned his elbows on the tabletop. No notebook and pen this time. There would be no paperwork for this visit.

"I want to ask you some more questions about your tutoring," Dale said.

Kovacs didn't respond.

"Kids you've tutored. In the past."

The last of the fire crackled in the other room.

"What about them?" Kovacs said.

"Just trying to get some facts straight. So, there's Sammy Cox every Monday."

"Yes. Was."

Dale crossed his legs. "You mentioned other kids you've tutored in the last year." Dale waited for Kovacs to answer, but he remained silent.

"Let's go further back. How about a boy named Corey Collier? Two years ago?"

The briefest expression flickered across Kovacs's face. Worry. Panic, maybe.

"Yes, I tutored Corey."

"At his house? Like the others?"

"Yes. For math. I worked with him for about two months, but then he and his mother moved."

"Why didn't you mention him before during our first interview?"

"You asked about kids I tutored in the last year. I tutored Corey nearly two years ago."

"I never said *last year*."

"Yes, you did—"

"No, I didn't." Dale's tone sharpened.

Kovacs clamped his lips together.

"Where did you move here from again?"

"Budapest, Hungary." He pronounced the name as Buda-*pesht*.

"No, I mean, when you first moved to Iowa."

"I don't understa—"

"I'm talking about West Des Moines," Dale snapped. "The fact that you lived in West Des Moines in September of 1982. Not far from where another paperboy was kidnapped."

"West Des Moines?" Kovacs echoed.

"Yes. Isn't the timing of that interesting?"

Kovacs shook his head, seeming confused. "I don't know anything about a West Des Moines boy."

"Does the name Matt Klein ring a bell?"

"I don't know that boy," he whispered.

"Stop lying!" Dale slammed his fist on the table.

Kovacs flinched.

"You don't know about West Des Moines. You don't know about the South Side. You don't know about Matt Klein or Chris Stewart or have anything to say about Corey Collier. You don't know much of anything, do you?" Dale took a deep breath to calm himself. "How do you pay all your bills, Mr. Kovacs?"

"What?"

"Your bills. How do you pay for them with just your

tutoring and piano lessons? Doesn't seem like you'd make enough to cover a mortgage, gas, water, electric, food. So, how do you pay for everything?"

Kovacs stood. "I think you should go," he said. "I won't answer any more questions without a lawyer."

Dale pushed out of his chair, tipping it over with a clatter. "You want a lawyer now?" he said. He moved around the table, and Kovacs backed away.

"No lawyer," Dale said, swinging his head from side to side. "You're going to tell me what you did."

Kovacs lifted his chin. "I know my rights," he said. "I won't talk to you anymore without a lawyer. You need to go."

For a brief moment, everything Dale was putting at risk flashed through his mind—his job, his family, maybe even his freedom—and he considered leaving. If he walked out of Kovacs's house now, it would be no harm, no foul.

But Dale had to know what was in that basement. He couldn't leave without seeing it. Dale knew Kovacs was hiding something down there with such certainty he would've staked his own life on it.

To hell with a search warrant, or losing his job, or even legal repercussions. He was getting into that basement one way or another.

"I'm not going anywhere," Dale said, "until you tell me what I want to hear."

"You're crazy," Kovacs said, backing even farther away. "I saw what you did at the library in front of your own son. I should call the police on *you*."

Searing anger tore through Dale's chest so hot that white stars exploded behind his eyes. He drew his gun from the holster at his hip and pointed it at Kovacs's face.

"I am the police, you son of a bitch."

Kovacs's arms shot above his head. "*Szaros*!"

The gun wavered in Dale's hand, but he kept it trained at Kovacs. "Don't you talk about my son," he said through clenched teeth. No turning back now. He wasn't leaving, he *couldn't* leave, until Kovacs admitted what he'd done.

"I know what you did to Corey and Matt and Chris," Dale said. "And what you've been doing to Sammy Cox. You hurt those boys. I *know* you hurt those boys."

Kovacs violently shook his head. "No, no, no!" His eyes glistened with tears. "I didn't mean to hurt him. I wanted to help him."

Dale snorted. "That's what you all say." Dale gestured to the basement door with a flick of the gun barrel. "We're gonna take a little tour. Open it."

Kovacs stared at Dale, arms still in the air.

"Now!"

Kovacs jumped and scurried to the bulletin board next to the phone. He unhooked a small skeleton key hanging from a tack and moved to the door. His hands shook so hard he fumbled to fit the key into the hole.

"It's just a basement," Kovacs said. "An old dirt basement. There's nothing down there. There's nothing—"

"Shut up!"

Kovacs finally inserted the key, released the lock, and opened the door. He stood back and raised his hands once more.

"Light," Dale said.

Kovacs flipped the switch on the wall, illuminating a dusty, dull bulb at the bottom.

Dale nudged Kovacs in the shoulder with the gun barrel. "Walk," he said.

Kovacs slowly started down the narrow steps, and Dale followed, the old wooden planks creaking beneath their weight.

As they descended, the air grew cold, musty. Decades of cobwebs coated every nook and cranny. Cool earth and dust filled his nostrils, and Dale felt as if he were descending into the belly of his childhood, that black hole of his memory he rarely allowed himself to visit. ·

At the bottom, Kovacs flattened himself against a wall. Dale squinted into the gloom, surveying the room. Low ceiling rafters, crumbling cinder block walls, piles of wood scraps, boxes, and a few rusted paint cans on a rickety shelf.

"Please," Kovacs said, clutching the key to his chest. "I—I don't—"

"Shut up," Dale said. "Don't talk unless I ask you a question." He kept the gun pointed at Kovacs as he continued to scrutinize the room. A corroding water heater in one corner, a decades-old furnace in the other. A foul-smelling drain in the center of the floor. No windows.

Dale twisted around and peered through the risers, making out the shape of a door in the dimness. Another room. His vision started to molder; his brain slipped sideways.

The long-ago voice wormed through his ears, slithering and slimy. *It's my secret hideout.*

"There," Dale said, pointing to the door. "What is that?"

Kovacs didn't move his eyes from Dale's pistol. "Storage," he said. His teeth chattered from the cold. Or fear.

Dale tilted his head. "What's *in* it?"

Kovacs glanced at the door, and Dale sensed his resistance to answer.

"Open it," Dale said.

"I can't."

"Open the fucking door!" Dale shouted.

Kovacs jumped. He retrieved a blue plastic flashlight from the shelf with the paint cans and switched it on. He directed the weak beam at the door and unlocked the knob with the same skeleton key he'd used upstairs.

Kovacs yielded, and stepped aside. The door slowly creaked open.

Dale braced himself for what he might see.

A starving, naked boy chained to a wall or tied to a bed. A rotting body. Bones.

I know you love trains.

He inched beneath the stairs, wiping his face with his free hand. He was panting, struggling to catch his breath.

I only invite special friends down here.

Dale swallowed down bile burning the back of his throat. Each time he blinked, it was like a camera shuttering back and forth between past and present.

"Get the light," Dale said.

Kovacs tugged on a cord in the center of the low ceiling and stepped out of the way.

With the gun still on Kovacs, Dale took a deep breath, and peered into the closetlike room. But instead of a terrified boy or a decaying body, he saw stacks of blue jeans with white tags still attached. Boxes of Adidas and Nike tennis shoes in different sizes and colors. Cassette tapes still in cellophane wrappers, boxes of diapers, canisters of baby formula stacked like blocks.

"What the…" he murmured, confused. The tension in his arm loosened. "What the hell is this?"

"I mail to family," Kovacs said, his voice quavering, his English breaking down. "Back in Hungary." He moved the flashlight over more bags of toys and electronic video games still in packages.

"In Hungary, everyone is in poverty, but it's worse for the Roma. My family, they sell to the black market to survive."

Dale bent over and picked up a pair of new Levi's blue jeans. Women's, size eight.

"I shoplift most everything," Kovacs continued, "then deliver to point man. We meet many mornings in the park, behind the library, for exchange."

Dale dropped the jeans and swayed, nearly passing out.

No.

Kovacs was *the guy*. Everything had pointed to him. Had led right to his doorstep. Dale pressed the butt of his gun to his forehead and staggered sideways. The room flipped upside-down.

"I can't let you get away again," he wheezed, struggling to breathe. He was losing his mind. This was how perfectly normal people went insane.

"Officer Goodkind?" Kovacs asked quietly.

Kovacs was a pedophile. A child molester. The monster in the basement Dale had been hunting his entire life.

He wouldn't let him get away again.

He lunged at Kovacs and pinned him to the wall, pressing the barrel of his gun to Kovacs's forehead.

"I'm asking one last time," Dale said, his jaw clenched. "What did you do to those boys?"

A strangled sob escaped Kovacs's throat. "There are no boys," he gasped.

Dale cocked the hammer back. "You hurt those boys! I know you did! Just fucking say it!"

Fat tears leaked from Kovacs's eyes and wet his cheeks. "I didn't help him," he cried. "*Istenem*…forgive me."

More lies. Dale's finger twitched on the trigger. One more millimeter and the bullet would explode into Kovacs's brain, killing him instantly. He'd never killed anyone before, but he could do it now. One less pervert on the planet.

"Our father, who art in heaven…" Kovacs moaned. "*Szenteltessék meg a neved.*"

Dale let off the trigger.

Kovacs continued chanting, the two languages mixing and jumbling. "Thy kingdom come, *te akaratod…*"

He released Kovacs and backed away. Kovacs slid to the floor, still moaning.

Dale looked around the tiny room, bewildered, as if he didn't know how he'd gotten there.

No boys. No bodies.

He'd been wrong about everything.

Dale collapsed to his knees and began to weep, his cries echoing off the bare cinder walls.

"And lead us not into temptation," Kovacs continued in a loud monotone, "but deliver us from evil." He calmly stared at Dale.

Dale pushed himself up onto his feet and holstered his pistol. Slowly, he backed out of the room.

"For thine is the kingdom, and the power and the glory," Kovacs finished, tears still streaming down his cheeks, "*örökre és örökké. Ámen.*"

Dale turned and ran up the stairs, tripping on every step. He staggered through the house and out the front door into the blanket of early darkness, the cold shocking his hot skin.

He kept running until he reached his car parked on the next street, and only then did he finally stop to retch into the pure white snow.

TWENTY-SEVEN

Three months, twelve hours missing

CRYSTAL HAD FLED Mr. K's house with no direction or destination in mind. Her only goal was to simply put as much distance between herself and the humiliation as possible.

He was *Mr. K* again. He had never truly been *Sebastian*. All the budding romantic feelings and fantasy scenarios had been completely one-sided. She understood that now, and the split-second crash into reality while sitting on his couch had inflicted devastating injuries.

As she trudged along the sidewalk, gusts of wind picked up the powdery accumulation and drifted it across the sidewalk. She started to cry fresh tears once again, and the salty droplets froze to the tips of her eyelashes. She pulled her knit scarf over the bottom half of her face. The grocery bag grew heavy in her arms, but she didn't want to go home yet, the pain from the fight with her mother still too raw as well. She kept walking, aimlessly, intermittently crying and fuming. Her anger vacillated among Mr. K, her parents, and even herself. The frigid air did nothing to cool her hot pain.

When Crystal found herself near the library, she decided to walk there and warm up for a bit, try to calm down and regroup. Then she would go home. At the corner of Tenth and Porter, next to Peace Evangeli-

cal Church, she stopped for a moment to wipe the wet
flakes smearing the lenses of her glasses and to switch
the heavy half gallon of milk again. She flexed and unflexed her fingers, so cold they'd crossed the physical
pain threshold to numb. Her head throbbed and small
squiggles were starting to bisect her vision, like blips
of static across a television screen.

She slipped her glasses back on and continued.
The library wasn't far now. As she passed Thirteenth
Place, she spotted a lone figure walking away from her
up ahead. She paused at the familiarity of the nylon
coat—navy blue with fat white-and-red stripes along
the arms and around the shoulders—and the matching
moon boots of the same color and stripe pattern. The
figure passed under a streetlight, illuminating brown
hair dusted with white flakes.

It was Sammy.

Crystal nearly shouted his name, but something
about his stride stopped her. He was practically march-
ing, with purpose and a destination, it seemed, not just
wandering or playing around in the snow. Curious as
to what he was doing and where he was going, she
turned onto Thirteenth Place and followed, keeping
her distance.

After one block, Sammy turned left, onto Southlawn
Drive.

Crystal blinked, confused. Wiped her smeary lenses
once more. "What the hell…" she whispered.

She shadowed him to the corner of Thirteenth and
Southlawn, where she ducked behind a large oak tree
in an unlit yard.

Sammy continued his quick pace along empty
Southlawn.

Crystal pressed her forehead against the tree, an acidic drop of dread eating a small hole in her stomach. She prayed he wasn't going where she suspected.

But at 1223 Southeast Southlawn Drive, Sammy turned and hiked up the driveway. He crossed behind the white work van and disappeared around the side of the tall garage.

Crystal set the paper bag down on top of her feet and waited behind the tree, shivering uncontrollably. She ran through a mental list of all the reasons he might go to Kenny Harris's house. To collect for his paper route. To deliver something for their mother. For a friendly visit.

A friendly visit? Not a chance.

She hunched against the trunk in an effort to quell her shaking.

After only a few minutes, the door of Kenny's garage yawned open, and Kenny and Sammy walked out together onto the driveway. They were having what looked like a normal conversation, nothing amiss. Kenny wore heavy denim coveralls with a name patch over his heart. Crystal clung to a sliver of hope. Sammy had probably just picked up his route money. That had to be it. And Kenny was clearly going on an emergency work call for some poor soul whose furnace had crapped out. It was all explainable.

Kenny ruffled the top of Sammy's head and climbed into the driver's seat. The van backed slowly down the driveway onto the street, and Sammy followed. When he reached the sidewalk, he started retracing his earlier path, in the direction of home, to Crystal's relief.

As the van's headlights passed and turned the corner, she crouched behind the tree. Pacified that Sammy had been on an errand, she picked up the grocery bag and brushed snow off the bottom. But just as Crystal was about to emerge from her hiding place, Sammy halted. He waited for a few seconds, then spun around and ran back in the direction of Kenny's house. He sprinted up the driveway, his thick moon boots throwing clods of snow behind him, and he once again vanished behind the side of the garage.

Crystal walked into the middle of the empty street and stood, baffled. The tiny sliver of hope and relief she'd felt just moments earlier vanished like a puff of smoke. She looked left, then right, as if the street itself might provide an answer to what Sammy was doing.

Her glasses became smeared with wet snowflakes again, but she didn't bother to clean them. She hurriedly crossed the street to the opposite sidewalk and loitered in front of Kenny's house, debating whether or not to go further. Every nerve ending tingled, sensing danger, warning her to go home.

But Sammy was her little brother. She had to know what he was up to. Whatever it was, she had to know.

After checking once more that no one was watching, she darted up the driveway to the back of the garage, sticking close to the perimeter of the building. The backyard was dark and shielded by a row of bushes creating a natural fence. She nestled the grocery bag between a gap in the hedge and approached the house. She mounted the deck stairs and peered through the glass slider into a small kitchen. Not a single light on. She tugged on the handle, but it didn't budge. It didn't appear that Sammy had gone inside.

Crystal next approached the back door to the detached garage. She tried the knob. It was unlocked. She slipped inside, warmth immediately blanketing her.

"Sammy?" she whispered, afraid a neighbor might hear if she shouted.

No answer.

"Sammy?" she said again, a little louder this time. "Are you in here?"

She waited a few seconds, but there was no sound, no movement. She closed the door and rubbed her frozen hands together, trying to restore blood flow and feeling.

Crystal's eyes slowly adjusted to the soft yellow glow of a Miller beer analog clock hanging on the wall. She squinted, identifying objects by the weak light—the silver muscle car, a push lawn mower, shelves and boxes, a tool bench. She moved to inspect the car more closely. Black interior bucket seats, just like the newspaper report had said. She made a slow circle to the front and crouched to read the chrome decal attached to the grille. She could just make out the letters.

Chevelle.

Not a Camaro.

Crystal stood, disappointed. She poked around the rest of the space. Rakes and shovels hanging on one wall, a pair of sawhorses with two boards lying across them, piles of sawdust on the ground below. On the opposite side, a solid set of wooden shelves crowded with paint cans, gasoline containers, and more boxes. But no Sammy. She tried the interior door to the house. Also locked. Maybe he'd gotten in another way. Or maybe he was hiding somewhere in the backyard, or even on his way home by now. She crossed her arms over her chest, puzzled.

The wind howled outside. She needed to go before Kenny came back and caught her. She'd never be able to explain why she was in his garage. As she turned to leave, the boxes on the shelves caught her eye. Close enough to read them now, Crystal immediately recognized the red lettering on the sides.

HVAC Parts and Supplies.

It was the same lettering on the box she'd found in Sammy's closet. The box with all the candy and the dirty magazine. And the Polaroid.

She gently slid one down. On the top flap, someone had scribbled in pencil, *Midwest Heating and Cooling.* The same name on the side of Kenny's van. His father's company. She opened the flaps. Inside was a jumble of mechanical parts. She checked another. More parts. Pieces of ducts and vents.

Crystal puffed out her cheeks. What had she expected? She nudged the box back into place.

Enough was enough. She'd let her imagination run wild for months to the point of being ridiculous. Kenny wasn't holding Chris Stewart hostage, and her brother wasn't here involved in some kind of nefarious activity. Sammy had probably dropped a glove or something when he was collecting his route money, had come back to retrieve it, and was now headed home through backyards. She felt stupid for even following him. She rewound the scarf around her face, pulling it back up over her mouth and nose.

As Crystal moved toward the door to leave, the ceiling above her creaked. She froze. Another creak. Then a shuffling sound, followed by a thump. The creaking moved from one side of the ceiling to the other, above the shelves. Footsteps. She yanked the scarf down.

There was an attic. And someone was up there. It had to be Sammy.

"Sammy?" she whisper-called.

The creaking stopped.

Crystal crept back to the shelves, and upon closer inspection, she realized they weren't flush against the wall, creating a gap of several feet behind them. She peered around the end of the shelving unit.

Stairs.

Another thump above her.

"Sammy! Answer me!"

With no response, she stepped onto the first tread, but hesitated. She stared up the dark, narrow staircase for a few moments, immobilized by the frightening possibility that it wasn't her brother, and what she might instead encounter.

No. It had to be him, and she had to know what he was doing. She couldn't leave until she did.

Crystal took another step, inching her way up. Adrenaline flooded her veins, accelerating her heartrate and shortening her breaths, like she might hyperventilate. But she couldn't stop. She *had* to see.

At the top, she peeked her head through the hole and surveyed a small loft space.

Crouched on the floor, illuminated by the red glow of a kerosene space heater on the floor, was Sammy. He was bent over an open *HVAC* box with a small flashlight clamped between his lips. He was trying to light something with a cigarette lighter, and the scent of burning paper wafted through the air.

"Sammy!" she shouted.

He pointed the beam directly at her, and she shielded her eyes. "Get out of here, Chrissie," he replied.

Crystal climbed the last steps. "What are you doing up here?"

She moved deeper into the room and saw a card

table scattered with bottles of glue, brushes, containers of paint, and model cars in various states of assembly. Next to the heater on the floor, a bare, dingy white mattress with blue vertical stripes. Bare wall studs, exposed pink insulation, low ceiling. This was where the Polaroids had been taken.

Sammy remained crouched on the floor over the box, watching her.

"What are you *doing*?" she asked again.

He finally stood, holding the flashlight limply in his hand. In the other, he clutched two small, flat items.

"This isn't your business," he said. "Just go home."

She snatched the items out of his hand.

"Hey!" he cried, trying to grab them back, but she shushed him.

They were two Polaroid pictures. In the eerie red light of the space heater, she could just make out the features of a shirtless boy holding a baseball bat in slightly different poses, like he was waiting for a ball to be pitched to him. He stood in front of a bed covered with an I-Cubs comforter. The bottom corners of the pictures were burned.

"Who is this? Where did you get these?" she asked, holding up the pictures.

He snatched them back. "Just leave, Chrissie," he repeated. "It's none of your business."

"How did you get in here?"

"I have a key."

"How…what…" Crystal shook her head, tongue-tied by which question of many to ask first.

"Why do you have a key to Kenny's garage? What are you doing in here?"

Sammy stared at the floor, his lips defiantly pursed.

"Why were you trying to burn those pictures?" She moved closer to him and stepped on the cigarette lighter he'd been using. "You'd better start telling me the truth right now," she said, "or I'll go straight home and tell Mom that I followed you and caught you up here, and then your ass is grass."

Sammy dropped the two photos into the open box and pointed at it. "I'm getting rid of the stuff in there."

"What stuff?"

He dragged the toe of his boot through a puddle of melted snow. "Bad stuff," he said quietly.

Crystal eyed the box warily, as if some dangerous creature might leap out of it at any second. She began to sweat beneath her heavy winter coat with the heater cooking right next to them. For a split second, she considered taking Sammy's hand and leaving. Getting the hell out of the attic and away from the garage. If she didn't ask any more questions or look inside the box, they could just go home and pretend like none of this had ever happened.

Sammy sniffed and wrapped his arms around himself, swishing the nylon of his coat, and for a brief moment Crystal saw the little boy he used to be in the profile of his face. The little boy who used to sleep with a stuffed panda bear, and climbed into bed with her whenever it stormed, and who'd coined her nickname *Chrissie* when he first learned to talk because he couldn't pronounce *Crystal*.

She'd spent so much time looking after him the last few years, being *responsible* for him, that she had to know what he'd been keeping from her. If he was in trouble, she would help him.

Crystal reached out and delicately pried the flashlight from Sammy's grasp, and he didn't protest. She lowered to her knees and removed her scarf, laying it on the floor, and unzipped her coat. With a deep inhale, she pointed the flashlight beam at the box, and looked inside.

First, she saw more magazines of naked women like the one she'd found in Sammy's room. The corners of the pages had been burned, like the two Polaroids. Beneath the magazines, a file folder of papers with typed lists of names, cities, and post office box numbers. Dozens of names, all male, and cities across the country. Small handwritten notations peppered the margins.

*blond hair only
*blue eyes only
*sports poses

Crystal flipped to the second page. More names, addresses, and notes. In the back of the folder, an envelope. She opened it and counted several hundred dollars' worth of cash.

She set the folder down and dug deeper into the box. At the bottom, a thick, rubber-banded stack of Polaroids. She slid the rubber band free.

Boys. So many boys.

She swallowed a sick lump down her throat. Most of the faces she didn't recognize, but a couple she did. More pictures of Corey. One picture of a kid from their street who'd sold them candy bars for Kenny's baseball team fund raiser. As she progressed through the pile, the poses became worse. She forced herself to keep looking, her hands shaking, until she found the small, round face and belly she'd feared would be there.

Crystal pressed her hand over her mouth. Hot tears streamed down her cheeks and dripped off her chin.

"Oh, Sammy," she whispered.

She turned the photo over, unable to look any longer, and choked on a sob.

Sharp pains splintered through her chest. In the deepest recesses of her mind, she'd known.

"I'm sorry, Chrissie," Sammy said.

Crystal gulped down wet, noisy breaths. "Sammy," she said. "How did this happen?"

He stuffed his hands into his coat pockets and kneeled next to her. "It's a secret club," he said. "He only invites special boys."

Crystal sobbed so hard she nearly wretched. "W-why didn't you tell someone? Why didn't you ask for help?"

Sammy pulled one hand free and opened it. In his palm lay a small brown pouch.

She gasped. "You told Mr. K."

Sammy tucked the pouch back into his pocket. "He said he couldn't do anything or it would get him in trouble, too. So he gave me the magic *bujo* instead." He shrugged. "He felt bad for not helping me."

Crystal turned away as her face crumpled. Her tears were a river now, flowing freely down her face and neck, dampening the neckline of her sweat shirt.

Mr. K. Another blow to her heart.

"Don't cry," Sammy said. "I'm not mad at Mr. K anymore."

The pulsing pain in Crystal's head had settled behind her left eye. Her scalp and face began to tingle.

"We need to go," she said, her words coming with difficulty now. "We need to tell Mom."

Sammy tilted his head and looked at her with a pity-like expression. "Chrissie," he said sadly. "I already told Mom. She didn't believe me."

Blinding white specks passed through Crystal's vision, and she dizzily tipped over onto her backside.

"When it first started," Sammy continued, "I told Mom he was always hugging me and it made me feel weird sometimes." From the box, he picked up a Polaroid of a boy with a large strawberry birthmark on his chest. The corners of his mouth turned down. "She told me I was being silly. That he was a really nice guy and his family did so much for people."

She pressed her face between her knees and closed her eyes, trying to quell a wave of nausea.

"This isn't happening," she murmured.

"It's okay, Chrissie." He patted her shoulder. "I'm not mad at Mom anymore, either."

Crystal lifted her head. "We need to call the police."

"No!" Sammy shouted. Crystal winced and cupped her head.

"I told you." His voice shifted into a calm, steady tone. "He said he'd make me disappear. He said he would kill you and Mom." Sammy picked up the cigarette lighter still lying on the floor. "But I have a plan to make it all stop."

Crystal started to argue but froze.

A vehicle motor approached. Tires crunched across snow. But Sammy didn't seem to hear. He flicked the lighter and held it to the corner of the Polaroid.

The motor cut. A door slammed.

Crystal switched off the flashlight and grabbed Sammy's forearm, jostling him. The flame extinguished, plunging them into the red glow of the heater. Sammy dropped the smoldering picture into the box.

Below, the back door groaned open, then clicked shut.

There was a queer intermission where the world felt as if it had stopped spinning on its axis. Crystal strained to listen but heard only the whoosh of blood in her ears.

Then, footsteps, climbing the stairs.

There was nowhere to hide in the small loft space. Crystal and Sammy remained on the floor, paralyzed.

A shadowy form ascended through the opening of the stairwell, like a monster rising from dark water. The figure of a man. Crystal was too terrified to even scream.

Blinding overhead light. Crystal flinched and clenched her eyes shut. When she opened them, blinking hard, she saw Kenny, standing next to the stairs, still wearing the denim coveralls with the name patch. *Kenneth.* The harsh overhead bulb flattened his features and created deep shadows around his eye sockets.

He propped one hand on his hip. "Hey, little buddy," he said. "What's going on up here?"

Sammy stood. Crystal remained cemented to the floor.

"Seems like I've had a break-in." Kenny wagged a finger at them. "You two are in big trouble."

Crystal's brain simultaneously lurched and froze, comprehended and denied. *Scream, run, hide, fight.*

Kenny turned to Sammy.

"I thought you went home," he said.

Crystal glanced at her brother. His face remained neutral.

"Seems like you didn't count on my call getting canceled." Kenny moved closer. His voice was disturbingly sweet, cordial. "I'm very disappointed in you, little buddy."

Sammy said nothing. He continued to stare at Kenny with a nearly tranquil expression.

He walked toward them, staring at the opened box on the floor next to Crystal.

"This is a secret club, Crystal Cox," Kenny said. "And you weren't invited. I don't like people poking around in my business." He curled his lips over his teeth, his eyes like black beads, dead.

"Y-you won't get away with this," Crystal said, and knew instantly she sounded like a stupid child.

Kenny laughed. "Sure, I will. Right, Sammy? You remember what I said would happen if you ever told anyone our secret, right?"

A terrifying realization flashed through Crystal's mind. Kenny was going to kill her brother right in front of her.

Crystal rose to her feet and opened her mouth to speak, to beg, to reason, whatever she needed to do, but before she could utter a word, Kenny's hands shot out and grabbed her by the throat. She started to scream, but the sound was cut off to a strangled wheeze.

A new horrifying realization. He was going to kill *her*.

His fingers squeezed the small bones of her neck, and they popped under the pressure, compressing her windpipe. Crystal tried to mouth words—*stop, please, help*— and clawed at Kenny's hands and forearms. Her eyes bulged and her lungs began to burn, desperate for air.

Kenny's beet-red face hovered inches from her own. She thrashed her legs, kicking the box over and sending the contents flying. Her glasses slipped and fell to the floor in the struggle.

She jammed the butt of her hand into Kenny's nose, catching him off balance, and he stumbled sideways, her neck still in his grip. Their bodies crashed into the card table of model parts, glue, and paint, and knocked over the heater. Crystal's vision narrowed, like a lens slowly shuttering to a tiny, distant pinpoint of color. She was losing consciousness. She could feel the life draining out of her.

A blur of movement passed behind Kenny, followed by a hard thump, and then the hands released Crystal's neck.

She dropped to the floor and drew the deepest, most blissful mouthful of air, like a newborn baby taking a first breath of life. She coughed, cradling her throat, and felt the beautiful rise and fall of her chest, the steady in, out, in, out. The basic bodily function was so satisfying, tears welled in her eyes and streamed down her cheeks.

Someone moaned, followed by the sound of scuffling, and a dull thud.

Without her glasses, everything was just light and blurry shapes. She groped around the floor, patting her hands like fingers on piano keys. Finally, she made contact with the smooth edges of plastic lenses. She slipped the glasses back on, but spiderweb cracks splintered the left lens.

Through her usable right lens, she regained focus. Sammy stood over her, panting. Next to him, Kenny knelt on the floor, his hands clutching the left side of his neck. Red liquid oozed between his fingers.

Blood.

Crystal scrunched her eyes, confused, thinking she'd caused it when she hit him in the nose.

But his nose wasn't bleeding. The blood was coming from his neck. Just above his collarbone, something hard and shiny protruded.

"*Saaaa,*" she croaked. "*Saaa.*" Her voice box produced nothing more than a hoarse whistle. She pushed up to her knees, wobbly.

Kenny pawed at his neck. He jerked once on the shiny object, and it released with a sickening *thwock*. He dropped it on the floor and stared at his blood-soaked hands.

Crystal picked up what had been stuck in his neck. Blue metal. Gold *DMPD* letters. Her pocketknife.

Kenny pressed his fingers back over the open wound, but it was bleeding faster now, pulsating. His carotid artery, Crystal weirdly recalled from an A&P class last year. Blood continued to stream down his arms, dripping off his elbows. A wet, gargling sound bubbled from his mouth with an explosive, bloody cough. He tried to stand and swayed, then staggered and fell onto his back.

Sammy loomed over him. Kenny reached out for Sammy's leg, his nails scratching at the denim, but Sammy kicked the hand away. He crouched next to Kenny's head, straddling the pool of dark blood spreading around it.

"Bag yer face," he whispered.

Kenny's skin grew mottled and gray, like molding clay. He gurgled one last time and went still, arm splayed.

Crystal crawled toward him, still wheezing and dizzy. Kenny's eyes were locked on the ceiling. She pressed her fingertips to the opposite side of his neck, waiting, feeling for any movement, the tiniest thump of a pulse. But nothing. He was dead.

She shook her head in shocked denial. No, he

couldn't be dead. This wasn't real. She was dreaming, having a nightmare so vivid she couldn't distinguish it from consciousness. She closed her eyes, commanding herself to wake up. Her throat tightened and sent a searing current of pain through her neck.

When she snapped her eyes back open, Kenny's unmoving body was still there in front of her. A creeping line of blood spread across the wooden boards.

"*Whaa...*" She cupped the damaged muscles of her throat and emitted a sound like a squealing piglet.

Sammy bent down and picked up her knit scarf where she'd shed it onto the floor.

"Whaa..." Crystal tried again. "Whaa you do?"

Before Sammy could answer, sparks popped behind them. They both turned at the sound. The space heater, still plugged into the outlet and blazing hot, was face-down on top of the bare mattress, sizzling and smoking. The fabric ignited with a *whoosh*.

Crystal struggled to her feet but sagged against the wall, steadying herself with her hand. Sammy approached the mattress, transfixed by the yellow glow spreading through the cotton stuffing, his eyes wide. Black smoke was quickly filling the small loft space, and Crystal covered her mouth and nose with the crook of her arm, fighting the agonizing urge to cough, and Sammy pressed her scarf to his face.

The flames spread to the edge of the mattress and reached the box, turned over on its side, and quickly devoured the cardboard and trail of flammable debris until it reached the exposed pink insulation, where it erupted into a snarling wall of flames. Crystal recoiled from the singeing heat.

The flames grew floor to ceiling, lashing and roaring like a living, breathing beast, driving them back against the wall.

She took one last look at Kenny's lifeless lump on the floor and grabbed Sammy's hand, dragging him down the stairs. As they reached the bottom step, something above popped, followed by a louder *boom*. Outside, in the falling snow, they ran across the yard and crashed through the hedge into a neighboring yard. There they crouched behind a garden shed, huddling and shivering in the freezing cold.

Black plumes of smoke rolled out between the roof joints. Within minutes, the sound of crackles turned into a dull roar as flames ate through the peak and engulfed the roof. Nearby, a dog began to frantically bark.

Crystal still held Sammy's hand tightly in her own, too afraid to let go. They watched the orange glow build until it set the night sky on fire.

Soon, all that would be left was ashes.

TWENTY-EIGHT

Three months, twelve hours missing

DALE HAD BEEN waiting in the nearly empty mall parking lot for over an hour with the motor of his car running, just watching the snow fall. The mall was dead because of the storm.

He was wasting gas, but he couldn't think of anywhere else to go. His head felt foggy, disconnected. Like he'd taken a dose of cold medicine.

His revolver lay on the seat next to him.

At the edge of the lot, there was a telephone booth, on Fifth Street, next to the bus stop. He could call Dr. Smith's emergency after-hours answering service. The answering service would then take a message and give it to Dr. Smith, and Dr. Smith would call him back at whatever number he'd provided. He counted the loose change in his console. He had enough.

But he didn't move. He just sat. Waiting.

Dale had parked next to her brown station wagon—one of the few cars still in the lot—and watched the north entrance doors.

His swollen left eye throbbed and had turned the shade of eggplant. He hadn't eaten anything since the stale doughnut for breakfast, and yet he wasn't hungry. The thought of food made him queasy.

Dale glanced at his revolver again.

He'd nearly shot someone tonight. He'd been so close. Within millimeters.

In the academy, he'd known a cadet who'd named his service weapon Betty Lee, after his mother, like the guy who dropped the bomb on Hiroshima. Dale had never named his weapon. Not in the Army or on the force, but he thought maybe he should now. His mother's name was Ann, which wasn't as snappy as Betty Lee or as pretty as Enola Gay. His grandmother's name was Lorna, but he'd never liked his grandmother.

He could name it Constance, after his wife. He touched the cold barrel.

"Hello, Constance," he whispered. "You nearly killed someone tonight."

A strange laugh bubbled up his throat.

Dale flicked his wipers to clear the snow from his windshield. A petite figure with long blonde hair emerged from the mall. He ran the wipers again, watching. Tina stepped off the curb, teetering through the deep snow. The plows hadn't been through yet, and her high-heeled shoes sank up to her ankles.

Dale moved Constance to the floorboards, near his feet, and got out.

"Tina!" he called.

She shaded her eyes against the blowing snow.

"Dale?" she replied. "What are you doing here?"

"Hoping to catch you after work. Do you have a minute?"

"Of course!"

Tina wobbled around her car to his and collapsed into the passenger seat. "Oh my god, it's so cold!" She held her hands up to the hot air blasting from the vent.

She smiled at him. "You weren't here for another haircut, were you?"

He shook his head, and the motion made him momentarily dizzy. "Not today," he said. "I just needed to…talk to you."

She cocked her head. "About the case?"

"Not about the case." He forced a smile, but the expression felt strange on his face, wrong and plastic.

"Okay." Tina wedged her purse between her knees and knit her brow. "So, what do you need to talk to me about?"

He ran his sweaty palms down the front of his slacks. "I guess I could use a friend right now," he said. "And you… I mean, I know we're not friends, but you seem like a really nice person."

"That's a sweet thing to say."

She unbuttoned her coat, and he caught a whiff of that powdery perfume.

"Did you get into a fight or something?" she asked, pointing to his eye.

He instinctively touched the puffy skin. "Oh, no. Occupational hazard. It's not a big deal. How—how was your day? Ruin anyone's hair?"

She laughed lightly. "No, but I still had a terrible day."

"Oh, yeah? Tell me about it."

Tina eyed him warily, and for a moment he thought she was going to get out of the car. He was relieved when she started talking.

"Um, well, I had to leave work for a few hours this afternoon to deal with a problem with my son, I had a terrible fight with my daughter, three appointments canceled tonight because of the storm, and I barely made five bucks in tips."

He opened his mouth to respond but closed it, his mind blank. His brain was on a time delay of some sort.

"Can I smoke in here?" Tina asked.

He cleared his throat. "Sure."

She pulled a velveteen cigarette case from her purse and opened it. "It's my last one." She cracked the window and lit the tip.

"I had a terrible day, too," he said.

"Oh, really? What happened?"

"I messed up a huge case."

Tina blew a plume of smoke. "How did you mess it up?"

"I got tunnel vision." He gripped the sides of the steering wheel. "I convinced myself someone committed a crime that he didn't commit, and I went after him." He squeezed hard, making the vinyl creak and strain. "I think I'm going to get fired."

Tina was quiet for a long time. "Why did you get tunnel vision?" she finally asked.

Dale closed his eyes. "I let my personal problems get in the way."

Tina patted his hand. "Everyone messes up sometimes. Even cops. You're not perfect, and you have an incredibly stressful job."

Dale closed his fingers around hers and leaned his head back against the rest. "It's not an excuse."

She cleared her throat and gently extracted her hand. "Maybe you should talk to your wife about this."

Dale stared at the ceiling. "I can't talk to her about my job. She wouldn't understand." He rolled his head and looked at her. "But you're easy to talk to."

Tina took a drag. "Thank you."

He was making her uncomfortable, he could tell. He sat up straighter, and his foot knocked the gun on the floor. Maybe Constance wasn't the right name after all. Maybe he could name her Tina. Or Christina.

"Is your name short for Christina?" he asked.

She turned back to him. "What?"

"Is Tina short for Christina?"

"No. Just Tina."

"What's your middle name?"

She finished her cigarette and tossed it through the crack. "Marie."

"Tina Marie! That's perfect!"

She drew her purse closer to her chest. "Are you sure you're okay?"

Dale reached down and touched the barrel again, a new tic, it seemed. "Sure!" he said. "I'm fine, really."

He'd nearly killed a man today, but he was perfectly *fine*.

Pressure began to build once more in the back of his throat, another strange laugh, or a scream.

Dale bent forward, pressing his forehead against the steering wheel, trying to swallow and catch his breath, but the pressure finally ruptured. He began to weep, violent, heaving, ugly cries that rocked the car.

"Oh my god," Tina said. "Hey, hey, it's okay." She scooted closer and rubbed the back of his shoulders with her small hand. "Dale, it's okay. Try to take a deep breath."

But he couldn't stop. The heaving continued.

She rhythmically shushed him like a parent trying to calm a child. "Dale, listen," she said gently. "If it makes you feel any better, I also messed up big-time today."

He coughed, his voice shaky. "Yeah? What'd you do?"

"I said some terrible things to my daughter." She paused and bit her lower lip. "I'm so ashamed to admit this, but I slapped her."

Dale lifted his head and sniffed. "What was the fight about?"

"College," she said. "I don't want her to go."

"Why not?" He wiped his face with the sleeve of his trench coat.

"I don't know. I keep telling her it's because we can't afford it, but..."

"But what?" he asked.

"Maybe I'm just jealous of all the possibilities she has that I didn't," she said. "So I'm trying to hold her back." She looked at Dale, and even in the darkened car, he could see her face was cloaked in sadness.

A snowplow rumbled by, finally starting to clear the lot.

"I'm not a very good mother."

"That's all right. I'm not a very good father."

"I doubt that." She laughed ruefully. "I'm such a mess that I sent my kids to the corner store for milk and my cigarettes in this storm. I'm so broke that I can't even fix the damn leak in my water bed, so I've been sleeping on the couch."

"Well, my wife kicked me out of the house and I've been living in a motel for the past month, so I win."

She smiled, seeming comfortable with him once more. "What a sorry couple of suckers we are."

The terrible Vise-Grip in Dale's chest loosened. Tina's smile was so warm and pretty. Everything about her put him at ease. He leaned over and kissed her, cupping his hands around her soft face.

She pulled away. "Dale, don't," she said. "You're married."

He shrank against the door. "I'm sorry."

"It's okay. You're upset. You're not yourself."

He squeezed his eyes shut. The vise returned, cranking even harder on his chest.

"Hey, hey," she said. "It's all right."

"I shouldn't have done that. I've just… I've felt so alone lately."

"No harm done," she said. "We all do crazy things when we're lonely or upset." She massaged the back of her neck. "I hate being alone. I have a terrible track record with men. I got pregnant and had to marry a deadbeat when I was still a teenager. He then cheated on me, so I had a one-night stand with his best friend just to get even, which effectively ended the marriage for good. Then, last year, I finally met a perfectly nice guy. Decent looking, made good money with his own business, owned his own home, was handy around the house, and was great with my kid. He, like, genuinely cared." She drummed her fingers on her purse. "But after a while, he just bored me to tears. No attraction whatsoever. So I broke up with him. I should've known better than to date someone else's leftovers."

"Leftovers?" Dale said.

"Yeah," she sighed. "He dated my friend Kathy first, and she just raved about what a nice guy he was. I went out with him after she moved. That's how I met him. He came into the salon."

Dale's mouth turned to dust. "Kathy Collier?"

"Yes, how did you know?"

"What was the guy's name?"

"What guy?"

"The guy you both dated." Dale worked to keep his voice calm.

"Kenny Harris."

"Where does he live?" His tone was getting impatient.

"Why?"

"Where does he live!" Dale shouted, making her jump.

"Southlawn Drive!" she replied. "Over by the library!"

By the library. Not on the corner of Tenth.

Dale steepled his fingers over his mouth. He had the sensation of falling. Like a black abyss had opened up and swallowed him and he was slipping through time and space.

Tina started to button her coat. "I think I should go."

He needed something to weigh him down, to anchor him. He picked up his gun and set it on his lap.

"Dale," Tina whispered, "you're scaring me."

Her tiny voice. So distant.

"Yeah," he said, "you should go." He turned the ignition, but the already-running motor squealed in protest.

Tina yanked on the door handle and barely scrambled out of the car before Dale put it in drive and sped away.

TWENTY-NINE

Three months, thirteen hours missing

THEY WALKED SLOWLY, stepping through small snow-drifts in some places, not speaking. Crystal couldn't move any faster because every deep breath of cold air caused excruciating pain in her throat.

As she stumbled along, Crystal weirdly thought about her mother, and a long-ago grocery-shopping trip to Hy-Vee. She'd been six years old and Sammy just a baby. He'd ridden in the cart in a little plastic chair Tina had balanced over the flip-up child seat. Crystal followed, trying not to let her foot touch any lines of the tiled floor. *Step on a crack, break your mother's back.* It was winter and still cold, so she was bundled up, but Tina wouldn't let her take her coat off when she begged and gave her the reason-that-wasn't-really-a-reason *because I said so.*

Whenever Crystal would try to walk ahead just a few steps to look at something, Tina would snap her fingers and tell her to stay close. But Crystal was impatient because all she wanted to do was get to the bakery section where they made fresh rolls, doughnuts, and cookies. Every Saturday, she couldn't wait to get to the glass display case and look at the giant sugar cookies decorated like frosted animal faces and flowers. The selection changed from week to week and she was curious to see what would greet her on the other side of the glass. Sometimes the bakery man gave her free doughnut holes.

Her father had once told her that kids got into trouble when they were either bored, impatient, or curious, and one of the three would inevitably lead kids to break rules. For the first time ever during their Saturday shopping trip, curiosity got the best of Crystal, and she broke a rule. When Tina had her back turned in the canned-fruits-and-vegetables aisle, Crystal slipped around the corner and walked across the store to the bakery without permission.

The bakery man was there in his funny white hat and apron, and she waved to him through the glass case since she wasn't tall enough to see over it. He held out a box filled to the brim with doughnut holes and told her he had extra, so she could take as many as she liked. Crystal plucked out three little round puffs, still warm and gooey, with her thumb and index fingers. As she ate, she examined the day's selection of decorated sugar cookies in the display case, which were sports-themed: footballs, basketballs, and baseballs.

Still nibbling on her doughnut holes, Crystal wandered to the cereal aisle. She browsed the boxes of Pink Panther Flakes, Dinky Donuts, and Sugar Smacks. But her favorite was Super Sugar Crisps with the bear on the front, and she wanted her mother to buy her a box. But they were up high where she couldn't reach, so she climbed the bottom two shelves. As she balanced on her tiptoes and stretched her arm over her head, she slipped and fell, pulling down dozens of cereal boxes with her. One of the tumbling boxes hit her face and knocked her glasses off, plunging her into a blurry world without lines and borders.

She dropped to her knees and tried to feel around for her tiny, pale-pink frames, but all she felt were the boxes, scattered everywhere. She started to panic. Without her glasses, she couldn't see anything. She stood and slowly walked to the end of the aisle with her arms held out straight in front her, but once she reached the end of the aisle, she couldn't tell where she was, or which direction she'd come from. Everything just smeared together into blobs. She turned and walked back to the cereal boxes, where she sat on the floor and started to cry.

By that point, she'd attracted the attention of several people and a small crowd had gathered, asking her name, where her mother was. This was where Tina finally found her, panicked and crying herself. Crystal couldn't remember what exactly was said, just that people had scolded her mother for letting her child climb the shelves and make such a mess, for not keeping a better eye on her own kid. And Tina had become angry and shouted at them, and Sammy had started crying from his little chair in the cart, and it was all Crystal's fault, because she'd broken a rule and wandered off.

This was what Crystal kept thinking about as she walked with Sammy. She'd let her curiosity get the best of her, and look what had happened.

At last, they reached their house. On the stoop, Sammy tapped her shoulder and handed her something. Her scarf.

She accepted it and wrapped it around her neck, and with one silent look, their agreement was made without discussion. They wouldn't tell.

When she and Sammy entered, their mother was in

the kitchen, wearing her burgundy velour bathrobe, heating up a can of soup on the stove.

"There you are!" Tina said. "I've been waiting for almost half an hour. Where have you been?"

They lingered in the doorway and a rush of freezing air blew past them, carrying in flakes of snow.

Tina stopped stirring the soup and set the spoon down. "I got home from work, and you two weren't here—close the door." She tightened the belt around her waist. "Do you know how worried I was?"

Sammy pushed the door shut. Crystal didn't speak, afraid of how her voice would sound if she tried.

"We were at the store," Sammy answered.

Tina looked back and forth at their empty hands. "Then where are my cigarettes and milk?"

Crystal and Sammy exchanged alarmed glances. Crystal had left the brown grocery bag beneath the hedge.

"I—we were on our *way* to the store," Sammy continued, "but, um…we got sidetracked. Playing in the snow."

Tina crossed her arms. "Playing in the snow."

Crystal shifted from one foot to the other. She would have to speak sometime. "Yeah," she said, "throwing snowballs and stuff." Her voice came out scratchy but audible. Better than she'd expected.

"Then where's my money?" Tina asked.

Again, Crystal and Sammy traded nervous looks.

"Um, I had it in my coat pocket and I lost it," Sammy said. "It must've fallen out when I was sliding around. I'm sorry."

He was so adept at lying, Crystal now realized.

Tina skeptically narrowed her eyes. The lies were

probably on their breath like stale beer. She stepped closer to Crystal. "What happened to your glasses?" she asked.

Crystal touched the spindly cracks on the lens and delicately cleared her throat. "They fell off when Sammy and I were playing. And then I accidentally stepped on them."

Tina pinched the bridge of her nose, and Crystal braced herself. Their mother wasn't buying their story. She somehow knew what they'd done. They were busted.

Tina straightened, switched off the stove, and said, "Come sit down, both of you."

She led them into the living room, where she sat on the couch with Sammy, and Crystal sat stiffly in the recliner, still wearing her coat and scarf wrapped strategically around her neck. She fiddled with the fringed edges, waiting for the guilty gavel strike. What would happen to them? They'd have to go to the police. Confess. Could they claim self-defense? That it was an accident? But Sammy going back to the garage wasn't an accident. Crystal following him wasn't an accident. They'd broken into Kenny's garage. And she'd left that damn bag of groceries in his yard.

Tina draped her arm around Sammy, and he laid his head on her chest. Tina started talking. "This has been such an awful day, and some really terrible things have happened."

Crystal gripped the arms of the chair. Sammy would go through juvie court, but Crystal was eighteen. An adult. She could be charged with real crimes. She could go to prison. Her entire future had gone up in flames with that garage. The events of the evening had so thoroughly fried her emotional circuits that she didn't even feel like crying anymore.

"It got me thinking," Tina said. "I've decided that we should move to Florida. The three of us."

Crystal's mouth dropped open, but Sammy's head popped up and his face brightened.

"Really?" he asked.

"Really," Tina said. "I'm ready. I think it's time for us to make a fresh start." She touched his cheek, still pink and chapped from the cold. "I think it would be good for you both to see your dad more, get to know Candy better, meet your new brother or sister." She slid her gaze to Crystal. "And go to college."

Crystal's brain struggled to catch up. They weren't busted. They weren't in trouble. What's more, her mother was saying all the words she'd been dreaming about.

Florida. College. Fresh start.

"Are you serious?" she asked weakly.

Tina nodded. "If you're okay with moving in the middle of your senior year and leaving all your friends."

The realization still wasn't penetrating. "You want me to go to college?"

"Yes. I really want you to go. If we move now, we can establish residency and you'll get in-state tuition. And you'll have a place to live next year while you're a student."

Tina patted the cushion, and Crystal moved from the chair to the couch, where she settled into the warm circle of her mother's arm. Her thoughts returned once more to that day in the grocery store, how she'd been blind and terrified, barely able to see her own hand in front of her, let alone the faces of the people around her, and yet she'd known her mother even from a distance by the sound of her voice, her scent, and her touch, and how safe and comforting it had been. Just as it was now.

"I'm sorry about our fight today," Crystal said. "I didn't mean the things I said to you."

Tina pulled her closer. "I'm sorry, too. I'm proud of you, Chrissie. I hope you know that."

"Can I be done with my paper route?" Sammy asked.

Tina kissed the top of his head. "Yes. You don't have to do the paper route anymore."

They sat quietly for a moment, watching the Christmas tree lights blink on and off.

In the distance, a siren wailed. Tina twisted around and parted the front drapes. She and Sammy looked out the window, but Crystal couldn't bring herself to.

"Wow," Tina said. "That's a big fire." She clicked her tongue. "I hope no one was hurt."

Crystal stood. "I'm really tired," she said. "I'm going to bed."

"You sound terrible," Tina said. "Are you getting sick again?"

"Maybe. Yeah. I don't feel very well."

"I'm going to bed, too." Sammy removed his coat and tossed it onto the chair.

Before Crystal climbed the stairs, she hugged her mother. "Thank you," she said.

Tina tightly returned the embrace. "You're welcome. And hey, we'll get your glasses fixed tomorrow."

Tina turned back to the window. For the first time, Crystal tried to picture what her mother's new life might look like in Florida.

Whatever it was, it would surely be better than her life here.

THIRTY

Three months, thirteen and a half hours missing

UPSTAIRS, SAMMY YAWNED. It wasn't that late, but he was exhausted. He and Crystal parted at their bedroom doors on opposite sides of the hallway. Crystal finally removed the scarf and touched the necklace of dark bruises dotting her throat.

"Does it hurt?" he asked quietly.

"Yeah." Her voice was still scratchy, like she had a cold. "I'll be wearing turtlenecks for a month." She started into her bedroom.

"Chrissie?" Sammy said. "Will we get caught?"

She glanced over her shoulder at him. "I don't think so," she answered. "No one saw us."

"What about the grocery bag?"

"It's under some bushes, probably buried in the snow. I doubt anyone will find it, let alone connect it to us."

"Okay." Her answer made him feel better.

"Hey," she said.

He stopped at the door and turned around. "Yeah?"

"What was your plan?"

Sammy pressed his cheek against the smooth doorframe. "He always turns his back when he takes his clothes off and folds them over the chair. When he's not looking."

Crystal hung her head.

"But he got a call and had to leave." He clicked his tongue. "So, I came up with a new plan and went back."

She closed her eyes. "And I followed you."

Sammy took his time responding. "It could've been worse, you know."

"I guess," she said, her fingers grazing her neck, "but wasn't it bad enough?"

She closed the door.

In his room, Sammy knelt on the newspaper spread across the carpet, his knees crinkling the Sunday funnies. He picked up the model he'd been working on for the last few weeks—a 1977 Pontiac Firebird Trans Am black-and-gold "Special Edition," immortalized in his favorite movie *Smokey and the Bandit*. Sammy's father had taken him to see it in the theater a few years ago, and the model had been the last gift from the Model Car Club.

Sammy gathered the newspapers and model parts and wadded them up. He grabbed his big delivery bag and stuffed the ball of paper inside, along with the walkie-talkie from beneath his pillow. With one swipe of his arm, he dumped all the model cars from his bureau into the bag and quietly carried it downstairs. Outside, barefoot and unnoticed, he buried the bag in the bottom of the garbage can, just as he had with the box of treats from his closet, and replaced the lid.

It was time to make a fresh start, just like his mother had said.

Tomorrow, he would call his dad and tell him the news: they were moving to Florida. He couldn't wait to see his father again, to meet his new stepmother and baby sibling. He hoped the baby was a girl. He'd like another sister. Sisters were good to have around.

Back in the house, as Sammy changed out of his clothes into a pair of fresh pajamas, he noticed a dark smudge of blood on the side of his wrist. He licked his thumb and wiped it away.

He pulled Mr. K's *bujo* out of the front pocket of his blue jeans. Mr. K's magic had kept him safe, even if everything hadn't gone according to the original plan and had gotten a little messed up. Turned out the people at the fair had been right: space heaters were really dangerous.

Everything Sammy had prayed for so many times had finally happened. He tucked the *bujo* beneath his pillow where he usually kept the walkie-talkie.

He hoped Curtis didn't stay mad at him forever. He hadn't stayed mad at his mother and Mr. K.

Sammy perched on his knees next to his bed and clasped his hands beneath his chin. When Mr. K had first given him the *bujo*, he'd told Sammy he was praying for him, and that Sammy should pray, too. Even though he'd been mad at Mr. K for not helping him, he'd taken the advice and started praying every night for the *bujo* to keep him safe and for God to help him.

Now, he asked God to forgive him for what he'd done to Kenny. Sammy wasn't a bad person. He'd just had to do a bad thing. And what Kenny had done to him was a lot worse. Surely that counted for something.

Mr. Tibbs scratched at his door, and Sammy let him into the room. He picked up the old cat and climbed into bed, tucking them both beneath the blankets.

"I'm sorry I was so mean to you," he whispered into Mr. Tibbs's fur. "I promise I won't be mean anymore. We're all just doing the best we can."

Mr. Tibbs purred.

Sometimes, being a human was so hard.

But then again, he supposed, being a bird was probably hard, too. Or a spider. Or a cat.

Just being alive was hard.

THIRTY-ONE

Three months, one day, two hours missing

DALE STOOD IN front of the remains of Kenny Harris's garage. Tendrils of smoke curled up from the smoldering pile of rubble. It had finally stopped snowing.

Bradley had caught the case and followed as the county ME and assistant carefully rolled a gurney carrying a black body bag down the slippery driveway to a waiting van. A scorched body, or what was left of it, was zipped inside the bag. Likely the homeowner, Kenneth Harris, son of Cliff Harris, the well-to-do businessman with his name and sponsorship all over the city. As soon as the ID came in, Chief Hagen himself had rushed to the scene to oversee the investigation. He and Cliff had been friends for years.

Small clusters of onlookers watched the activity from across the street. A next-door neighbor had already reported seeing Harris arrive home in his work van sometime between six and seven last night, park it in the driveway, exit, and walk around the back of the garage, where he presumably entered. Approximately thirty to forty minutes later, the neighbor spotted the first flames burning through the roof and called 911. No witnesses saw Harris escape or could locate him. No one else had been spotted entering or leaving the residence.

Dale moved aside as the ME team rolled the gurney

by him and loaded the body into the van. He'd told no one about the events of yesterday and last night. He was still trying to make sense of it all, and so far Kovacs hadn't reported it either. He wandered around the smoldering mess once more, studying the ground as he walked. Charcoal tracks marred the white snow on the ground, and pieces of ash and wood littered the yards surrounding the house.

Bradley and his team had already walked through the interior of the house and found nothing out of the ordinary. A typical bachelor pad. One bedroom, one bathroom, no basement, minimal furniture, a fridge full of condiments and beer, cabinets stocked with canned beans and soup. When the fire inspector pulled the blueprints for the garage Harris had filed with the building permit application several years ago, the team saw that the heavily insulated one-car garage had been designed with a small loft accessible by an oddly concealed set of stairs.

I'd get my kid away from Southlawn Drive if I were you.

That's what Corey Collier had said.

Harris had lived just seven houses away from Kathy and Corey Collier. On South*east* Southlawn Drive.

Not South*west* Southlawn, where Sebastian Kovacs lived.

Such a sloppy oversight. One of Dale's many mistakes. How many times had Kenny almost been revealed, only for Dale to stubbornly keep looking at Kovacs? All along, he'd been so close to the truth.

Sebastian Kovacs wasn't a child molester. He was a petty thief who happened to live on a street with the same name as a serial pedophile.

Southeast. Southwest. Dale had nearly killed an innocent man over a simple direction.

He continued walking the perimeter of the hedge and stopped, spotting something beneath the shrub. He bent over and brushed the snow away. A paper grocery bag.

He peeked inside. A half-gallon carton of milk.

Dale frowned, unsure what to make of it. He glanced around, but no one was paying him any attention. He discreetly tucked the bag under his arm and carried it to his car parked on the street.

Inside, he rested the bag on his lap and searched deeper. Next to the milk was an unopened packet of Capri 120 super slim cigarettes. His stomach sank.

In the very bottom of the bag, beneath the cigarettes, a folded square of paper. He carefully opened it so as not to tear the delicate, damp seams. The ink was slightly smudged but still legible.

Hi Judy,

Please sell Crystal one pack of my usual Capri 120's Super Slim Lights hardpack.

Thnx! T. C.

Finding a piece of evidence was usually like finding a puzzle piece that filled in a mysterious picture just a little more. Snapping it into place was exciting, one step closer to completion, to victory.

But this piece—the bag and its contents—filled in a picture Dale didn't want to see, didn't want to be true. If it meant what he thought it meant, there would be no victory with completion.

Had it been both of the kids? Or just the girl? Had there been a confrontation? A thwarted assault? Self-defense?

Dale moved the note and bag into the passenger seat. Bradley and Hagen stood just a few feet away, talking. All he had to do was call them over. Tell them what he'd found, and what he suspected.

He ground his fists into his eyes. He was so tired of this job and of seeing all the horrible things human beings could do to each other.

Whatever had happened in that garage, Dale didn't want to know anymore. He was just too damn tired.

He rested his hands in his lap and stared out the windshield, buying time before the inevitable.

Bradley knocked on the window, and Dale got out of the car.

"You can go," Bradley said. "Inspector's pretty sure the fire was started by a kerosene space heater. Accidental. Me and the chief got it covered."

Dale glanced at the front seat of his car. He couldn't put it off any longer.

Bradley watched the ME van pull away. "You know," he said, "the timing of this case is kind of strange."

"Why's that?"

Bradley gingerly touched the white bandage over the bridge of his nose. "I gave you that tip yesterday morning about the Stewart case."

Dale tensed, unsure where Bradley was going with this. "Yeah?"

"I kind of…omitted a piece of information."

"What information?"

"The caller mentioned Kenny Harris by name, but I didn't write it down. On the tip sheet." Bradley shifted away as if Dale might hit him again. "He's a really good guy, you know. Gives a lot of time to the community. His old man is really generous, too. Just didn't seem fair to drag the guy's name through the mud again."

Dale couldn't have heard Bradley right. "What do you mean, 'again'?"

Bradley dismissively waved his hand. "Just some crazy bitch a few years ago spouting a bunch of horseshit. Some jilted ex or something. Long before your time. Hagen squashed it." He gestured to the charred garage. "Anyways, just seemed like a weird coincidence that this happened."

A weird coincidence.

Dale dropped his head. It felt like fatigue was eating away his bones. Only yesterday he'd been so keyed up about the Stewart case he'd punched Bradley in the face. Now he just wanted to curl up under a blanket and sleep forever as the last ounce of fight drained from his body.

"I gotta get back," Bradley said. "See you tomorrow."

Dale said nothing as he watched him walk away.

He was done talking about these cases. No one would listen anyway.

Mr. Parkhill had been a respected teacher at his middle school for years. Everyone loved him. Even Dale, at one point. It hadn't mattered when he'd told someone. People saw only what they wanted to see.

Dale opened his car door, gathered the grocery bag items, and tossed them into a nearby dumpster. Then he unclipped his badge, removed his gun from his holster, walked them over to Hagen, and shoved them into his hands.

The chief blustered, started shouting at him, but Dale

didn't stop, didn't hear a word. He just got into his car and left.

He drove to the corner of Tenth and Hillcrest and parked in front of the retired sheriff's house, facing the corner where Chris Stewart had been rolling his papers ninety-three days ago.

Matthew Klein and Christopher Stewart would never be found. The clock would never stop running on their cases unless some farmer turned up bones one day while plowing a field, or hunters stumbled across a skeleton in the woods, but the chances were slim, so the clock kept ticking. Whoever had taken those boys had hidden their bodies and hidden them well, and knew how to keep it a secret.

People kept secrets all the time. It wasn't that hard, actually.

He thought about the Sevastopol map at the precinct.

The City of Respect.

What shaped and defined a city? he wondered. Topography, at first. Rivers and shores and mountains and plains. The ground on which the city was built. The rhythm of the seasons and weather. But then, over time, a city became shaped by its people: their wants, their needs, and oftentimes their fears.

The car motor shuddered in the cold. He slid the gearshift into drive and started for home. He would tell Connie everything, let the chips fall where they might.

The corner of Tenth and Hillcrest was just a corner again. A woman walked by with a tiny dog on a leash. She waved, and Dale waved back.

One respectful South Sider to another.

THIRTY-TWO

Three months, one day, two hours missing

CRYSTAL SLEPT FOR a few hours, then awoke with a start, her heart pounding, her nightgown damp with sweat and sticking to her body. She'd been dreaming. A pain-laced nightmare of heat and fire and a menacing orange sky. She rose and crossed the hall to Sammy's room. He lay sprawled on his back with his mouth agape, his damp hair plastered to his brow, as if he slept so hard it physically taxed him. Mr. Tibbs was curled on the pillow next to his head.

Sammy stirred and rolled onto his side, throwing his arm over his face.

They would both go back to school today like nothing had even happened.

Crystal quietly closed the door and returned to her room. As she changed out of her pajamas, she moved slowly, her muscles and joints sore, like she'd run a marathon. She stood before her full-length mirror and cataloged her injuries: the angry purple lines around her neck, a tiny scratch on her temple, a thick lump on the back of her head, and a flowering bruise on her right hip and thigh. She leaned closer to the mirror. The whites of her eyes were bloodshot. She'd have to come up with another excuse.

Crystal dressed in jeans and a thick turtleneck

sweater that reached her chin. She hobbled downstairs and poured herself a glass of orange juice. Swallowing was excruciating, so she dumped the rest of the glass out.

Her throat just needed time to heal. Everything needed time to heal.

A fresh start.

She thought about what she'd be leaving behind when they moved to Florida and knew her list was short and had shallow roots. Somphone, the yearbook staff, the school newspaper.

And Mr. K, of course.

She didn't want to part on such unpleasant terms, didn't want her last words to him, spoken in such anger, to lodge between them for one more second. The sudden desire to fix things between them, to make them right once more, was overwhelming.

Crystal glanced at the clock. If she hurried, she'd catch him on his walk, before she had to leave for school. She slipped on her boots and coat, which still faintly smelled of smoke, and stepped outside. The air, too, bore the scent of acrid smoke.

As she walked, she purposefully kept her gaze away from the east.

THE WINDOWS OF Mr. K's house were dark. No lamp in the picture window. The front screen door sat slightly ajar, and snow had collected in the jamb. It had been open for some time.

Crystal pulled the screen wide open and knocked on the wooden interior door, but no answer. After several seconds, she cupped her hand and peered through the small diamond window into the dim living room but saw nothing. She tried the knob. It opened.

Inside, the house was still. The large pieces of furniture remained, but every smaller personal item was gone—the lamp, the colorful afghan from the back of the couch, the cuckoo clock on the mantel. In the kitchen, the teapot and all the delicate teacups. No papers, no clothes, nothing.

No trace of Mr. K left anywhere.

On the counter lay a silver house key. Next to it, an old-fashioned skeleton key.

BACK HOME, CRYSTAL LAY on her bed in her clothes watching the occasional car headlights streak across the ceiling.

She felt oddly unchanged.

Even though Mr. K was gone, and Kenny was gone, and Crystal was finally getting her greatest wish to move to Florida and go to college, she and the rest of the world felt exactly the same. Sammy and Corey Collier and all the other boys in those pictures would bear scars for the rest of their lives. Chris Stewart and Matt Klein were still missing. They hadn't been among Kenny's photos. Their abductor was still out there. Maybe even looking for his next victim.

A small, hard acorn of anxiety was still lodged in her chest that had been there since the moment she'd found the first Polaroid in Sammy's room. Kenny's death had done nothing to budge it.

She wondered what Kenny had been thinking about in his final moments of life as he choked on his own blood—if he'd seen the hatred and pain in Sammy's eyes, and been sorry for all the terrible things he'd done.

She hoped so, but doubted it.

Most people were only sorry for getting caught, not for what they'd actually done.

Kenny would be thought of in death exactly the same way he'd been thought of in life, as a good guy. Nice, generous, great with kids. Any evidence to the contrary had burned up with the garage. Kenny was gone, but all the men on his mailing list were still left.

It had all been for nothing.

The Kennys of the world continued to hide in plain sight because people let them.

Crystal bolted upright. The words of the essay started to form in near-complete sentences. By the time she rose and pulled the chain on her lamp, the words were practically tumbling out of her brain and onto the paper.

She opened her red notebook to a clean page. The house was still quiet except for the sound of her pen scratching across the paper.

After the disappearances of paperboys Matt Klein and Chris Stewart, the editor of the Des Moines Register *newspaper wrote, "A sinister shadow darkens our doorways and our lives."*

Crystal's handwriting filled one page, then another.

But what if that "sinister shadow" isn't a shadow at all? What if that "shadow" has always lived here amongst us, not as a shadow, but as our very own neighbor, friend, or even family member?

When we give a criminal the label of "evil," or categorize them as a "monster," we give them power through camouflage. We allow them to hide

*in plain sight while doing what they do behind
closed doors, in secret.*

*I met a monster once, face to face. He didn't
have green skin, or sharp teeth, or long, scary
claws. He was just a man who everyone thought
was a "good guy" because he was nice and
looked like them. No one questioned why he sin-
gled out young boys, eager to spend time with
them, or why kids constantly came and went from
his house. And it's in these unasked questions that
we all become complicit.*

Six pages filled, then seven. Her hand cramped from
writing so much so fast, but she shook it out and kept
going. Finally, she reached the ending. She tapped the
cap of the pen against her bottom lip. Then she wrote
the last lines.

*Perhaps we resort to labels when something hor-
rible happens because the truth is too difficult to
face: we are all capable of evil.*

*There is no "sinister shadow." There are no
"monsters."*

There is only us.

Crystal stopped and laid the pen down. She stared
at her sloppy handwriting, and the hard acorn started
to dislodge.

She couldn't undo what Kenny had done, but she
could write about it. She could make people think about
it, talk about it. And maybe, start asking the unasked
questions.

She crossed the room to her window and parted the

curtains. Dawn had broken cold and bright. The snow-covered street was empty. On the opposite side, rolled editions of the *Des Moines Register* dotted stoops and porches. Her head and neck throbbed in time with her pulse, and she pressed her forehead to the cold glass. It felt as if she'd lost and regained everything important to her in the span of a few hours.

She returned to her desk and laid her hands on the pages of the notebook, rippled from the markings of her pen. It was a good essay. The best she'd ever written. A strange sense of confidence washed over her that she was going to win the scholarship. It was important writing, the kind of writing she'd dreamed of doing—where words and the truth mattered.

If she got married and had a family someday, she tried to imagine what it would be like to raise children now, knowing what she knew, after everything she'd seen that could happen to children. She would never be able to let them walk to school alone, or go into public restrooms alone, or to the movies or the mall or the park without adult supervision. Lord only knew how it would eventually affect her generation as adults.

Generation Paranoid.

She would type up the essay and mail the application later today. She flipped the pages of her notebook to the beginning of her handwriting. Her essay needed a title.

She neatly printed the words down at the top of the page.

The Monsters We Make: A Community of Abuse

SATURDAY, MAY 31, 1986

ANOTHER BOY.

His mother watched from the front picture window as he left his modest South Side house on Thornton Avenue. It was after dinner, and she'd asked him to walk to his grandmother's house two blocks away to let her dog out. His grandmother had undergone hip surgery recently and still couldn't get around very well. He didn't mind, though. He loved his grandmother, and she'd give him candy once he got there as a thank-you. One of those new Push Pop suckers.

He headed down the driveway and turned to wave at his mother just before he passed behind a late-blooming lilac bush. She waved back and closed the window drapes.

His family was new to the South Side, having moved to Des Moines from Minneapolis only a few weeks ago, just after his thirteenth birthday, after his grandmother broke her hip.

He set out on his street, and goose bumps pimpled his slender arms and legs in the unseasonably cool May air. He wore cutoff jean shorts and his favorite Pac-Man T-shirt despite the chill, impatient for summer to arrive. But at least it got warmer here earlier than it did in Minnesota.

His street was quiet as dusk descended, few cars and people to be found. But he liked the quiet. So far, he

liked the South Side. He was looking forward to starting school in the fall and making friends.

He walked at an easy pace, unaware of the corner
just seven blocks away made famous less than two years
earlier. And he'd never heard the story of the other boy
in the neighboring suburb, on a different corner, or the
connections between the two. Folks had mostly moved
on from those stories by then. There was nothing new
to say.

So the boy didn't notice a lone car approaching him
from behind, rolling along the street, slowly, hugging
the curb. The driver's side window rolled down, and
the car stopped.

The driver called to the boy, asking a question.

The boy turned around. *What did you say?*

The man repeated himself, asking for directions to
the airport. *I'm really lost. Can you help me?*

The boy approached the open window.

Timothy Allan Pearson
"Tim"
Case #86–13444
4 hours missing.

* * * * *

AUTHOR'S NOTE

WHILE THIS BOOK is a work of fiction, I was heavily inspired by the real missing-persons cases of Johnny Gosch, Eugene Martin, and Marc Warren Allen.

John David "Johnny" Gosch disappeared in the early-morning hours, around sunrise, on Sunday, September 5, 1982, while delivering the *Des Moines Register* in a West Des Moines, Iowa, neighborhood. He was twelve years old.

Eugene Wade "Gene" Martin disappeared in the early-morning hours, around sunrise, on Sunday, August 12, 1984, while delivering the *Des Moines Register* in a South Side Des Moines neighborhood. He was thirteen years old.

Marc Warren Allen disappeared in the early-evening hours, around sunset, on Saturday, March 29, 1986, while walking to a friend's house in his South Side Des Moines neighborhood, just blocks from the site of Eugene Martin's disappearance. He was thirteen years old.

To date, all three boys are still missing and believed to have been abducted, with no solid leads or suspects in any of the cases. Neither West Des Moines nor Des Moines law enforcement have ever officially linked the three cases, though informally, many individuals who worked closely on the cases strongly believe they are connected.

When Johnny Gosch was abducted in 1982, I was

seven years old and lived two hours away in a small southern Iowa town. I was too young to understand that case when it happened. But when Eugene Martin was abducted on August 12, 1984, I was nine years old, and in Des Moines on vacation—a rare trip to the capital city for my family—and staying in a motel on Fleur Drive, mere blocks from where Eugene went missing on my sister's fourteenth birthday.

After the news of Eugene's disappearance broke on Monday morning, I have a distinct memory of standing in the motel parking lot, looking at the downtown Des Moines skyline and thinking, *Someone out there is stealing children*, and it terrified me. Before Eugene Martin, it had never occurred to me that people even did such a thing. Thus, the paperboy cases—Eugene's in particular—have both haunted and fascinated me for over thirty years.

In preparation for this book, I extensively researched the three Des Moines cases, as well as child abductions nationwide in the 1980s, to understand their timelines, and how they were handled in that era. I started by reading hundreds of *Des Moines Register* articles about the Gosch and Martin cases archived at the Des Moines Central Library on microfilm. I studied Paul Mokrzycki Renfro's graduate thesis *Lost in the Heartland: Childhood, Region, and Iowa's Missing Paperboys (Annals of Iowa, 74, 2015)*; the memoir *Why Johnny Can't Come Home* (Johnny Gosch Foundation, 2000) by Noreen Gosch, Johnny's mother; and the documentaries *Missing Johnny* (MSNBC, 2012) and *Who Took Johnny* (RumuR Inc., 2014).

I conducted interviews with retired *Des Moines Register* reporter Frank Santiago, who wrote about the cases throughout the 1980s, and retired DMPD senior police officer James Rowley, who worked on the original Eugene Martin case, and I spoke with several former South Side Des Moines paperboys who delivered papers during the time of Martin's abduction, as well as a former classmate of Johnny Gosch. I also visited with an adult survivor of a childhood abduction and sexual assault.

While the main characters of the novel are purely fictional, I did incorporate many of the real-life details of the three cases into the story, such as Eugene Martin's abduction in front of a retired Polk County sheriff's house, the *Des Moines Register*'s H.O.P.E. decal program, and the faces of missing children on the backs of milk cartons—a campaign originating in Des Moines at Anderson Erikson Dairy in late summer of 1984, where a friend of the Martin family worked and suggested the idea to the plant manager. (Anderson Erikson Dairy also happens to be the company that my dairy-farmer father sold milk to for forty years.) Other cases mentioned throughout the story are also real—the two murdered paperboys in suburban Omaha, the case of Kevin Collins in San Francisco, and the Atlanta Child Murders.

It's also important to note that Noreen Gosch has been highly influential in changing how law enforcement searches for missing children, despite the doubt and criticism she received at the time of her son's abduction. She lobbied for the Johnny Gosch Bill, a piece of state legislation that mandated an immediate police response to a report of a missing child. The bill became law in Iowa in 1984, just a few months before Eugene's abduction, and directly impacted his case, as there was no waiting period before law enforcement launched an investigation and got the FBI involved. Similar laws were later passed in an additional eight states. In August 1984, the same month as Eugene's abduction, Noreen testified in Senate hearings on Capitol Hill, speaking about organized pedophilia and the role she believed it had played in her son's abduction. She also testified before the U.S. Department of Justice, which eventually provided $10 million to help establish the National Center for Missing and Exploited Children, an organization that is still in operation. At the time, Noreen was invited to the White House by then-president Ronald Reagan for the dedication ceremony. She continues to work for and speak on behalf of missing children and their grieving families to this day.

I've visited the locations where the three Des Moines boys—Johnny, Gene, and Marc—were last seen alive, and today they're just regular streets and corners, with no memory or trace of the terrible events that took place decades earlier.

It's difficult to quantify how much those cases impacted future generations of parents who were children, like me, when the boys went missing. Former latchkey kids who grew up in the shadow of these abductions with lost faces staring at us from the backs of milk cartons, grocery sacks, and public bulletin boards. We were the first generation of kids taught to fear every stranger who was just a little too friendly, to avoid every corner that was just a little too dark, and suspect every passing van that drove just a little too slowly. And because of that, we grew up to be equally paranoid, vigilant parents.

Perhaps writer Paul Mokrzycki Renfro summed it up best in his dissertation: "The Gosch and Martin cases continue to loom large in the Iowa consciousness. They fractured, at least in the public imagination, a pristine past."

ACKNOWLEDGMENTS

IF IT TAKES a village to raise a child, then it took a village to write this book, and I have many villagers to thank.

First, a heartfelt thank-you to my agent, Julia Kenny, for believing in this story and being such an invaluable teammate.

I was so lucky to work with astute editor Chelsey Emmelhainz, whose insight and suggestions made this book far better than I ever could have on my own, and the rest of the excellent team at Crooked Lane Books: publisher Matt Martz, Jenny Chen, Ashley Di Dio, Melissa Rechter, and copyeditor Rachel Keith.

Thank you to developmental editor Maggie Morris, who helped dig me and an ailing draft of this book out of the bottomless black hole we'd both fallen into at one point.

Thank you to retired Des Moines senior police officer James Rowley for answering my many questions about the Eugene Martin case and DMPD police procedures in general, to *Des Moines Register* reporter Frank Santiago for chatting with me about covering the Johnny Gosch and Eugene Martin stories, to Eric Herman for sharing childhood memories of former classmate and friend Johnny Gosch, and to Marc Francisco and Linda Francisco for answering questions about Des Moines South Side paper routes in 1984.

I owe an extra-special thanks to C.B. for so openly

and generously sharing his harrowing personal story of childhood abduction and abuse with me.

I'm indebted to the Des Moines Public Central Library for the treasure trove of archived *Des Moines Register* articles from the 1980s that helped inspire and shape this story. Love your local library, people.

I'm also indebted to the Midwest Writing Center and director Ryan Collins, the sponsors of the Great River Writers' Retreat, and the sisters of St. Mary Monastery for giving me invaluable, uninterrupted time to work on this book in such a beautiful, peaceful environment.

Thank you to Paul Mokrzycki Renfro for answering my questions about his illuminating University of Iowa dissertation *Lost in the Heartland: Childhood, Region, and Iowa's Missing Paperboys*.

During what has been a challenging few years, I'm grateful for my community of fellow writers who read drafts, gave suggestions, and offered fellowship and support. My Iowa community: Wendy Delsol, Calla Devlin, Dawn Eastman, Catherine Knepper, Carol Spaulding Kruse, Jenny Moyer, Kimberly Stuart, and Jennifer Wilson. My VCFA family, especially Mathieu Cailler, Jennifer Cohen, Courtney Ford, and Donald Quist. Rich Farrell, for talking me out of an insane number of point-of-view characters, and Dave Jauss, for answering my early questions about point of view. (I'll forever be your devoted Padawan.)

And an additional thank-you to Donald Quist, whose searing essay "The Animals We Invent" inspired an important thread in this book, not to mention the title.

Thank you, Julie Stone, for making a New Year's resolution with me that turned around our bad writing mojo and attitudes.

Humble thanks to authors Heather Gudenkauf and Robin Oliveira, both above-and-beyond-generous writers, for giving this book early promotional quotes.

Thank you, Jackie Jensen, my favorite beta reader, my hopelessly unpaid editor, my cheerleader, but most importantly, my friend.

I'm so grateful for Jenni Gilbert Hobbs, my bestie and my person for thirty years now; for my parents, Myron and Sue White; and for my husband, Troy Van-Baale, for over two decades of unwavering love and support through all the ups, but especially the downs.

And finally, thank you, dear reader, for holding this book in your hands, and making words and stories matter.